The Tattered Eagle

Geoffrey Rex Collis

The Pentland Press Limited
Edinburgh • Cambridge • Durham

First published in 1994 by
The Pentland Press Ltd.
1 Hutton Close
South Church
Bishop Auckland
Durham

ISBN 1 85821 222 7

Typeset by CBS, Felixstowe, Suffolk
Printed and bound by Antony Rowe Ltd., Chippenham

The Tattered Eagle

My deepest thanks to Robert Bremner, 'Brem', now a sufferer of Altzheimer's disease, without whose Celtic canniness my life would have been some fifty years shorter.

My thanks also to the typing skills of my one-time long-suffering secretary Diane and my friend Eric Marshall.

Voyage of the
"Warwick Castle"

Voyage of the
"Duchess of York"

EUROPE

SPAIN

AFRICA

Freetown

Durban

MADAGASCAR

Aden

INDIA

Bombay

CEYLON

Colombo

Penang

SUMATRA

MALAYA

Singapore

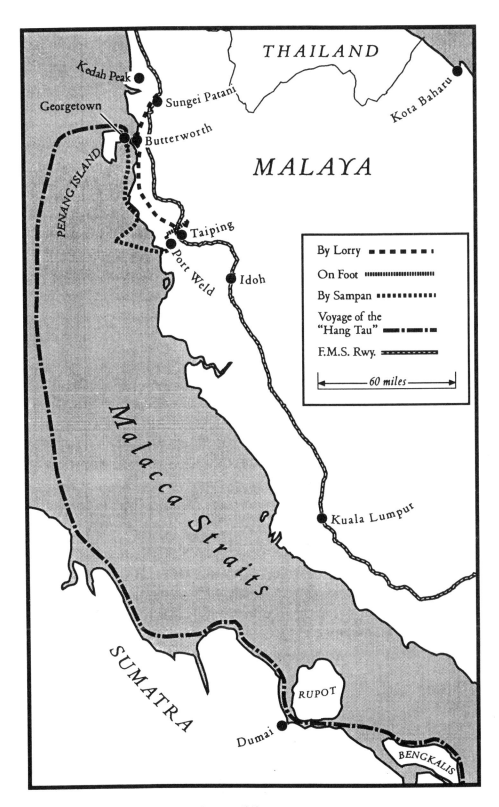

THAILAND

Kedah Peak

Sungei Patani

Georgetown

Butterworth

MALAYA

Kota Baharu

PENANG ISLAND

Taiping

Port Weld

Idoh

By Lorry
On Foot
By Sampan
Voyage of the
"Hang Tau"
F.M.S. Rwy.

60 miles

Malacca Straits

Kuala Lumpur

SUMATRA

RUPOT

Dumai

BENGKALIS

The Retreat – 10 December 1941 – 27 January 1942

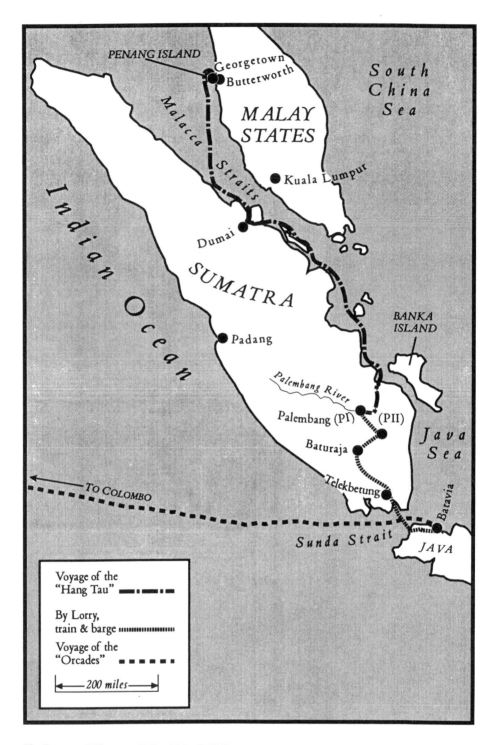

The Retreat – 27 January 1942 – 1 March 1942

Chapter I

The date was 22 March 1941 as I emerged from the sweating depths of this newly converted troopship on to the deck, taking in great lungfuls of salty spray as the vessel dipped and rose with the swell of the cold forbidding waters of the Firth of Clyde.

As the first glimmer of dawn spread from the east, somewhere over Glasgow the sun was struggling to perform its daily duties above banks of forbidding cloud. On the starboard bow could just be made out the mountains of the Isle of Arran, and dimly beyond them the Mull of Kintyre, many years afterwards to be immortalised in song by Beatle Paul McCartney.

All around us, as daylight spread across the Firth, could be made out the shapes of other great ships that somehow had assembled during the night. All were painted in their wartime coats of battleship grey, camouflaging the proud colours of the various shipping lines that had distinguished them in the pre-war years when the big liners reigned supreme in inter-continental transport. By straining my eyes I could make out four rows of five, twenty of Britain's finest commercial vessels pressed into wartime service to move the troops to places they knew not where. Beyond the liners, which would have been so vulnerable to Hitler's lurking U-boats, were the Royal Navy's destroyers, some four or five bustling around the perimeter of the convoy, for all the world like hens shepherding their chicks, lorded over by two great battleships, one of which I learnt later to be the redoubtable *Nelson*.

To me, who had just celebrated my twenty-first birthday, maybe a man in years, but still a callow youth in worldly experience, this all seemed like a great adventure stretching before me. The old sweats at the embarkation camp had said it would be for four years at least, or until the war ended; at that time it looked like continuing for ever. I gave no thought at all to what might lie beyond. In my naive way it seemed that I was being wafted away from the war and, provided a German submarine did not home in on us

1

during the next week or two, I should be savouring the delights of a world cruise at the Government's expense. Within a few short months I was to find out just how wide of the mark were my musings when cold realities shattered my rosy dreams.

I could not but feel a little guilty about leaving my ageing parents to suffer the brunt of the blitz in the Smoke, which I had learnt from my new mates from other parts of Britain to call London. I knew of the mixture of fear, depression and bravado as one suffered the nightly bombings of Hitler's aerial fleet, for I had lain prostrate at home in North London during the previous autumn having been stricken by broncho-pneumonia as I went on leave after passing out from my technical training course. The nearest bomb demolished two houses, only two doors from where we were crouching beneath a table. I remember seeing the roof and frontage of one crumble and subside into the road in a cloud of dust. Luckily our neighbours were able to scramble out of the back.

Two days after Christmas Day 1940 came the worst of the raids on the City of London, when most of the area now resurrected as the Barbican was set on fire. I recall standing near Moorgate Station the next morning, as blackened firemen still fought the blaze, and wondering how the City could ever rise up again.

My father, who had spent his whole working life as a stockbroker's clerk in the City, still struggled up to the City each working day as best he could, denied the retirement he had planned for 1940 because the business simply could not have continued had not the old men been prepared to soldier on. Could he have rolled back the years I am sure he would rather have been on that ship, as I was, heading out into the unknown. Unknown, that was, to the lowest forms of life in the RAF such as myself.

After two months on a night fighter squadron, sandwiched between six months of technical training, I had finally passed out as a Fitter IIA. In theory I knew how to look after all parts of an aircraft except for its engine. I did not have a great deal of confidence in my ability to help keep the Air Force airborne, and had not exactly excelled myself in the passing-out exam; but the RAF, which was starting to flex its bombing muscles over the Ruhr, was still fairly desperate for skilled ground crews; an AC2 who at least knew how to handle a spanner and screwdriver was better than nothing at all.

Some nine months earlier, still pimply and very green about the ways of

2

the world, I had passed through the blue iron gates of the RAF Number One recruiting base, up the High Street from Uxbridge Town Station, after the long one-way ride on the Piccadilly line from Bounds Green.

As I clutched my call-up papers in my hand I did feel a certain amount of pride, but not a thought about the dire things that might happen to me in the years ahead. It had not occurred to me to volunteer for service in the months of the 'Phoney War', for I knew before the outbreak of war that I was going to be one of the first to be conscripted.

I had always nursed an ambition to fly, as did most boys of my age I suppose, spurred on by a five-bob flight from Portsmouth to the Isle of Wight and back in 1937. My vague thoughts were to become a navigator, for I did not consider myself daring enough to be a pilot; anyway I was quite good at geography, having acquired my highest marks in that subject for the College of Preceptors exams.

However, I knew on that June morning in Uxbridge that I was not destined to be plotting a course across the North Sea to Bremerhaven, for I did not meet the specified standard of vision. It had not occurred to me that I was anything other than A1 physically, and was completely unaware that I had astigmatism of the right eye, inherited from my father before me, and now passed on to my son.

The surrender of the French government was announced as I entered the recruits' interview room at Uxbridge, and the education officer seemed to redouble his efforts to conjure up some sparks of talent from the motley throng of twenty- and twenty-four-year-olds whose surnames began with A to D, who were being pushed before him that Monday morning. As I wasn't able to fly it must have seemed the next best thing, in the eyes of the powers that be, that a lad from middle class background and private school education might be turned into a ground mechanic.

My only qualification seemed to be that I could drive a car; even then I was unable to answer the question: 'Can you describe a four stroke engine?' My solutions to arithmetical problems weren't too hot either, and the prospects of being earmarked for cook house duties looming larger. In desperation the EO popped the topical question: 'Did I realise what the surrender of France meant to us?' Stifling back the urge to answer: 'No more Folies Bergère or Normandy onion salesmen,' I tried to stiffen up my quivering upper lip, and croaked something from my parched mouth about being 'alone now to

3

uphold the freedom of democratic government'. I can't believe that I was at all convincing, for in my heart I really thought we were going to lose the war, in spite of Winston Churchill's wireless rhetoric. I don't think the EO was convinced about me either, but such was the country's obvious plight that any able-bodied young man might just be moulded into a tool of war. So I was earmarked to be an Airman Rigger.

The four months at Number Six Technical Training School, Hednesford, through that eventful and sunny summer of 1940, were a mixture of hard graft; sweat, as we ground round the drill square for a solid week; pain, as the needles went in for inoculations; and comradeship.

From a sheltered suburban life, with a cosy little circle of friends, I was suddenly pitchforked into hut 52, on top of the hill above Hednesford, with some thirty other assorted males aged twenty and twenty-four, whose only common denominator was a surname with initials A and D.

It did not take long to elect our hut foreman; even on the gruelling struggle, with full equipment, up what was known as 'Kitbag path', from the halt on the Walsall to Rugeley branch line, Joe had stood out as a leader of men. His loud voice, bushy moustache, and claim to have been earning the princely sum of £7 a week as a salesman, put him head and shoulders above the rest of us.

His right-hand man was the even louder voiced Fred Cockle. With that name he just had to be an East End barrow boy. I can only once remember him short of words; that was on the first day, when we handed our particulars in to the headquarters' office. He was told he couldn't classify his religion as 'Atheist'. 'Wot's C of E, for Gawd's sake?' was all he could get out. I can still remember the day when he stamped up the steps into the hut, stopped, sniffed the air while he paused, then bawled out at the top of his voice, as if announcing the price of Brussels sprouts down the Commercial Road, "OOZE SHIT?' as the pungent whiff of a surreptitious fart wafted across his ample nostrils.

From Fred I learnt that every sentence should be liberally sprinkled with expletives, mostly of four letters, or seven when used as an adjective, which they usually were. One soon got to know that no one of the rank of Corporal or above had parents, and they in turn accepted that situation when dealing with us new recruits.

Then there was the little Brummy lad 'Ollie'. He was twenty-four and one

4

of the few married men in our entry. A silver-edged sepia photograph of a rather wan plump girl had pride of place on his locker. He was renowned for his down-to-earth pithy comments. The one that springs to mind was the occasion he came in from ablutions, easing himself back into his white webbing braces, and exclaimed in his Erdington whining prose, 'There's only one thing better than a good shit.'

Gilbert Critchley might easily have been a West End matinee idol, both by name and appearance; but his only connection with theatreland was his wife, who walked the streets around Shaftesbury Avenue, with Gilbert presumably doing a spot of pimping. He should have been in an earlier entry than number 52, for at the age of twenty-five he could hardly claim exemption for a reserved occupation; but his entry into the Royal Air Force was delayed whilst a small dose of the pox was cleared up.

Gilbert used to say that he couldn't see a goodlooking woman without wanting to seduce her. Every night that he could get out of camp he would try his luck with the local talent around Hednesford and Walsall, relating his latest conquest with relish next morning to all us sex-starved mortals.

I remember particularly his story about the young teenager whom he persuaded to take him home, only to be confronted by her mother. In order to safeguard her daughter's maidenhood she offered her services instead. Quite willingly, it seemed to Gilbert, as he tackled her long satin black drawers, for hubby was sweating it out on the Libyan sands with the Eighth Army. So well did she defend her Shirley's supposed virginity that Gilbert fairly crawled back to the billet on his knees at two o'clock in the morning, and didn't go out of camp again for the next two nights. It was from Gilbert that I learnt that a shag was not just a scraggy-necked bird that liked sitting on rocks off the Cornish coast.

But there were some true friendships that were forged during those training days. Stan, Harry, Ray and I formed a close quartet who would each put themselves out to help one another whenever possible.

Stan was, and I believe still is, a 'salt of the earth' Londoner, although we have drifted apart since the war, as indeed have the others. His was an old head on young shoulders, and his peacetime occupation of garage mechanic put him ahead of the rest of us when it came to handling tools; but he was always willing to pass on the benefit of experience to those he considered his friends.

5

Harry was the same age as myself and, judging by his home address in Shoreditch, ought to have been a Cockney: but his deep BBC voice belied his home environment. He was single and unattached, and he and I would spend our off-duty hours strolling around the park in Walsall eyeing what skirt there was on parade. There did not seem to be any shortage of talent, also strolling in pairs, but such was my shyness of the opposite sex at that time that I cannot recall ever having got anywhere, and I don't think Harry did either.

Ray was twenty-four, and the handsomest of our quartet; he earned his nickname from his likeness to Ray Milland, who was then a young heart-throb of the silver screen. Ray could have picked up any local lass he pleased, had he been so minded; but his heart was promised to Elsie, an attractive brunette from London, and socially beneath him in his rather snobbish mother's estimation. That did not discourage Ray, and they were married on his first seven-day leave from the RAF. Ray, with his soft spoken voice and classical features, melted into the ranks to the extent that no one, other than his close friends, seemed to remember him in later years.

From the first day at Uxbridge, the four months at Hednesford, two on 604 Squadron, then a further two on a fitter's course near Cheltenham, we four remained together. At the end of the fitter I2A course we were told we were going to be posted straight overseas. We knew then that it would be the parting of the ways for the quartet, and when we met up again for the last time at the embarkation camp we made a date to meet up together again in Piccadilly Circus on the fifth anniversary of the date on which we had joined up, 17 June 1945. It was an accurate prediction that the war (in Europe) would be over by then, although we were all in the service for the best part of another year afterwards.

To my shame I did not make the effort that I might have done to keep that date. Indeed, the only one to keep that appointment in 1945 was Harry, and to him it must have seemed most unlikely as he wiled away his time for 3½ years in the Nazi Stalag Luft III. Harry was not posted overseas from the embarkation camp, by some curious quirk of Air Force administration, and to return to ground duties on a bomber squadron must have seemed to him to be a bit humdrum, so he volunteered to remuster as a flight engineer. It was quite a new profession for aircrew, and had been introduced with the new four-engined bombers to relieve the pilot of the responsibility of nursing his engines and fuel supplies when he had rather a lot of other things to occupy his attentions on a night bombing run over Germany.

When Harry volunteered to be a flight engineer I don't know if he was aware that the RAF was losing them rather fast; for in their cramped seat in the centre of the aircraft, between the main spars, they had rather less chance to get out in a hurry should the aircraft be doomed. In fact, Harry's new career did not extend beyond the first half of his very first operational flight. He was lucky that he did get out of the burning aircraft and open his parachute successfully; but not so lucky that he broke a leg landing in a tree and was soon captured by the Bosch.

The only one of the other three to accompany me on the midnight train journey from Wilmslow embarkation camp, as we steamed away into the unknown, was steady Stan. As the loaded train chugged its way through the night I deduced from the long and labouring hissing of steam from the exhausts that we must, after an hour or two, be heading up to Shap summit towards Scotland; the halt for refreshments at Carlisle, as dawn was breaking, proved this theory to be correct. To me, who had never been north of Carlisle before, even the prospect of entering Scotland was exciting.

For some strange mixed-up reason the last thing I had done before marching out through the gates at Wilmslow was to post a letter to my steady girl friend in London in which I told her that I did not expect her to be available when, or indeed if, I returned from four years or more overseas, and therefore our friendship should be considered at an end. I did not deserve to find her still uncommitted to anyone, as proved to be the case when I returned after those four long and eventful years, during which time life for me hung by the merest single thread on several occasions.

In 1946 we married, and she bore me four children, the first of which died soon after birth. At the time, the infant's death seemed a hard cross to bear; but not nearly so shattering as the sudden death of my dear wife after only ten years of marriage.

Chapter 2

Those two months at sea, from March to May 1941, still remain vivid in my memory. It was a truly awesome sight as the great ships veered westwards round the Mull of Kintyre. About every twenty minutes the throaty roar of the ship's sirens signalled a veering of several degrees to port or starboard. This zig-zagging was intended to lessen the chance of enemy submarines plotting the course of the convoy.

From the deck of the *Warwick Castle*, a passenger vessel of the Union Castle Line that had plied the Cape Town run throughout the thirties, it seemed all the other ships must be smaller than ours. In fact it was rather like viewing the planets from Earth; as I was to discover some weeks later, when transferring from the *Warwick Castle* to another ship in Bombay Harbour, we were in fact one of the smallest ships in the convoy.

Within a couple of hours the mainland, then the Western Isles, had fallen astern and out of view. So ended my brief flirtation with Scotland, and I had only set foot on its bonny land to march from the Harbour Station in Glasgow to the ship's gangplank, a distance of a hundred yards or so! I promised myself that, should I survive this war, I would return and dally in the Scottish hills and heather. The glimpse of the Kilpatrick Hills to the north, and beyond them a peep at Ben Lomond, had whetted my appetite to return, as we were towed ignominiously stern first down the River Clyde to the Firth of Clyde. Our sea trials, necessary after conversion into a troop carrier, had been carried out in the Firth the day before sailing. As snow squalls swept across the bleak grey sea it seemed a far cry from the warm tropical waters that we hoped we would reach in a few days.

Sometime during that first day at sea the great armada must have passed Mallin Head on the port side, although invisible to those on board; no doubt the convoy had kept out of sight of prying Irish eyes which might not always be friendlily disposed towards the Allies.

As darkness fell that night we headed out into the hostile swells of the Atlantic rollers, and those who were not good sailors began to lose their appetites, if not their breakfasts. The next day was even rougher, as the winds whipped up to gale force and the ships bucked fore and aft, bows disappearing into the rollers and re-emerging amid vast showers of spray. It was a fascinating sight as each great liner in turn dipped down into the churning sea, as if in salutation to the mightiness of the ocean, and arose again showering clouds of white spray back as far as their funnels.

For two whole days the storm raged, seemingly unabated, as the convoy headed out into mid-Atlantic. I was glad to discover, the hard way, that I was a good sailor; the fact that I was the only one of the twelve on my mess table sitting down to breakfast on the second day proved the point.

At least during the storm it was less likely that enemy U-boats would be able to mount an attack on the convoy. On the fourth morning, as daylight spread across the grey bulks of the liners, we noticed there were only nineteen remaining out of the original twenty. At first we thought that one had been picked off by a torpedo in the night; but a knowledgable deck hand said one vessel had stayed on westward course, to run the gauntlet for Canada, while the convoy veered round to the south, heading towards the Azores.

For the next two or three days the waves became less fearsome, as the stormy weather moved to the east and the temperature began to rise; and with it our spirits. Every nautical mile seemed to remove us further from the Nazi predators that might be lurking just beneath the surface, and indeed from the war itself. It did not seem to bother me that the Government was hardly likely to be financing a world cruise without something unpleasant developing before long. Enough to enjoy the day and the ever strengthening sunshine beating on the deck; tomorrow could look after itself.

New friendships began to develop amongst the 1500 or so souls thrown together on the *Warwick Castle*, from all parts of the United Kingdom and many different walks of life. Some were musically talented, and I became fascinated by a three-piece band that chanced to come together around an old upright piano, no doubt a left-over from pre-war cruising days. Hearing the young pianist practising his syncopation, someone else produced from his kit bag a much treasured clarinet and joined in, together with a drummer who had raided the cookhouse for an empty Crawford's biscuit tin on which to beat out the rhythm with his wire brushes.

Some ten days after leaving the Firth of Clyde we sighted land for the first time; just a few mountains on the horizon, which we guessed were the Azores. A couple of days more and we spotted birds, presumably foraging out to sea from the West Coast of Africa to see what they could devour from edible flotsam thrown overboard from the liners. On waking next morning there was much excitement as the sun rose above some low hills, which was all we could see of the massive African continent. It was my first glimpse, at close quarters, of foreign shores, although we weren't to be allowed to set foot on dry land. The land proved to be Sierra Leone, and the few odd buildings we could see straggling along the shore-line, interspersed with palm trees, was Freetown. A strange aroma that was not entirely unpleasant wafted out from the land, making a change from the salty spray that had filled our lungs on deck for the past couple of weeks.

With the tropical smells came the gum boats. They were mostly canoes, paddled by the men, usually accompanied by two or three small, brown, naked boys whose job it was to dive overboard to retrieve any coins that might be tossed into the water by the men leaning over the ship's rails above. It was worth a few pennies just to watch the boys weave around in the water to grasp the coins before they sank too deep below the surface. The boats were laden mostly with tropical fruits that could be bought for a few pence, and were hoisted aboard in a basket suspended from a rope thrown across the rails by the vendors.

It must have been quite a boost for those maritime barrow-boys to have the great wartime convoys calling in every few months for refuelling. Although the customers were rather less refined than the passengers aboard the peacetime cruising vessels the quantity was much greater, and it must have been financially worth the indignity of the odd missile, such as an empty beer bottle, being aimed at the canoes.

On 3 April, after some three days while the whole convoy was visited by the refuelling tanker, we pulled up anchor and headed out again into the Atlantic, by now much friendlier than the first foray round the Mull of Kintyre. In the estimation of the Admiralty we no longer needed the protection of HMS *Nelson* which, together with its sister battleship, had turned about when the convoy nosed its way into Freetown harbour, heading back for the northern waters of the Atlantic to perform more vital tasks, no doubt.

As we steamed again south-eastwards the sun at midday was now almost directly above our heads, and apart from being told always to wear our pith helmets on deck it was announced there would soon be a 'line crossing' ceremony for those who had not crossed before into the Southern Hemisphere. I had heard vaguely about the ceremony of being shaved by Neptune then tipped into the briny, but had not expected many potential customers. I expect that the captain thought it would help to relieve the boredom, as indeed it did. It was healthy slapstick fun, in which the warrant officer, decorated with a beard something like Father Christmas's and wielding an outsize wooden razor, seemed to be thoroughly enjoying himself in the guise of Neptune, sentencing each victim to a ducking in the pool, which was carried out with lusty abandon by two attendant sergeants. It was not quite so funny when it came to my turn to find myself struggling and gasping for air at the bottom of the temporary ducking pool. I can imagine how the village witches felt in medieval days of yore when sentence was passed on them at the local duck pool.

Over the next week or so life developed quite a pleasant pattern as we steamed southward at a steady fifteen knots per hour, still zigzagging at intervals, although to us World War II was something taking place on another planet. There would be no aircraft for thousands of miles on which we would have to sweat and toil. The sun shone brightly on the sparkling water as the bow of the *Warwick Castle* parted the now friendly ripples of the South Atlantic into furrows of fluorescent foam through which the flying fish performed their antics. We leaned across the deck rails for hours wagering on how many seconds each fish would stay airborne over the water before finally flopping back into the ocean.

More formal entertainment was a boxing contest, and clay pigeon shooting for those who prided themselves in the handling of guns. One night as we neared the Cape of Good Hope, there was a concert party, after supper, in the main lounge, attended by the captain and senior officers of the Services. The quality of the amateur talent on board was really surprising; our friends with the upright honky-tonk piano, clarinet and biscuit tins were quite a hit. One thing that was novel to most of us when we first boarded the ship was a hammock. Those of us who were quartered in the mess room had to familiarise ourselves with the able seamen's sleeping habits, and there were many hilarious moments at first as we attempted to lay ourselves horizontally,

11

suspended between the beams. When we reached warmer climes we had an advantage over those lucky enough to be assigned to bunks in cabins in that we could erect our beds in the cool air on deck, provided the hammocks were stowed away in the morning before the deck hands came to swab down the decks. If you didn't it meant waking up to a blast of salt water from their hoses.

Towards the end of the second week in April we could just make out on the portside the flat top of Table Mountain, appearing like a cloud on the horizon. It was the first landfall since Freetown, although we had kept quite close to the West African coastline, but just out of sight of eyes on the shores that might not be friendlily disposed towards the Allied cause. However, we were given to understand that should the vessel happen to be struck by a submarine torpedo there was a chance of being able to get close to shore before sinking. It was not a great comfort.

Because of the number of large vessels descending upon the Union of South Africa, berthing was divided between the three main ports, Cape Town, Port Elizabeth and Durban. Some six ships veered away to port, to spend the next four days refuelling and re-victualling: South Africa was still the land of plenty.

The *Warwick Castle*, together with another five vessels, was due for another two nights at sea before docking at Durban. Foolishly I spent those two nights, in the manner I had done since Freetown, with my hammock slung between two convenient stanchions on the upper deck: I had overlooked the fact that we had now moved some 40° south of the Equator, and although the autumnal days were quite hot the nights became decidedly chilly. The canvas of a hammock provides scant protection from the wind, and it must have blown up strongly during the night. At dawn on the morning we were due to dock at Durban I woke frozen to the marrow, with sharp stabbing pains in the stomach. It was as much as I could do to roll up my bed and crawl down to the sick bay.

My temperature was over the hundred mark so I was whipped straight into bed, where I had to remain while my mates filed down the gang planks to sample the delights that South Africa had to offer.

Chapter 3

After two days in the sick bay I was feeling much like my old self again, raring to stretch my legs on dry land once more. It had been exactly one month since we climbed up the gangway on that cold cheerless day in Glasgow.

My old Cockney mate Stan and I felt we were stepping into a different world as we made our way from the docks towards the centre of Durban. We ignored the trolley buses that reminded us so much of London, although all public transport was free for servicemen. It was sheer joy just to step out and keep walking in one direction after a month in the confines of a ship. The calendar was rolled back two years as we gazed into shops full of goods and food that we had not seen for many a day. Large American cars were everywhere, and a general air of opulence prevailed.

Of course, the blacks were hardly living the life of Reilly, mainly because they were not allowed to, even if they had the money. At this time it did not worry us in the least that the black man was not allowed to enjoy the pleasures of the white man, or even to join in his activities. We simply thought it rather quaint that the blacks had separate queues for buses, and then could only occupy the wooden seats at the back. After all, we had been brought up to think of the black man as an inferior form of life.

We spent the day sampling the delights of the Service Club, where a sumptuous repast could be savoured for only a few pence, followed by free seats in a very modern, air-conditioned cinema. As darkness began to fall we gazed in wonderment as the neon signs blinked into life, just like the pre-war Piccadilly that we would not see again probably for years, if at all.

As we stood just gazing around a car pulled up; the driver leaned out and beckoned us, extending an invitation to dinner with him and his wife at their apartment a few blocks away. I had heard, while lying in the sick bay bed, that the whole population of Durban had been asked over the local radio to make the British servicemen welcome, and to invite them to their homes. After two days in port, and with thousands of men swarming out of the five liners, I had expected we would be too late to catch up with any hospitality; but either the population of Durban is much greater than I thought, or we were just lucky.

We were led into a modern and well furnished flat, to be greeted by our host's young wife, who was clearly intent on making us at home. A splendid meal was served up by their black servant, and drinks were not in short supply. It was hard to believe that our host was merely employed as a garage mechanic. Perhaps we should emigrate after the war, was the thought foremost in our minds as we waved our new friends goodnight at the dockside, just before the harbour clock struck midnight. Next day, to be our last in South Africa, we were taken on a conducted tour in and around Durban.

There was something unreal about that day: like a Bank Holiday joy ride, but under conditions that neither of us expected to experience at first hand. The abundance of sweet scented flowers; the palm trees; the monkeys and other animals roaming around that we had only ever seen in zoos. Returning, after a picnic lunch in the hills, we found the city of Durban bustled with life, and displayed the sophistication of modern civilization: it was hard to believe that it had all come about well within the last hundred years.

We cast away from the quay at Durban next morning, 21 April, saddened to be leaving this beautiful city, and filled with gratitude for the hospitality shown to us by its citizens. As we pulled away slowly from the dock side one lovely lady began to sing in a clear resonant voice 'Land of Hope and Glory'. The men crowding the rails fell silent, and many seemed near to tears. In some way it reminded us that we were not just embarking on a cruise, and there would be many who would never return to their homes. I have often wondered since who that lady was who felt she just had to let the world share her patriotic fervour for the Old Country.

When clear out to sea from Durban we steamed nor'-east at a gentle speed while the rest of the ships formed up again in convoy. There, waiting for us already, were the liners that had put into Cape Town and Port Elizabeth, only there weren't so many now: just fifteen plus two escorting destroyers. We assumed that the other vessels had remained in port for some reason or other.

For the best part of the next week we steamed uneventfully in a generally

14

northward direction, again keeping out of sight of the coast of Africa on the eastern seaboard. Somewhere along the route we must have passed on the starboard side the island of Madagascar, in area about the same size as Great Britain. We could not see that coastline either, so must have been steering midway between the island and the mainland, a distance of some 250 miles at the closest point.

Up until this time we assumed that the *Warwick Castle* would disgorge its human cargo somewhere around Suez, and that we would be reinforcements for the squadrons battling it out in and above the sands of North Africa. The influx of Rommel's Afrika Korps, to bolster the flagging Italians, was making life much more difficult for the Allied Eighth Army. Certainly the odds were that we would end our sea voyage at the top end of the Red Sea. Indeed, when we reached a point in the Indian Ocean somewhere off the Horn of Africa, ten of the convoy turned due west for Aden, whilst the *Warwick* was one of the five that veered to the east. I had no doubt that the skipper knew all along where he was supposed to dock, but the information didn't filter down to the likes of us.

At that point we bade farewell to our sister ship the *Stirling Castle*, which had travelled alongside us most of the way from Gourock; it was rather like losing an old friend. Once again we were north of the equator, and the heat was pretty oppressive as we steamed for the next three days across the Arabian Sea towards Bombay.

As the *Warwick Castle* drifted into the harbour we could make out the shape of the great arch, supported on two columns, built in the Victorian era and known as the 'Gateway to India'. One could picture the days of the last century when columns of soldiers in pith helmets and colourful uniforms and with fife and drum bands would head towards the trouble spots to the north, or on the North-West Frontier, to quell some mutiny or troublesome tribe.

On going ashore the first thing one noticed, apart from the pungent aromas, was the abject poverty. The sight of deformed and crippled scraps of humanity holding out scrawny hands for money was sickening in itself. The road into the city was lined with such beggars crying out for alms. My first visit to the sub-continent left me feeling disillusioned about the Imperial presence in India. How could a comparative handful of white men, however well intentioned, act in the best interests of the teeming millions, comprising

15

many creeds, that swarmed throughout their vast country? Although these thoughts disturbed me, as we wandered through seedy streets and crowded bazaars, brushing aside persistent salesmen eager to prise our few rupees from our pockets, I knew there was nothing that I could do about it, but I was left with the feeling that the British Raj would not last very much longer once this was over. I daresay the Japanese hierarchy had similar thoughts, at that very time, as they pieced together their plans to wrest the grip of the British from the Far East. Before that year was out all the world would know of their imperialistic intentions.

I was not sorry to return to the ship that night. In the early hours of the next morning I was sick at sea for the first time since leaving Glasgow. It could not have been the motion of the boat, for the harbour was like a mill pond; it was either the kipper for supper, or the Indian meal in Bombay. It was lucky that my hammock was roped up to one of the rails at the side of the ship, so the sea birds were able to take immediate advantage of my *mal de mer*.

Indeed, that was to be my last night in a hammock. To the common erk, working on an aircraft, the Royal Air Force adminstration moved in mysterious circles. Of all the hundreds of men aboard the ship why was I to be one of thirty to be transferred to the one vessel destined to travel on further to the east?

I recall the shock at hearing my name called out over the Tannoy system to report to the Orderly Room. Whoever had stuck the pin into the list against AC2 No. 1252987, Fitter 2A, was to alter the whole course of my life in the months ahead.

It became apparent that all the airmen aboard the *Warwick Castle*, and probably those in the other three ships remaining in Bombay, were intended as replacements for experienced personnel who had been marooned in India since the start of the war, unable to return to England when their allotted period of service abroad was spent. All were long term servicemen who had joined the RAF in peacetime as a career. Doubtless, many were disillusioned by now, having probably accepted the King's shilling during the depression of the thirties, with the prospects of learning a trade. In the eyes of the RAF overlords these men, with their three years of apprenticeship followed by years of experience in a squadron, should be far more use in the pursuance of the war against Germany than a bunch of green rookies like us, conscripted

16

into the service without much option, and with a bare eight months of training behind us. In fact, I am not so sure it worked out as the Air Marshals expected.

As we, the selected thirty, clutched our kitbags and shuffled in single file to the ladder down to the Naval cutter alongside, we were not aware that we were destined to join the renowned No. 27 squadron, stationed on the North-West Frontier for years, but moved to Malaya during the time we were on the high seas.

It was farewell for four years to Stan, the last of our friendly quartet who had been together since the first day at Uxbridge. I must confess that my sadness at losing the steady companionship of Stan was overshadowed by the exciting prospects of voyaging on to Malaya, a country I had always wanted to visit since school days and the stories of one of the teachers who had spent much of his childhood there.

In the services, particularly during wartime, friendships are made, then lost, and others forged. As the thirty, of assorted air force trades, stepped into the cutter, there were only two others I had known previously, Fruity and Brem. We did not know it then but we three were destined to share the most harrowing weeks of our lives together, from which only two would survive.

Fruity had actually joined up at Uxbridge on the same day as me, but we were very different in our ways of life, and in temperament, so had never considered ourselves close friends; but here we were thrown together again. His nickname suited him well from two angles: firstly, his surname was Date; secondly, he had a penchant for the opposite sex which could almost be described as an obsession, and generally they fell about him. In the summer of 1940, whilst we were both training at Hednesford, we had met up together at a hop in Walsall. I had two left feet when it came to dancing, and a tongue tied in knots when it came to chatting up a bird. Fruity was in his element, toes twinkling to quick-step, waltz and tango – they all came easy to him – with the best of what Walsall had to offer in the way of comely wenches eager to hang around his neck. I managed to grab one scrubber eventually, and then only in a Paul Jones; but her attentions were plainly elsewhere, so when next time the music stopped she was away like the wind to throw her arms around the neck of Fruity who happened to be fairly free at the time. The experience did not do much for my ego concerning the

17

opposite sex. Within the year Brem and I were to be very grateful that Fruity had what it takes to charm the girls.

Brem was quite different, not that he did not appreciate the opposite sex. He was basically shy, which was one thing we had in common, and could scarcely be described as ruggedly masculine, in spite of his upbringing in a Caithness croft. His father farmed a smallholding only six miles from John O'Groats. The sparsely populated countryside in that part of the world was probably the main reason why he did not mix easily with the other airmen, although he was quite prepared to use the usual four-letter words with the best of them. But somehow it never sounded quite the same coming out of his mouth, with the accent of the northernmost counties. He always claimed that the most perfect English was spoken by those from north of Inverness; a fact I would not dispute. Indeed, it always gave me pleasure just to hear him speaking. Basically he was lazy, but clever enough to be able to get away with it. His cut-glass accent and waspish wit never exactly endeared him to the NCOs, who had usually come up the hard way. He had volunteered for service in the RAF some months before he would have been conscripted. His reason for enlisting prematurely was quite simply because he did not want to run the risk of being drafted into the infantry.

As the naval cutter chugged across the bay leaving the *Warwick Castle* in our wake, there was a tinge of sorrow at leaving the vessel that had been our home for the past six weeks; but I was glad to be given the opportunity of living in Malaya, and seeing something of the Far East.

The liner that was going to take us there was now looming up closer ahead of us. The *Duchess of York*, for such was the ship we were to board, was rather larger than the *Warwick Castle*, and in peacetime had been employed on the North Atlantic route to Canada. Because of her normal voyages in a cool climate she was not ideally ventilated for plying in the tropics. The ship was already more crowded than the *Warwick Castle*, mostly with army personnel. There being no cabins or sleeping quarters for us we were each issued with a mattress and told to lie at nights wherever we could find a space. As we would be heading back south towards the equator it would be quite comfortable sleeping up on deck, for it very rarely rained at night.

It was 3 May when we hoisted the anchor and headed out of Bombay harbour, veering to port along the western seaboard of southern India.

On the third day out from Bombay we were steaming due east again, as

18

we rounded the southernmost tip of India and headed straight for Colombo, where a contingent was to be put ashore. From our anchorage about a mile offshore Colombo did not seem the busy town that I later found it to be. We could only see the line of palm trees beyond the shoreline, with some stately-looking colonial buildings further back. On the horizon, some fifty or so miles inland, could be seen the blue mountains that rose more than eight thousand feet above sea level. One particular mountain stood out from the rest, presenting a perfect dunce's cap apex. This was the holy mountain of Adam's Peak: I was to become quite familiar with this pinnacle some while afterwards.

Our stay off the coast of Ceylon was only a matter of hours, and we were off again on the last leg of the voyage. Rounding the southern seaboard of Ceylon we headed again due east across the Bay of Bengal, passing the northernmost point of Sumatra on the starboard side after two days.

For the final day and a half of the long sea voyage we steamed gently south-east down the Straits of Malacca, past the island of Penang, that we were soon to know so well, on the portside. On the morning of 11 April, after eight weeks at sea, we could just make out, across the port bow, the buildings of Singapore. As we drifted slowly nearer to land we could make out also the gleaming barrels of the great naval guns that guarded the entrance to this British bastion of the Far East. Their very presence was to us, in all our innocence, reassuring. How the Japanese generals must have been laughing up their sleeves!

Chapter 4

As we boarded transport at the Empire dock, for the five miles to Kallang, my first impression of Singapore was the strong oriental smells, particularly foul as we crossed over the creek that divides the western part of the city from the eastern side, where stood the cathedral, and beyond it the equally imposing edifice of the Raffles Hotel. It seemed difficult to comprehend that all had been developed on a swamp in less than a hundred years.

Kallang was the old civil airport; in peacetime Imperial Airways planes would touch down on the long flight from Croydon to Sydney. Amy Johnson had stayed briefly, back in the early thirties, on her record-breaking flight to Australia. Now it was requisitioned by the RAF; and the mark I Blenheims of 27 squadron had come to rest at Kallang after the long flight from the North-West Frontier of India. But they had not stayed long enough for our band of thirty to catch up with the squadron, for they had flown north again, some four hundred miles, to the newly opened airfield at Butterworth, near Penang. We were told we would join them within the week, after being kitted out with our tropical kit from the main RAF stores at Seletar.

I had expected that we would hand over our 'blues' in exchange for the cotton khaki drill that would be worn in these parts. On the contrary, we were simply issued with another kit bag, and seemingly were expected to carry our normal gear around for the next four years. As a single man the span of duty overseas was four years, and three for the married man. In fact, it was not to be many months before I had lost the whole of my kit.

An important piece of the equipment was the mosquito net, a new experience for all of us, and still very necessary in Singapore, in spite of widespread spraying of insecticides on the mosquito breeding grounds.

Our temporary quarters were tents that had been erected in one corner of the airport. Not having been in the Boy Scouts it was yet another new experience for me to sleep under canvas. Almost everything was a new experience in those early days; not least was the servant boy to undertake the more menial chores of camp life. The prestige of the white man had to be upheld, even though we were the lowest form of life in the Air Force.

I soon found out that it rained for two hours every day in Singapore: at least, it did during the week we were there. Not just rain, but drenching thunderstorms that broke the heavens regularly at twelve o'clock each day. By two o'clock the tents were virtually flooded out; but by three o'clock the sun was shining fiercely again and the puddles rapidly drying out.

During the few days in Kallang we ventured into town most evenings, gravitating to one of the large dance halls, either the New World or the Happy World. For me it was a great frustration; I was not much good at dancing, for the very good reason that I did not really enjoy it. I did enjoy the chance of female company, especially the close proximity that dancing offered; but was not much good at chatting up. Unlike the town hall at Walsall there was no escape for the girls at the Happy World; for the payment of 10 cents one was entitled to three minutes dancing to the strains of electric guitars. The hostesses were all Chinese, and must have been bored stiff, particularly with the likes of me, too tongue-tied to utter a syllable.

The following morning there would be bawdy comments bandied around about last night's conquests, some of which may have been true; but most likely they had spent their last dollars at one of the many red light establishments. What I do know is that I boarded the *Penang Express* at the end of that week still a virgin.

Trains had always fascinated me, and this was my first railway journey abroad, a whole day and night of it. For me it held great magic from the moment we chugged across the Johore Strait causeway to the mainland of the Asian continent and began our leisurely journey northwards. The title *Penang Express* seemed somewhat misplaced, for it rarely exceeded 35 miles per hour, and the many halts along the route allowed ample time to wash and brush up, if so inclined. At Kuala Lumpur, the capital city, there was plenty of time to take a meal in the magnificent station building.

Throughout the afternoon we steamed steadily northwards, the line of hills on our right-hand side that formed the backbone of Malaya, like the Pennines in England, serrating higher and higher towards the Cameron Highlands. As the sun sank across the Malacca Straits the mountains took on

21

a purple cloak, swallowing up the green of the jungle, and etched sharply against the blackening eastern skyline.

Darkness had fallen well before we reached Ipoh, a town that I never saw, the rhythmic swaying of the coaches having soon induced sleep and dreams of faraway home.

I awoke as dawn was breaking, on what was to be the last day of over two months' journey, to realise that the train was stationary, the engine gently hissing steam across a jetty. Across a stretch of water, of mill-pond calm, the outline of mountains could be made out. This proved to be the island of Penang, with the town of Georgetown, as yet invisible to us, nestling on the eastern side of the main mountain, facing towards the mainland of Malaya.

We were jerked back to the realities of life by the raucous bark of a mustachioed sergeant: 'Pick up your kit and fall-in on the platform.' By the time we were 'fell in' most of the civilians from the train had shuffled across the jetty to board the waiting ferry for the short trip across to Penang, a journey with which we were to become very familiar in the months ahead. For us it was a ten-minute drive, in the back of two 30-cwt lorries, to the newly opened RAF Butterworth camp.

The living quarters were situated on a narrow stretch of land between the coast and the road to the north. The quarters resembled those of a holiday camp, rather than the usual barracks or huts of a military encampment. Indeed, it had been built to provide accommodation for lepers! Each little white painted wooden hut was isolated by some ten feet from the next and was intended to house two patients. As far as I could find out it had never been used for its original purpose when the RAF stepped in to requisition the camp to provide quarters for its airmen.

The influx of thirty new 'bods' meant that room had to be made in the cosy little huts for a third person. Resentment over a third person sharing the shower was, I believe, compensated for by the bringing of first-hand news from 'Blighty'. For those who had already served four or five years abroad the new influx were greeted with open arms, for it renewed their flagging hopes of soon being repatriated.

Chapter 5

Having been in the RAF now for nearly one year I was at last beginning to feel that I belonged somewhere. For eleven months I had either been training or travelling, not to mention four weeks down with broncho-pneumonia. Shortly I, and my mates among the thirty new 'sprogs', as the older hands called us, would have to button down to using spanners and screwdrivers on a real aircraft; I was not too sure that the Blenheims Mark I of 27 Squadron would stand up to the shock.

Down on the maintenance area, which was a lorry ride of a mile from the living quarters, we new boys were soon made to feel inferior to the old hands, for they had all spent three years as apprentices at the RAF number I Technical Training School at Halton; and with their years on the squadron gaining experience were all one or two ranks above us lowly AC2s. From my first meeting with the Squadron Engineering Officer it seemed likely that I would remain an AC2 for the foreseeable future. Clearly he was not impressed with my meagre squadron experience, totalling three weeks on 604 Squadron on Salisbury Plain. Flying Officer Edwards, for such was his name, was keen to know all about the new technical developments and the new types of aircraft that were being pressed into operations in England. He was clearly envious that I had been on the famous night fighter squadron, equipped with the hush-hush Radar in its new Bristol Beaufighter. Unfortunately this AC2 hadn't realised at the time, as he stood around shivering in a bleak hanger on Salisbury Plain in December, with sleet lashing horizontally through the gap made by a Jerry bomb that had blown off the hangar doors, just how lucky he had been to work on a Beaufighter. F/O Edwards had hopes that 27 Squadron would one day be re-equipped with 'Beaus' to replace the ageing short-nosed Blenheims, for both were the product of the Bristol Aero factory. It was most unfortunate that I did not know the answer when asked what engines were fitted to the Beaufighter; I feel sure that the name I blurted out had no connection at all with the Bristol Aero Company.

Anyhow, work on the maintenance flight of 27 Squadron was not too arduous a matter, for the squadron was still on a peacetime footing. Work on the aircraft began at 7.45 and ceased at 12.45 with a leisurely half hour or so for a tea break in between. The rest of the day was one's own. The old hands, having spent years in India, usually retired to their *charpoys* (beds) after *tiffen* (lunch) for a couple of hours or so. Our 'sprog thirty' soon found that we had to learn a new language, which was probably a mixture of Hindi and RAF slang interspersed with frequent four letter words usually starting with F. Whenever we sprogs attempted to argue a point we were told to 'get your knees brown'. How I longed to be an old sweat, with two or three years of overseas service behind me, and a battered pith helmet on my head. We soon discovered that our khaki drill tunic, shirts, shorts and slacks should be tailored to fit: our baggy knee-length shorts soon earned us the nickname 'moon-men'; and it really was quite appropriate, for we did look like nothing on earth.

Personal hygiene was something we had to adjust to in those equatorial climes. We had already found out that one showered at least once a day, instead of the once a week that was considered quite fastidious in England, back in the thirties. I can remember the goading my father needed from my mother to bath every two, or even three, weeks in winter time; and we were living in a house with a bath and a geyser to heat the water. I could recall the occasion when, as a joke, I festooned bunting left over from the Coronation of King George VI along the landing leading to the bathroom awaiting my father's emergence after his long delayed scrub-up. And those were the days before under-arm deodorants were even thought of!

At first I did not appreciate that one's clothing and towels also needed their daily douse. I remember the embarrassment I felt when taking a shower during that first week with 27. My towel was slung casually over the *atap* partition, as I was enjoying the water trickling over my body in my little cubicle. In the next cubicle were two long-serving members of the squadron sharing a shower and discussing their *dhobying* arrangements. One was saying to the other, in a loud voice that I knew was raised deliberately for me to hear, 'I usually send two towels a day to the *dhobi wallah.*' It was a lesson in hygiene I never forgot for the rest of my days in the tropics. Being of a rather miserly nature I had been reluctant to give up hard earned dollars just to

24

have the washing done. An AC2 Fitter 2A's pay packet didn't go very far – only an AC2 'General Duties' got less. I could not see myself ever earning any more while Flying Officer Edwards was my boss. The two other men in my chalet were both employed in lower grade occupations, and would have been earning less than me had they not been twice promoted over the years to the dizzy heights of Leading Aircraftsmen.

LAC Atkins, nicknamed Tommy of course, was the squadron postman, as well as doing various other odd 'general duties' clerical jobs in the Orderly Room. As such he was one of the more popular men in the squadron. He was only a small man, twenty-six years of age, from somewhere in the industrial Midlands of England.

'What made you join the RAF, Tommy?' I asked him one evening as we sat on the chalet verandah after dinner, watching the sun setting low across the Straits.

'It were better than ten bob a week on the dole,' he replied in his slow whining voice. 'I was only nineteen in 1934, my father had lost his job in the local clothing factory as the slump of the thirties hit the industry. I had only had the occasional odd job, errand boy and such like, since leaving school at fourteen. The RAF seemed a steady job, and a chance to see something of the world; so I signed on for twelve years.'

'How do you feel about things now, after seven years in uniform, and at least another two before you see home again?'

Tommy gave a couple of puffs on his Will's Gold Flake. 'I'm happy enough, there's nobody particular waiting for me back in Brummy, or anywhere else; my father died of TB not long after I joined the RAF; mother married again and has another family to look after. My sister married at eighteen, while my brother, serving in the Army, is engaged to be married; so I heard in the last letter from Blighty.'

'Is there not someone waiting for you, whom you might set up home with after the war?'

'I thought there might be, until the war started; then she started going out with some sod in a reserved occupation, so my sister wrote and told me, and the bastard's put her in the club.'

I mumbled my condolences as best I could: something about 'It's happening all the time, with women lowering their defences, and their knickers, thinking they may not get many chances of fulfilment with most of the able-bodied

25

men going away to the war.'

'That's true,' said Tommy. 'I was saving myself for Brenda, until I got the news a few weeks ago. Me, twenty-six, and never had sex with any woman in my life. Where better than Singapore to put that matter right? I went out that night, with my $10 in my pocket, for the nearest brothel. By the way, it's not true what they say about Chinese girls!'

In some way I was pleased to hear this; at least I was not quite so self-conscious about being *virgo intacto* still at twenty-one; I had another five years to fulfil my desires before breaking Tommy's record!

Sex, of course, was usually the main topic of conversation after sundown in the canteen or billet. The braggers, much in the majority, were always happy to find a receptive ear, and my sexual education, so lacking before I joined up, was advanced considerably as I listened to the lascivious love yarns of the lechers: and most of the old hands were proud to be known as such. In Malaya there was much more scope for amorous adventure than the North-West Frontier of India, where most had languished for years. Now they were making up for lost time with a vengeance. There was not much male competition in Penang; the Army and the Navy were not in evidence, and the RAF had only recently set up camp. There seemed to be a plentiful supply of Chinese girls who were quite willing to co-operate, or so I was told, and the brothels were always pimping for business.

From early days in training one was constantly being lectured about the effects of VD. I remember that I was fascinated the first time we were ordered to attend the MO's lecture in the canteen at Innsworth Lane, specially cleared of female NAAFI staff for the occasion. It was the week that the camp was to start being used as an intake centre for WAAFs. No doubt that had some bearing on the matter, for they were lectured similarly the next day. I had never even heard of VD, let alone knew what the letters stood for, and what they meant. I was somewhat taken aback when some of the more extreme examples of the disease were flashed on to a screen.

Nevertheless, I was surprised how many macho types passed out cold at the sight. Sex can be a wonderful thing, but I suppose every silver lining has to have a cloud.

The CO of 27 squadron had long since given up lecturing the airmen about the terrors of venereal disease. It was just general knowledge that contraceptives could be had free from the MO's orderly, when embarking on a dirty night out; and there was a wash room, with medical aids, behind the guard room when you got back. It was quite surprising to the naive ones, like myself, just who was prepared to make use of the facilities. The extrovert types, who were far in the majority, bragged about their experiences next morning. But there was one wireless operater sergeant with a neat clipped moustache and smoothed down hair above an aquiline nose which emphasised his aloof expression: one would have thought him above sexual vices. Not a bit of it. As we followed him up the ramp of the Penang Ferry one Saturday his attaché case knocked the guard rail, bursting open the fastening of the case; out tumbled his pyjamas, shaving kit, tooth brush, and three little flat cylindrical containers that could only have contained one thing. It was impossible to contain our merriment as he groped around on the quay, red-faced and most undignified, his story about going to listen to a concert burst wide open.

Although it may have seemed like it, all was not beer and sex, such as the various expeditions that I, and one or two colleagues, set out to accomplish on free weekends. The first of these was to reach the top of Mount Penang, some two and a half thousand feet above sea level. I have always had an urge to reach the highest geographic point near where I happen to be at the time: sometimes the ambition has been thwarted, or has ended in disaster. It was the easiest of mountains to reach the summit of, unless you were deliberately looking for a difficult route, something that one was not inclined to do in temperatures hovering in the nineties. In fact, it was some ten degrees cooler at the top of Penang Peak, which was reached in a highly civilised manner by trolleybus and funicular railway. A touch of the Swiss there. Had we not got caught out shelterless in a sudden and vicious thunderstorm all would have been well.

Then there was the expedition to Kedah Peak. At three and a half thousand feet, and thirty-five miles north of Butterworth Camp, that was rather more ambitious. We had a bone-shaking ride on a native bus to start with, then a seven mile climb, excluding short cuts through the jungle, to a rest house at the summit. There was something forbidding about the Peak, which rose up stark from the plains around it; in primeval time it must have been a volcano. In the months ahead I was to remember the foreboding I felt as we trudged up the track through the jungle, with apes gibbering around us and the constant singing of cricket-like insects and raucous birds. It was the giant

27

spiders' webs, with hosts to match, that scared me most. Again we were caught flat-footed by a deluge on the way down. We never seemed to learn the lesson that in Malaya the heavens invariably open up every day. Three dripping rats boarded the bus back to camp.

Some four weeks after our arrival the men we had come to replace were 'on the Blighty Boat': a phrase used for the home posting. That was one hell of an excuse for a binge. Indeed, it never needed much excuse; pay day or a delivery in from the brewers, were well accepted reasons for pushing out the boat.

The quaffing of beer provided the setting for the airmen and NCOs to air their repertoire of dirty songs. I was really quite spellbound at first by the apparently inexhaustible supply.

I learnt all about Salome:

> Standing there, with her ----- bare,
> waiting for someone to slide it there.

The 'Good Ship Venus' was quite a favourite, with its immortal lines about the cabin boy:

> Who stuffed his-----,
> with broken glass,
> and circumcised the skipper!

The more ambitious vocalists would plump for the adventures of Ivan Skavinsky Skivar, and Abdul The Bul Bul Emir, whose prodigious sexual feats were the wonder of all; and ended the last verse with one jumping on the other's back when he was down on his knees – which wasn't surprising.

The general format of proceedings, as the beer began to loosen tongues, was a spontaneous shout from some quarter calling on old so-and-so to give us a song: 'Sing you bastard sing, or show your f-----g ring.' I can only remember one person plumping for the latter and that was the much despised Engineering Officer, who was incautious enough to be passing by in the latter stages of one beer night. 'We call on E/O Edwards to sing us a song,' and then the usual chant, shouted by everyone at the top of their voices, so that it could be heard in Georgetown across the water. The luckless E/O

Edwards, seeing no ready escape route without considerable loss of face, decided to bluff it out. Jumping up on to the table he began to unbutton his belt, banking on the fact that no one particularly wanted to gaze up his fundamental orifice, which many had been accused of crawling up in the past: he was right.

I was fascinated with it all, but lived in constant terror that one night I would be called upon to face the option of song or ring. Fortunately, they invariably called on someone they knew could be relied upon to belt out a ditty, and all had their favourite verses ready. It was only after several weeks, hiding behind my beer mug in a dark corner, that someone slurred out my name; most of them were too legless even to think of a name by then. My rendering of the first two verses of 'Salome', in a voice squeaky with fright, had them doubling up in laughter at me, rather than the song, which they had heard countless times before anyway.

When we joined 27 Squadron we were told that the role of our unit in Malaya was to open up new airfields throughout the peninsula, then to return to a base in India. Nobody ever said anything about trying to stem a Japanese invasion. Even in the unlikely event of the little yellow bastards trying it on, these fine upstanding men, with the spearhead of skilled and experienced pilots, would soon send them packing back to Nagasaki with fleas in their ears. Anyhow, their aircraft, so we were told, were only poor imitations of those we had discarded as obsolete years ago. Everyone knew that when a beer night ended with that ringing alliteration shouted at the top of everyone's voice, 'We would rather ----- than fight', it was a complete reversal of the truth. I was to remember that in the dark days ahead.

On 22 June came the news that Germany had invaded Russia. One's first reaction was that it must relieve the pressure on our loved ones in England: the mighty blitz could be expected to end. But looking deeper it seemed that the Wehrmacht, flushed with victories throughout Europe, must soon overcome the Russians, however vast the terrain that must be conquered. Surely Hitler could not make the same mistake as that other corporal dictator by not finishing the job before the winter snows swept down from the Steppes.

Whichever way the war in Russia went it seemed likely to me that the Japanese would be fully paid up members of the World War II club before Christmas. If Russia collapsed before the snows Japan would want to come in for the pickings in Siberia and the Russian territories on her northern doorstep. If Russia held out until wintertime Germany would exert her influence on Japan to relieve the pressure in the East. In this event the Japanese would be sure to take the opportunity to absorb the coveted British possessions on the southern fringes of her territorial gains to the south, particularly the key port of Singapore. That was my thinking: possibly naive.

Having thought all that out I promptly forgot it again and got on with enjoying myself; for life was too short, and might be much shorter than expected: I was only twenty-one, after all.

Tropical climates are said to render the male more randy, and I don't suppose we new lads were any exception. However, my first experience of a brothel took me by surprise, and I ran a mile. Fruity and I had ventured into Georgetown to see what was to be had, before finishing up, after dusk, at the Elysée dance hall. Whilst strolling through one of the bazaar areas in a less salubrious part of the town, we were buttonholed by a young Chinese man who beckoned us to follow him. He dived into a rather sleazy doorway and started up a staircase covered with linoleum. At this stage I was all for turning round and bolting, pointing out to Fruity that we hardly had the price of a meal with us, let alone anything else.

'Come on, Ken, let's go and see what they have to offer,' was Fruity's enthusiastic comment. Much against my natural instincts I followed to the top of the stairs, along a bleak corridor and into an equally bleak room which contained just two beds, neither of which looked at all comfortable; which was probably because they weren't meant to encourage prolonged occupation. A single white sheet on each appeared to cover plain boarding.

'You wait here marters,' (the letter 's' appeared to be missing in Chinese English). 'I go fetch girls.'

'How much?' said Fruity.

'Ten dollars – short time,' said the pimp.

'Too much: five dollars,' rejoined Fruity.

'You see girls first – I go fetch,' and off he went down the corridor.

'You steaming idiot, Fruity, we haven't got ten dollars between us, even if I wanted to get my leg across, and I don't much in these dismal surroundings.'

'Wait on,' said Fruity, 'at least we can see the goods; they may settle for a fondle for five!'

After a few minutes a young Chinese girl came slowly and shyly into the

30

room; she probably was no more than fifteen years of age, and really quite pretty, as Oriental lasses go. She was probably the sister of the pimp, I thought.

A few paces behind came an older woman; that's the mother, I thought. She was plump and doing her best to cover the pock marks on her face with an ear to ear smile of welcome. That in itself was enough to put me off – a cert dose of the clap from that quarter, thought I; and I knew which one I would get if it came to the crunch.

That was the point at which I took fright and headed fast for the stairs, mumbling something about not having any money. Fruity could do nothing but follow, protesting all the while, for he barely had the ferry fare back in his pocket.

When we were on Penang Island we would quite often be approached, sometimes in the street, sometimes in a bar, by white folk, usually English or American, who had spotted the RAF eagle flashes on our tunics. The RAF was new to that part of the world, although they had had a large base in Singapore for some while. To meet men who had actually served in the Royal Air Force in England during the Battle of Britain, and suffered the blitz that followed, brought wonder and admiration into their eyes, and many free drinks and meals to us. I hated to shatter their illusions by telling them that I had been training in a place well inland during the whole of the Battle of Britain; and although I had served for three weeks on the airfield at Middle Wallop, one of the airfields bombed by the Luftwaffe in 1940, it all happened while I was laid up at home with broncho-pneumonia. True, I had been in London during the blitz, but was not there for some of the worst raids.

The truth was that I had great difficulty in convincing myself that England had won a great victory in the Battle of Britain, when the phrase was first announced to the world by Winston Churchill in October 1940. To me it was just a big propaganda exercise; the pilots and airmen were just doing the job for which they had joined the Service, and getting the experiences and excitements they had sought. I think, nevertheless, it is true to say that patriotism played its part.

When Germany turned its back on England in June 1941 and faced eastwards towards Russia, it began to dawn on me that perhaps Churchill was telling the truth after all; it was not just propaganda: the Old Country had achieved a real victory in the Battle of Britain. In terms of dog fighting the German doberman had failed to wrest the bone of England from the British bulldog. I did not know then how soon it would be before I was to experience, at very close quarters, just how important to a military force was air superiority. Only fifteen short months after the climax of the Battle of Britain the Royal Air Force was to suffer its most humiliating defeat, leaving the Eagle in tatters on the ground. In fact, we let down badly those generous and starry-eyed people who wined and dined us on Penang Island.

Chapter 6

B y mid-July it became knowledge, by way of what was always referred to as jungle drums, that we would be moving some miles north in about a month's time to open up another new airfield.

In the time left to us at Butterworth, with its easy access to the fleshpots of Penang, we decided to try and make the most of our time, to the extent that money would allow. I had just committed myself to pay M$17 for the purchase of a tennis racket, remitted in fortnightly instalments each payday. I was due to pay the final instalment, and take delivery of the racket, about the time we were due to move northwards. As we had been told the new camp was to be in the middle of a rubber plantation, and nowhere near a town of any size, my much prized racket did not seem likely to get much use. As it turned out I never *was* able to play with it. I have often wondered since whether the Japs brought in any tennis balls. I fully expect they used it for filtering their rice. What a waste of $17; I could have had two bangs in Penang, had I been so minded, or even an all night session for the price of that tennis racket. Still I was a virgin when we left Butterworth.

If I wasn't able to play tennis, at least I was able to play cricket, which was something I did know how to do. I imagined myself being the hero of 27 Squadron, who had been challenged to a match by the Planter's Club in Penang. In fact, our team was comprised of eight officers and only three airmen, one of whom, a medical orderly who was the third person living in my chalet, had opened the bowling for a Yorkshire Colt's XI before the war. He bowled through most of the innings, taking seven wickets, and I was not even asked to turn my arm over. When it came to batting the officers batted from numbers one to eight, and were all back in the pavillion for about 50. I came in at number ten and carried my bat for nought not out! Still it was a 'right royal do' afterwards, with real English girls (officers only of course) to ply us with food and drink in the sumptuous surrounding of the clubhouse. I suppose our hosts thought that they were making some small contribution towards the war effort by providing a few hours' relaxation for a few of those who were there to defend them. What a rude awakening they were to get in the not too distant future.

On one of the last Sundays before moving north Brem and I decided to explore inland, perhaps as far as the Thailand border. What we would now refer to as mini-buses were really quite efficient on these country journeys. By midday we had penetrated some fifty-odd miles to the small town of Baling, in the State of Kedah. It would have been like any other small Malayan township were it not for a vast column of rock that seemed to tower, sheer on one side, some two thousand feet towards the sky. There was something eerie and sinister about it; I daresay our primeval ancestors thought so too, as they carved out their caves that could still be seen in the lower reaches. At the base was a cavern that clearly had been some sort of temple for a religion no longer practised, for Buddhism was the generally accepted religion of both Chinese and Malays, and this cavern contained no statues of the Buddha. It was easy to imagine that brontosauruses and pterodactyls still occupied the summit, which appeared to have no visible means of access.

From Baling we covered the few miles to the Thailand border, just for the kick of looking across the border gate to a country that was still, in theory at least, neutral. Technically we would have been interned had we ventured past the gate. When the invasion came I expect that the little yellow men swarmed across the border at that spot on their way from the east coast landings around Kuanton and Kota Baharu, to reach the west coast of Malaya and the south.

It was on that same day that Brem and I journeyed to Baling that Fruity found himself a girlfriend in Penang. Next morning he could not wait to tell us about her. She was Chinese, twenty years, very pretty, and her name was Wong Befung. According to Fruity she was a cut above the Chinese girls who were dance hostesses in the Elysée ballroom. He had walked her home from the dance hall to her home in the northern outskirts of Georgetown. It was quite a large house where she lived with her two younger sisters, two brothers, and her widower father, whom she described as a sea captain plying his vessel along the trading stations and ports between Assam and Java. Fruity was introduced to him, and came away with the impression that

34

he was favourably disposed towards the English, whose language he spoke quite well.

It was clear that Fruity was quite smitten by Befung (Chinese for beautiful), and could hardly wait for the next opportunity to develop the relationship. He even offered to introduce us to the two sisters, who were just as pretty and, he thought, were twins aged about sixteen. It was an invitation that was to have considerable influence on our future lives, but not the next Sunday, for on that very Monday we were told we would be moving next Monday to Sungei Patani, in the State of Kedah, and the next weekend all would be confined to camp packing up. Fruity, Brem and I were all named in the first party to go.

In fact, we didn't move next Monday, partly because an eminent visitor was due to visit the squadron in order to inspect the aircraft for which he had donated money. I suppose it had to be the CO's plane, for which I was the airframe fitter, that was hastily decorated, underneath the pilot's window, with the coat of arms of the Maharajah of Patiala. He was an impressive figure of a man with a pointed beard and Svengali moustache, topped with a turban to match his army officer's uniform. In spite of his fabled millions he didn't slip a tenner, or anything, to the ground crew as he was shown around the aircraft. The CO took off, putting the kite through its paces up and around the airfield, which did not seem to excite His Highness very much – I suppose he had seen it all before.

Another bit of excitement that week was the visit to a Royal Naval cruiser, HMS *Danae*, at anchor off Penang. It was my first visit to a warship, and we were shown all around the vessel, including the near steam heat of the engine room. I came away feeling rather glad that I had joined the RAF and not the Navy. It was all a bit claustrophobic; and if fired upon at sea there was nowhere else to go.

One of the things I would miss was the dip in the sea after work. From our chalet it was only one hundred yards to the water. Admittedly the water was a bit grubby, as it was not very far from the moorage of Georgetown harbour, and the numerous boats of all shapes and sizes that used the harbour were in the habit of discharging their wastage and dirty oil, which would tend to drift our way. I was no great swimmer when I came to Malaya, but I improved a lot with practice at Butterworth, and this was to stand me in good stead later.

35

On the night before we were due to leave, with everything packed up and ready to go, Brem and I took a stroll along the beach at dusk, watching the sand crabs scuttle away to their holes – always a fascination, for some were quite large, and fearsome-looking in the twilight, with their little glinting eyes stuck up on stalks above their shells.

Just inland from the dunes we espied a lamp around which we could make out several shadowy figures. Our curiosity got the better of us and we moved closer. In fact, there were two little circles, all men who presumably were employed through the day on the various construction jobs being carried out around the camp.

One group of about six seemed to be Chinese, and playing a game which I believed to be Mah-Jong. Money was changing hands fast as they slapped what looked like counters on to an improvised table amid much clatter and shouting; so much so that they did not even notice us.

However, we were noticed by the outer circle of men, who were probably Malays. I did not know what the population division was between Malays and Chinese in Malaya. The Chinese were certainly more industrious than the Malays, and tended to congregate in and around the urban areas, which was where we usually were; so to us there seemed to be more Chinese than Malays.

As we were led into the circle we could see what was occupying them. In the middle was a contraption resembling a kettle, with a long flexible pipe leading out of it, the end being held by each man in turn while he took a long drag of the smoke within before passing on to the next man. So this was the hookah, about which I had heard, purported to be used by opium smokers. There was no going back now, for the men clearly showed they considered it a privilege to be asked to take a puff at the pipe. We in turn, just as clearly, must show that we appreciate being so honoured. I would not have fancied being around if they turned nasty. I took a swig which hit my lungs like a tornado, forcing me to cough and splutter, much to the merriment of the assembled company. I don't know if it was opium that we inhaled; if so, we did not become addicted.

On 20 August we finally swung out of the gates of Butterworth camp, a column of some thirty lorries, mostly laden with stores and some forty of us, armed with rifles, supposedly guarding the valuables.

I was sorry to be leaving Butterworth camp, the living quarters of which still retained the air of a holiday camp, particularly with its adjacent beach and view of Penang Island and its spectacular mountain, on the top of which the lights of houses twinkled at night. A thing of beauty most evenings, for all to see, was the spectacular sunset across the Straits of Malacca; on occasions it was difficult to believe it was real. We would miss these simple things, for we had been told that the new camp of Sungei Patani was more primitive, lacking many of the pleasures we enjoyed at Butterworth.

As the wheeled convoy moved along the road to the north on its twenty-one mile journey, the inhabitants of all the little villages lined the roadside, the younger ones waving uninhibitedly, their elders just curious to see what all the noise was about. I daresay there were a few odd Japanese spies amongst the spectators, but we never gave it a thought. Anyhow, I am sure we could not have differentiated between a Chink and a Jap.

Chapter 7

My first impression of Sungei Patani was one of gloominess. Maybe it was the fact that nearly all of the Air Ministry land, apart from the actual airfield, was beneath the rubber trees.

Rubber trees, which usually grow some sixty to seventy feet high, are not the most beautiful of nature's arboreous plants, even in their natural state, which they are not permitted to accomplish in Malaya for the sake of commerce. Like vast regiments of soldiers they stand upright in evenly spaced rows across the undulating ground. Side-shoots are shorn off to the height of a two-storey house, and the precious bark is thinly scraped each day, diagonally around the trunk, to enable the sap to bleed into a cup.

Our living quarters consisted of two-storey timber constructions, covered with roofs of *atap* (a type of thatch made from interwoven palm leaves), designed to house comfortably about fifty men. The billets were dispersed around the rubber plantation, only two or three rubber trees being uprooted for each building. The leaves from the trees on either side of each billet must have rendered them almost invisible from above. From the point of view of camouflage that may have been a good thing, and it helped to reduce the burning rays of the sun; but in other respects it was always gloomy, engendering a feeling of foreboding which was always with me during those weeks at Sungei Patani; and which proved to be well founded.

The airfield itself, which from necessity was cleared of trees for several acres, was a more cheerful place. Those were the days before concrete landing strips, and it was only necessary to provide a lump of ground where water would drain away quickly in order not to bog down the aircraft after rain. Flying was still a fair-weather thing: it did not seem to be envisaged that our Blenheims, which were light enough to be able to land on grass, might have had to operate in monsoon conditions.

The airfield stretched across a gentle dome of land, from our aircraft dispersal points and maintenance areas on the west side, to the eastern extremity which was bordered by the Federal Malay States Railway line. No longer could we see the sea from the camp, but we had a good view of Mount Kedah, only a smudge on the horizon from Butterworth, but now within five or six miles.

By mid-morning on that first full day at Sungei our calm was shattered as the full squadron of Blenheims roared in echelon formation across the airfield, some two thousand feet up, breaking formation in turn to the north of the airfield and swooping over our heads at tree-top height, before gliding in to land. It was nearly an hour later before the last engine was switched off and peace and quiet reigned again.

We were not yet, in those late August days, on a war footing, so most Sundays were free to do as we wished. Brem and I, always keen to explore, took the first opportunity to 'beat the bounds'. The barbed wire of the boundary fence proved more extensive than we had expected, taking us a good five miles to circumnavigate, and covering some fairly rough terrain. From a vantage point on the northern side, Brem, who had scrambled up ahead of me, suddenly exclaimed, 'There's a wide estuary over there, and what looks like the sea beyond.'

'A fine view, yes,' I responded, 'but so what?'

'Don't you see? If the Japs come, and we get cut off, we could have a little boat hidden in those mangrove swamps down there, and paddle our way across to Sumatra.'

'That all sounds delightfully simple,' I replied with no real conviction in my voice. But the seed of thought had been sown, and it was an idea we were, or rather Brem was, to resurrect some weeks later.

I was always the one to think that the worst would never happen. I can't think why I never got killed because of it. Brem was an ideal foil to my super optimism, for he always expected the worst. I was to be very very grateful for his attitude to life in the months ahead.

Sungei Patani provided fewer opportunities for socialising. The small town near to the RAF camp was no more than one main street with a couple of dozen shops and stalls down each side, and no cinema or bars. After a few weeks some enterprising and patriotic Europeans opened up a serviceman's canteen in the local Planter's Club, and it proved a pleasant venue to relax and have a rather better meal than we would get back in camp.

A much bigger problem at Sungei Patani was the mosquitoes. On landing at Singapore we were first introduced to the mosquito net, which was standard equipment for everyone, and it was an offence if not used, for an attack of malaria meant a week or more off work. By all accounts malaria was none too pleasant, so you didn't forget to tuck your net under your mattress at night. Even one mosquito that had somehow found its way inside the net could ruin a night's sleep. In Sungei Patani camp the mossies swarmed every night in their thousands particularly after heavy rain, which meant most days. I was wont to write quite a lot, and often it became difficult to see the paper clearly for the mosquitoes that swarmed in the lamplight. I was one of the lucky ones who were not affected badly by mosquito bites and certainly I never caught malaria throughout my stay in Malaya.

As the month of September drew to a close I was transferred back from 'the Flights' to the servicing section in order to help in a programme of modifications to be carried out on the Blenheims. All planes were to be fitted with armour plating behind the pilots' seats, and self-sealing petrol tanks. Various other technical jobs, that were not too easy to do in a jungle station, were carried out in order to put the planes on a better war footing, benefiting from lessons learnt during the Battle of Britain and the bombing of the Ruhr. It all proved to be a monumental waste of time in the event of what was to happen.

As September gave way to October we began to think less about the prospects of war. In any case, surely the Japanese would not dare to take on the might of the British Empire in the Far East, personified by Singapore with its mighty Naval base. Surely we only had to sally forth with a couple of battleships like the *Prince of Wales* and the *Repulse* to put down any ideas of establishing beach-heads on the east coast of Malaya. True, we in the RAF knew the air cover was a bit fragile; we really needed Spitfires and Hurricanes, but they were required for more urgent duties nearer home. Then there were the Americans, with their much trumpeted Pacific Fleet, based at Pearl Harbour in Hawaii. How could the Japs invade in the Malayan Peninsula without bringing down the US Navy on to them like a swarm of hornets? Such thoughts would bring comfort to us in those October days as we fiddled with our little modifications to the ageing Blenheims – Mark I – thinking all the while that our efforts were doing little towards ending World War II.

However, by mid-October there was the first of the invasion scares, causing us to work all the night through. We never knew what information started it, or indeed how we came to be 'stood down' after a couple of days. Nevertheless, the minor jolt in our normal routine was enough to trigger off thoughts, at least with Brem, of trying to construct our escape craft.

Brem was the one with practical experience of the sea; living my life in North London my first-hand knowledge of boats was confined to those one hired, at sixpence per hour, on the Alexandra Palace boating lake.

Brem's formative years were spent on the family croft near John O'Groats, which was within a stone's throw of the sea. In summer months, when the Caithness climate permitted it, he would be out in a dinghy fishing in the bay. I would kid him it was really coracles that they used in those parts, like the Ancient Brits.

Indeed, the craft we planned was something like a coracle, but elongated. It had to be constructed of light materials or we would not be able to lower it down from the first floor balcony near to our bed-spaces, where we planned to construct it, to ground level. Nor would we relish humping it the not inconsiderable distance to the nearest river if it weighed more than a few pounds. So the basic construction was to be a keel of 2" x 1" timber, some eight feet in length, with a prow at each end of similar material. The ribs, both lengthwise and at intervals across the beam, were to be strips of bamboo cane. These materials could easily be acquired from the local building labourers for the cost of a few cents left on the seats of their contractor's lorries, which were still busy around the camp. The RAF stores provided screws and rivets unknowingly. We were using thousands of rivets carrying out our modifications to the aircraft, so that a couple of hundred or so weren't going to be missed.

It was the rivets that somewhat strained what goodwill we had built up with our 'oppos' in the billet. They thought we were nuts building a boat anyway, especially during the after *tiffin* 'heads-down' on *charpoys*, the Indian name for a wood framed bed interwoven with coarse coconut hemp. Only mad dogs and Englishmen worked between 2 and 4 p.m. Screws can be secured silently, but we did not need very many, just for the main frame. Drilling with a hand-brace was a fairly quiet operation; but no way could you secure rivets without generating quite a racket. After ten minutes or so of riveting the chorus of hopeful snoozers would throw such remarks as 'belt up' or 'stop that f----g racket'; usually followed by a flying boot. Hence the job was taking rather longer than we had hoped.

By 25 October we had started to cover the completed framework with fabric, which was, in fact, a couple of surplus bed sheets wheedled from the stores clerk for the price of two beers in the canteen. When the material was only roughly tacked in position there came an urgent message for all personnel to report immediately to their places of work. This was it, we thought, the Japs have crossed the border somewhere the other side of Kedah Peak and are swarming southwards. It looked as if all the sweat and toil we had put in on our boat was to be in vain. But it all turned out to be a false alarm; or maybe it was just a ruse by Air Headquarters to see how quickly we could react.

By the last but one day of the month we had completed the construction work on our boat, but had been unable to misappropriate any dope, the stuff used for covering aircraft fabric, as the flight paint store was well padlocked, and the flight sergeant kept the key. We considered that he was incorruptible; so there was nothing for it but to go down to the village and buy paint. Paint would be inferior to aircraft dope, because of the astringent qualities of the latter which helped to stretch tight the fabric as it dried; but beggars couldn't be choosers.

We were further delayed the next day when we came to open up our tins of green paint, to find that one had deteriorated beyond use because of air getting into the tin where it had corroded. However, by sundown on the first Saturday in November the job was completed. The next day, Sunday 2 November 1941, was to be the occasion of the grand launching.

After breakfast, with the last coat of paint still sticky to the touch, we lowered our baby down from the upper floor balcony, and with an end each on our shoulders Brem and I commenced the long trek down through the rubber trees to find a suitable stream, amid derisive shouts from above. Nevertheless, I am sure they were glad to see the backs of us with our boat; at least they would now be able to resume their after *tiffin* naps in their 'pits' – provided the Japs allowed them to do so.

We did not exactly send out invitations to attend the launching ceremony, or indeed encourage anyone to follow us. For one thing we did not really know the venue nor could we be over-confident that the boat was going to be seaworthy. We could imagine the merriment and derision if it tipped us into the water – which is exactly what did happen. It was not exactly *us* who got wet, for Brem had adhered strictly to his maxim, which stood him in good stead right throughout his service career, never to volunteer for anything.

In the green, well watered country of Malaya one never has to travel far without finding water. The ditches of the rubber plantations disgorge each day's rainfall, which is sometimes several inches, into streams which soon become wide rivers, usually bordered by jungle or swamp. At the edge of our plantation there was a causeway with sufficient water to test the floating qualities of our little vessel. Marvellous; it floated and remained upright. What we did not take into account was the fact that the water only just about covered the keel. In other words it was badly in need of ballast. As soon as I stepped on to the flimsy base board it was rather like trying to walk a tightrope, a skill in which I had no practice. After two or three wild lurches the obvious happened, my thunderous splash creasing Brem up into convulsions of laughter as he perched high and dry on the bank. One does not much mind getting a soaking in equatorial climes, for we only wore shorts, but my Baby Brownie also got a ducking, and so eliminated the chance of capturing the launching ceremony on film for posterity.

'Cut out the cackle,' I remonstrated to the still smirking Brem, as I tried ruefully to dry out my Brownie. 'What do we do next? – you're the skipper.'

In the course of my desperate flailings during the brief few seconds in the canoe a large rent had appeared in the bottom, either caused by my foot or a submerged root. Whatever it was, the craft wasn't going to float properly without repairs and a fair bit of ballasting, neither of which could we do then and there.

'Let's see if we can get it down nearer to the creek, which will give us more water and should not be far away,' was Brem's considered advice. Unfortunately, it did not prove to be the best advice, for the streams led us into some fairly impenetrable jungle, and not a little swamp, before finally disgorging into the tidal creek. By the time we had hacked our way through several hours later, the boat had suffered further damage as we hauled the waterlogged hulk on to a bank, and we were well plastered in mud. We did not need to bother about that for it was soon washed off by the usual mid-afternoon deluge.

However, our journey was not wasted, for we espied in the creek nearby, secured by ropes to roots of trees, two sampans. There was not a soul in sight, and no habitation visible, so we could not resist casting off on one of the little crafts, not unlike the aforementioned boats on the Ally Pally lake, and paddled our course quietly, so as not to arouse any owner who might be within earshot, down the mangrove-bordered creek.

With the sampan safely tethered back again Brem uttered the thoughts that were in the minds of both of us: 'If the Japs come before we can repair our canoe, perhaps the sampan owners, whomsoever they may be, won't mind us borrowing one of their boats for a short sea trip.'

'Even if we do get the canoe repaired,' I rejoined, 'I would rather paddle to Sumatra in a sampan.' In fact, I didn't much relish the prospect of either alternative, but didn't like to hurt Brem's feelings too much by telling him so. As it was to turn out, our experiences that day were to prove vital in our fight for survival later.

By the middle Sunday in November, the 16th, Brem and I felt in need of a change of scenery and occupation; perhaps the boat building could wait for a bit. Had we but known it we were into the period of calm before the storm.

We had heard about the town of Alor Star, some thirty miles further north. The name was put on the map, as far as the rest of the world was concerned, in 1930, when Amy Johnson made it her last touch-down for refuelling before Singapore on her record-breaking flight to Sydney.

As it turned out the day proved to be rather disappointing. After the first five miles the road passed the base of Mound Kedah, from whence it ran almost straight for about twenty miles, bordered by dykes across marshy land not unlike the Cambridgeshire Fens, but a great deal hotter and steamier. When we reached Alor Star I was not surprised that Amy Johnson only wanted to top up with a few 4-gallon cans of high octane, and couldn't wait to get in the air again. We had to wait three hours for a bus back. Come to think of it, the Japs didn't hang around Alor Star too long either. It is one of those places that just does not match up to its romantic sounding name.

Alor Star was the furthest north in Malaya that we were ever to reach. During the following week we were told that we would soon be leaving to set up another camp at a place called Cyrenaica. Maybe that was further north for I was unable to find such a name on a map. If it was I am sure that the Japs were able to make good use of it, for we never did.

On the last Monday in November, we learnt that we were going to get reinforcements, in the shape of a Royal Australian Air Force squadron of

44

Brewster Buffaloes. On the Wednesday they duly arrived.

I don't think any of us had set eyes before on the American built radial-engined Buffalo, sometimes referred to as the flying beer barrel. We could see the likeness, as the squadron buzzed noisily across the 'drome before landing; rather like a swarm of bees, escorted by the queen bee in the shape of an all-American Boston twin-engined light bomber. From the racket their single engines made, considerably more decibels than our twin-engined Blenheims, I could see we were going to enjoy little peace while they were around.

I suppose that the Brewster Aero Company had designed the Buffalo as a fighter plane, but it had no great speed, with its short stubby wings and body to match. It was something like a monoplane version of the venerable Gloster Gladiator, with its radial engine that kicked up such a din on take-off. I would think that the US Department of War were quite glad to get them off their hands.

By the last weekend in November the storm clouds of war were beginning to gather. There was to be no Sunday jaunt on the last day of the month, or messing about with our boat; we had to work. It was a question of working on and on, night and day, until either every aircraft was serviceable or we dropped out from exhaustion. By the afternoon of Tuesday 2 December we had finished the work; every aircraft was fit to fly, and we were able to crawl back to the billets for a long sleep.

Right up until Friday 5 December I was firmly convinced that Japan could not, and would not, risk a war against the combined might of the Allies and the United States of America.

On Saturday 6 December, in mid-afternoon, a 'number one' state of emergency was declared. The aircraft engines were all warmed up ready for take-off at a minute's notice, black-outs were put up throughout the camp, and we were told to pack in readiness for moving within four hours' notice. Those such as myself, who had no immediate task to do, were told to return to billets and get as much sleep as possible.

By dawn next morning nothing had happened, but there was an ominous calm, and a tension in the air that you could almost feel. No one felt like talking very much. On that Sunday, 7 December 1941, the daylight hours ticked slowly away and darkness again covered the rubber trees around us. Unbeknown to us the Japanese were on the very brink of the invasion that must have been planned in detail for many a day.

Far to the east of us, across the International Date Line in the Pacific, dawn was beginning to break on what was to be one of the most momentous days in the history of World War II and, in magnitude, of all wars in history. As we slept that night, the holocaust that was the attack on Pearl Harbour was taking place. As soon as the Japanese High Command knew the main US fleet was crippled and out of action, the fleet waiting in the Gulf of Siam was given the green light to move. Before dawn had broken in Malaya, landing craft were moving in towards the east coast beaches around Kota Bahru and Kuantan; aircraft were taking off from carriers and airfields within range of the southern tip of French Indo-China, recently conquered by the Japs. A token raid by a small number of long range bombers was carried out on Singapore itself. The citizens of Singapore were asleep and unprepared, with lights still blazing unshuttered.

One of the first Japanese aims was to eliminate the risk of the Royal Air Force hindering their seaborne landing; and so the first flights of bombers took off as dawn was breaking to immobilise the key airfields of Kota Bahru, Sungei Patani and Butterfield.

In our maintenance section billet we were blissfully unaware of all that was going on. In our sleep we thought we were dreaming that our aircraft had taken off in the dark. It was no dream; the flight crews had all been called out in the night, and most of our planes had taken off by dawn. This we were told as we made our way that morning through the rubber trees to the cookhouse. Within a hundred yards of the mess-room we could hear the drone of aircraft approaching above the canopy of rubber tree leaves. Our aircraft returning after another false alarm? But you don't live with your aircraft week in, week out, without knowing instinctively the sounds of their engines. By the time the planes were overhead we detected a more metallic sound in the rhythm of the engines. Too late: as the thought struck home that the planes might not be ours, so did the bombs. In those first few seconds it seemed inconceivable that bombs were really falling on the camp, until I saw through the rubber trees the lethal orange flashes as another stick of bombs hit the ground. With the next stick whistling on its way Brem and I dived for the nearest ditch.

In a couple of minutes the immediate danger was past; for several men on other parts of the camp there would never be another day. As the noise of the aircraft engines faded away we picked ourselves up, still clutching knife, fork and spoon and tin mug; instinctively, like beheaded chickens, which we might well have been, our legs carried us on into the cookhouse.

We were now at war, with a vengeance; but the true desperation of our situation had yet to sink in.

Chapter 8

I no longer had much of an appetite by the time we reached the cookhouse counter; which was just as well, for the cooks had all disappeared. As Brem and I sipped our mugs of tea a second wave of bombers swept across the 'drome, unloading their bombs, which mercifully fell on other parts of the camp, the most spectacular result of which was the ignition of a petrol dump, sending flames and billowing clouds of black smoke several hundred feet into the air. It was a grim beacon for our returning planes which flew low across the airfield, circling round to find a clear strip between the bomb craters sufficient for landing. The seven planes that had taken off during the night all returned safely, the pilots claiming to have shot down four of the Jap bombers on their way back. However, two Blenheims that were not used in the raid had been set on fire by the bombing.

There were several casualties in the first raid, particularly amongst the coolies working on the camp, for there had been no warning, and many did not know they should throw themselves flat on the ground. There was the gruesome sight of one poor man staggering around, blinded, and with much of his face missing.

Down on the 'drome the first priority for us, the maintenance flight, was to fill in the bomb craters that had straddled the airfield. So green was I about active service, after two hours of total war, that it never occurred to me how vulnerable we were out there in the middle of the airfield. Although the enemy had inflicted a great deal of damage on RAF Sungei Patani I suppose it was hardly likely he was going to leave it at that. Around 11 o'clock we were left in no doubt.

Percy Prosser, one of the fitters in our gang, was blessed with rather better eyesight than most. Pointing towards Kedah Peak he gave a strangulated shout, dropped his spade, and began haring off like the clappers down the slope towards the jungle, some quarter of a mile away. At first I could see

48

nothing; then I could just make out a thin black line stretching across the sky just to the right of the Peak. It was the most terrifying realisation that these must be Japanese bombers; and in force. The thought of that moment still brings me out in a cold sweat, for there was no doubt that they were heading for us, and our little group was smack in the middle of the target area, with no shelter particularly near.

Percy had set off at right angles to the approaching planes, and was by then some hundred yards or more away, clearly intent on bettering Jesse Owen's 200-metre record; his flailing footwear sent up little clouds of dust as he receded rapidly into the distance. I carried out a very swift mental calculation that I was unlikely by then to outstrip the outside right of the bomber formation if I followed the same route. There was nothing for it but to run before the enemy, back to the airfield perimeter where there were a few slit trenches. By the time that I, and two or three others, hurled ourselves into the nearest trench, which seemed woefully inadequate, the drone of the aircraft engines was audible.

I glanced up, just as a startled armourer shot out of the flight hut and landed on top of me; I must confess I was quite glad to have another body between me and the enemy. The planes droned nearer and nearer relentlessly, at a convenient bombing height of about ten thousand feet. There was not a single plane of ours up there to distract them from aiming their bombs, although I could hear a couple of Blenheims desperately taxi-ing out to try to take off; but it was all too late.

With the adrenalin flowing through my brain I recall calculating how many bombs were likely to be falling on us, any one of which would be sufficient to bring obliteration. I counted twenty-seven planes, in perfect formation of three squadrons of nine, each with three flights of three, in perfect V formation, that would have done credit at the pre-war Hendon Air Displays. I reckoned that each plane probably carried six or eight anti-personnel bombs; that would be an average of 189 bombs. How could they possibly miss killing every one of us in those three trenches?

When the formation was nearly overhead I saw the bomb doors were already open. There was an eerie rattle of a machine gun, presumably as a signal from the Wing Commander to release bombs. I saw them all leave the planes almost simultaneously, trailing behind each aircraft, rather like pregnant herrings emitting their eggs in water. At first the bombs seemed to hang

49

there above us, wobbling a bit at first as they gathered speed and the tail fins directed them straight towards us.

I suppose it was only a matter of seconds, but it seemed like hours, as they began to grow larger, and then whistle, developing into a sickening shriek. There was a terrible urge to move to another shelter, anywhere, but I knew that was no use. An old sweat in my trench murmured, 'Heads down boys, and God be with you.' I did not have a religious upbringing, or I suppose I would have prayed at that moment. I can only remember thinking how grossly unfair it was that I should be dying at the tender age of twenty-one, never even having had a woman! I wondered if my mother, six thousand miles away, would know at that moment she would see me no more. Then all hell was let loose.

So many things happened in a split second. I was conscious of a sickening explosion across the airfield, silencing the desperate roar of Blenheim engines as one of our planes was actually hit by a bomb when taking off. Poor devils, I thought, they stood no chance.

At the same time debris was showering in on us. The armourer who was half on top of me let out a scream as a piece of phosphorus bomb burned through his shorts. I can't recall ever seeing him again.

I stumbled out of the trench expecting to see my mates injured or dead; but by some miracle we all seemed to have survived intact in spite of everything. I later counted twelve bomb craters in a radius of about twenty yards. Everything around seemed to be on fire, and the air hung heavy with the acrid smell of cordite and phosphorus. But I was alive and unscathed, and I had a most tremendous feeling of exhilaration.

I knew then how men came to win Victoria Crosses, albeit often posthumously. When you have a lucky escape the adrenalin runs high and a feeling of immortality leads you to think you can do anything and not be harmed. I, and a couple of others, dived into the nearby flight hut, by then well on fire, and started throwing outside all sorts of tools and things that we considered precious: as it turned out they never were used again. It was a most foolhardy thing to do as there was a stack of oxygen bottles in the corner of the hut and when the flaming roof caved in we only just jumped clear, and the bottles started exploding at regular intervals, sounding more deafening even than the bombs. We were driven back to a large shelter on the edge of the rubber trees and watched as all that remained of the squadron buildings was reduced to charred timbers and ashes. Several of the grounded aircraft seemed beyond repair as well.

Again we completely forgot that the enemy bombers might be circling round to inflict further damage. In fact they must have jettisoned all their bombs and considered their mission well accomplished. They were not wrong either, for the air station could no longer be considered operational. In the afternoon of that first day of the war the remaining seven serviceable Blenheims of No. 27 Squadron took off from Sungei Patani for the last time, heading back for Butterworth where it was hoped we might be able to consolidate and reform the squadron. It proved to be a forlorn hope.

The Australian Squadron of Brewster Buffaloes had already departed in order to operate from Ipoh, some fifty miles south, which had not yet been bombed, and where they could operate off the small civil airstrip, as they needed only a short take-off run.

As the sun set at the end of day one of the Japanese war it was difficult not to feel a little demoralised. We in the maintenance flight were lucky that no one had been killed, or even seriously injured. But many others had died, and throughout that night I believe most slept fitfully, with the feeling of death all around, and the prospects for us all pretty slim. England, that night, seemed very very far away; a place we could hardly hope ever to see again.

Only about half the squadron remained behind when the planes left for Butterworth, which was dispiriting in itself. We no longer had any electricity, the cookhouse staff had departed, and the canteen was closed. Our billet was one of the few left standing, so many had to sleep out under the rubber trees, at the mercy of the mosquitoes and anything that crept and crawled.

There were stories being told that did nothing to boost our morale. Of pilots declaring their aircraft unserviceable for some trifling fault, rather than take off again after the first raid. Of ground crew who were qualified air gunners; having trained in the peacefulness of India they had not been needed as aircrew up to now, and were more use to the Royal Air Force in their original capacity as fitters. On nights out in Penang they had worn their jackets bearing the AG brevets with obvious pride. Now we heard of these jackets being furtively disposed of.

There was one pilot in the squadron who was nothing like the others; in fact, he stuck out like a sore thumb. The ground crews nicknamed him Buffalo Bill. He was probably in his early thirties, but looked older, probably

51

because of the open-air life in hot climates. Born in Australia he had earned a living in the thirties big game hunting, just where I never found out. We did not question him, for he was not the sort that you doubted. He was of average height, but square and muscular, with arms like legs and legs like hams.

The first time Brem and I met him, when he joined the squadron about a couple of weeks before the war started, he waddled towards us as we were working on a plane, doing a 90-hour inspection, with modifications. His pigeon-toed approach reminded me of Denis Compton, my cricketing hero, walking out to bat at Lords.

'This is going to be my plane', he drawled in a sand-papered voice. 'What are you doing to it?'

'Just a minor servicing, and a few mods, Sergeant,' I replied.

'None of that sergeant, or sir, bullshit,' he rumbled. 'I'm just plain Bill and I'm here to kill Japs.'

'B-but we're not at war; not yet anyway.'

'You bloody well soon will be,' assured Bill. 'Jappo's not massing in thousands south of Saigon for the summer holidays.'

We were soon to realise that Bill really relished the prospect of trying to ward off an invasion.

'What mods are you doing then?'

'Fitting armour plating behind the pilot's seat and one or two other smaller jobs, like a container at the side of the cockpit to take maps and escape equipment in case you are forced down behind enemy lines.'

He paused for a moment. 'Maybe the armour plating might be some use, but you can stuff your escape gear; nobody's going to lose me if I prang in a jungle, I've spent too much of my life in them.'

Just how Bill had managed to enter the Royal Air Force to train as a pilot, for a reasonably good educational standard was required, and then to persuade Headquarters that he could fly Blenheims, I do not know. One thing was certain: the man had guts, and this he showed on that very first day of war. He was piloting one of the planes of the dawn foray on enemy barges landing on the east coast beaches. By all accounts he lashed into them again and again for as long as his fuel supplies would allow, but he still had enough ammunition to claim having shot down two Mitsubishi bombers on the return journey. How he managed to land safely was something of a minor miracle. The fuselage was liberally peppered with bullet holes; one of the engines was glowing red hot and petrol was seeping steadily out of the port wing. At least the self-sealing tanks had done their stuff, preventing a complete flood. His parachute, which doubled as a seat for pilots, was ripped open by enemy fire; and we were gratified to note that our time spent fitting the armoured plating had not been wasted.

The pilots had not long landed, and were mostly flaked out on chairs in the flight dispersal hut when the pencil-thin line of twenty-seven bombers was sighted over Kedah Peak.

'Which of you bastards is going to lend me his plane? I don't think mine's going to take off in a hurry on one engine,' roared Bill.

'Take mine,' was the chorus, 'if you must be a bloody hero.'

'Who's going to crew for me then?' shouted Bill, as he struggled into his Mae West and moved to the door. Not a soul spoke or stirred.

'Right, you lily-livered bastards, I'll go on my own; f---- the regulations.'

So saying he charged across the dispersal area to the nearest plane, signalled the ground crew to disconnect the lead from the bowser that was refuelling, shouted to remove wheel chocks, and roared away to find a take-off path between the bomb potholes. Luck was still on his side. He had just pulled off the ground and was retracting wheels as the first of the bombs exploded. The one pilot who was shamed into following him was not so lucky, and was just starting his take-off run when a bomb exploded just in front of the Blenheim's nose, killing pilot and navigator instantly. We had heard the sickening explosion as we lay in our slit trench.

Buffalo Bill's bravado was all in vain, for his tanks had only been a quarter filled when he took off, and there was not sufficient juice for him to gain height in order to engage the enemy, so he just had to return to base. It couldn't have surprised him that the other pilots avoided his eyes. He asked for an immediate transfer to the RAAF to pilot Buffaloes, but he was too late for that; the whole squadron was just leaving Sungei for the last time. I could never imagine Bill, who liked his beer and a coarse chorus or two, ever shouting out the last verse of the ditty that went, 'We would rather ----- than fight.' It was a saddening thought that perhaps the others did mean it after all.

The second day of the war was anti-climactic, inasmuch as no enemy aircraft attacked the aerodrome, although we saw planes flying past, presumably to find other targets. No doubt the Japanese spy network was highly efficient: how could we be expected to know the difference between Chinese and Japanese? Doubtless they knew by sundown on that first day that RAF Sungei Patani was out of action, and no longer needing their lethal attentions. So the Nips turned their attentions to Butterworth, where the remains of 27 Squadron had joined forces with what was left of No. 34 Squadron's Blenheims, previously stationed at Alor Star, which was rumoured to be in the land fighting area. As dusk was falling we learnt that Butterworth airfield had been pattern bombed, and the greater part of our squadron's planes, together with those of 34 Squadron, had been destroyed on the ground.

Twice during that second day we were told to be ready to move out within ten minutes, taking only as much kit as we could conveniently carry; the remainder would have to be abandoned. Twice the order was rescinded. All day we were salvaging what we could of the squadron's equipment. At least, by so doing, we avoided burial parties.

Wednesday 10 December started peacefully until around midday we spotted a squadron of nine Jap aircraft heading north. They were bi-planes with fixed undercarriages, not unlike the Swordfishes flown by the Fleet Air Arm. I expect these planes were operating from carriers too. At first they seemed to be passing us by, until the leader broke from the echelon formation with a banking roll heading straight towards us, machine guns blazing, with the rest of the squadron following. It was the first of many strafing raids that were intended to mop up anything that had been left by the bombers. The truth was that there wasn't very much. One of the two remaining planes, grounded for repairs, was peppered again, making quite sure that it would never again take part in the war; and the MT shed, empty of all vehicles, had several more holes drilled through its roof and sides.

By mid-afternoon came the order to report to where the squadron HQ was, before being burnt down, carrying only bare essentials; we were to leave in ten minutes for Butterworth. We did not need hustling, for the few of us who were left at Sungei were heartily glad to be away from the place which had always seemed gloomy, and filled with foreboding of disasters: which was how it turned out. I did not have time to grieve about leaving my tennis racket, still unused, or the many little bits and pieces that I had accumulated and treasured over the months.

Within the stated ten minutes we were aboard the lorry, and soon moving out of the main entrance of Sungei Patani for the last time.

So began the retreat that was later to earn me and my colleagues the nickname of 'Singapore Harriers'.

Chapter 9

The return to Butterworth was rather different from our arrival there the previous May. For one thing, all the chalets were full up; indeed, there was not even a spare bed anywhere. Several of our advance party were sleeping on the floor of the HQ hut, as well as the personnel of 34 Squadron from Alor Star, who had reached Butterworth just before us.

In spite of the discomfort of kipping on concrete we were in a much happier mood. The cookhouse was functioning and we were able to enjoy a square meal, the first for three days. We were reunited with our buddies who had left Sungei on the Monday. What's more, the living quarters, which were about a mile from the airfield, had not been bombed: we were away from the smell of death that we had left behind at Sungei.

The first priority after sunrise the next day was to dig more slit trenches for the additional bods that had descended on the camp. The obvious place was the top of the beach, mid-way between the billets and the sea. There were a few odd coconut palms that gave some protection from the sun, not to mention from the distinct possibility of a strafing Jap fighter.

It was rather like digging on the beaches of Cornwall as a small boy, but much hotter work as the sun got up. By noon we reckoned we had done enough; and none too soon. The first formation of enemy bombers – twenty-six in all – headed straight for us from the east. It was not until they were directly overhead, completely unopposed by Allied fighters, that we realised, with a colossal sense of relief, that we were not to be the target of the day. Again we heard the one burst of machine gun fire from the leader as the signal to release bombs. Clearly it was going to be the turn of Georgetown, Penang, to receive attention. One mile across the water we watched helplessly as each stick of bombs exploded in a line across the town. Each flash of orange flame sent a puff of smoke upwards until, within minutes, almost before the roar of the explosions reached our ears across the strait, a pall like a white shroud gathered above the town, punctured here and there by billowing black smoke as fires began to spring up in many places. Nor was there to be any let-up for nearly an hour. Wave after wave roared overhead – 77 machines in all – each unloading its messengers of death until the whole town seemed like an inferno.

Fruity was concerned about Befung, the eldest daughter of the Wong family, whom he looked upon as his Oriental girlfriend. 'If she is in town she will surely have had it. I can only hope she was at home with her sisters, for their house is on the outskirts to the north, and the bombs seem to have been concentrated on the dock area and the town centre.'

'I doubt if you are going to get the chance to go and find out, or even to see Befung again,' I told him, 'for it seems unlikely that we are going to stay here very long.'

When the enemy planes eventually left us in peace we made our way down to the airfield where the destruction of the past two days was all too evident. Burnt out and mangled wrecks lay all around. On our own squadron alone there were only four planes that could still fly, compared with fourteen the previous Sunday. At Air Command in Singapore the decision must have been taken to withdraw what remained from Butterworth to Seletar, the main RAF depot on Singapore Island. Three of our planes, all bearing the scars of red doped fabric patches over bullet holes in the metal skin, took off that afternoon heading south. The last one would follow later when urgent repairs were completed.

That evening we were able to relax for a while in the canteen which still had some beer, but rationed to two mugfuls per person while supplies lasted. It seemed unlikely we would be getting any more. No one felt like singing any of the dirty ditties that had been so much a feature of beer nights in the canteen of 27 Squadron over the years.

We got talking to two chaps who had been in Singapore the previous Sunday night when the Japs launched their token bombing raid on the city, coinciding with the destruction of the US fleet at Pearl Harbour. They said there had been no air raid warning, and all the lights in the city were still blazing a few minutes after midnight when the first bombs struck.

There had to be a sexual connotation to their story, of course. It was said that a couple on the top floor of a building had actually been killed whilst on the job.

'What a marvellous way to go,' said Fruity, 'just at the point when you are going to come, your lot!'

'I am not so sure I would want to go any way, whilst still in the prime of my youth,' rejoined Brem. Then after some reflection: 'Perhaps it wouldn't be so bad if I was nearing seventy, particularly if I knew I wasn't going to make it!'

'I doubt if you will make it at half that age,' I felt I had to contribute. 'Come to think of it, the chances now of reaching more mature years seem pretty slim anyway.'

Next morning three Brewster Buffaloes touched down, having been sent up from Ipoh. No sooner had they landed than a squadron of Stuka-type Jap bombers began dive-bombing shipping in and around Penang harbour. Without waiting to re-fuel the Buffs took straight off again, roaring up towards some handy cloud cover. For a while we lost sight of them behind the clouds, and we held our breath, hoping the Japs had not seen them; but they were too busy concentrating on the bombing of the ships below to notice what was happening above. One, two, three, the Buff roared down out of the clouds, and two Jap planes immediately spiralled into the water as the Buffalo cannon shells found their marks.

More enemy planes had now appeared and a general dog-fight developed, almost like the summer days of 1940 over the Kentish countryside. Heavily outnumbered and nearly out of fuel, the Buffs had to land again. Only two now; but we had seen at least three enemy planes destroyed, and one limping off with black smoke pouring from it. For us, with our grandstand view, it had been a thrilling sight, enough to raise cheers from the trenches and to raise our morale for a while from the low level to which it had sunk.

That night, I and one or two others slept out under the stars. For me it was the first time in my life, but it was not to be the last. We did not relish the thought of another night on concrete, and a hollowed out stretch of sand was preferable. We no longer had any mosquito nets to protect us, but the off-shore breeze at night seemed to be enough to discourage the pestilent insects.

By the Saturday I was getting a little bored with digging slit trenches, so I volunteered for repair, crash and break-down party. I know that old sweats would always say that you never volunteered for anything in the services: I always was one for sticking my neck out! It promised to be more exciting than trench digging, although I did not much fancy having to extricate any mangled pilots out of crashed planes.

Since the remaining Blenheims had departed for Singapore there were no planes based at Butterfield after the first five days of fighting and the Japanese Air Force had gained complete supremacy. Once again three Buffaloes from Ipoh touched down to re-fuel and soon took off again as a squadron of Zeros approached from the north. Again a dog-fight ensued as the Zeros attempted to strafe the airfield. They were faster than the Buffs, but could not turn so tightly. We saw two Zeros shot down, either by cannon fire from the Buffaloes or by anti-aircraft fire from Bofors guns around the camp. We saw one Buff in a shallow dive, with smoke pouring from its engine, disappear towards the trees to our right. We set off in our wagon as far as we could go over the rough ground round the perimeter of the airfield. At least the plane had not caught fire on hitting the ground, but we feared for the pilot. It took us nearly a half an hour to locate the plane, not too badly smashed up, in marshy ground between some palm trees. When we reached the cockpit we were amazed not to find the pilot still in the plane, for we were sure he had not baled out; he would have been too low to attempt it anyway. By some miracle the fuselage had missed the tree trunks which had ripped off the port wing, thereby reducing speed drastically as the pilot slid down the other wing and landed in the bog. By the time we got there an ambulance had already reached him from a shorter route, and he was on his way to have a broken leg set in the hospital.

On the next day, Sunday 14 December, we were out on the aerodrome again, awaiting any action that might arise. We did not have long to wait for the enemy, who circled around the area, as many as twenty-eight at one time we counted, looking for targets, presumably hoping to engage in aerial combat with any planes we might have left; but by now there were none to do battle.

I was getting a little blasé by now with the odd plane that peeled in to strafe targets. Somehow it brought back memories of school days and the strip of land at the back of our playground where we often indulged in stone fights. I had a peculiar fascination for ducking and swaying as stones were hurled. The inevitable happened one day, of course, and I was struck just about the right eyebrow during the afternoon break. My RAF pass-book recorded the scar as an identification mark on body.

I recalled the remainder of that afternoon in 1935, when I sat at my desk dazed, with my head throbbing, trying to staunch the blood trickling down to my neck without the master catching sight, or there would have been hell to pay, both for me and for those throwing stones. I remember thinking again of this incident in those far-off school days as a Japanese strafing plane backed round to approach in a shallow dive. I could see that he was aiming to shoot up an empty hut that another airman and I had just left. About twenty yards towards the cover of the trees I could see he was committed to his run in, and would not be able to deviate his course to target on me, so I stopped where I was and turned round. It gave me a strange thrill as the line of bullets ripped across the grass, then spattered the corrugated metal side of the hut. I could see the pilot very clearly as he pulled out of his dive about sixty feet above the ground, and not much further from me; it was the closest I had been to the enemy at that time.

I don't suppose he saw the two-fingered sign, with arm fully extended, swivelling round for a Winston Churchill Victory Vee; but it gave me a good deal of satisfaction.

By that evening, with none of our planes having appeared all day, morale was beginning to wane again. We had only recently heard of the devastating loss of those two famous battleships, the *Prince of Wales*, and the *Repulse*. At first we thought it just another rumour, but rather more cruel than most. How could two great warships, with their power and armaments, be sunk simply from the air? I think we all felt ashamed that the Royal Air Force had not been present to provide air cover, for surely it could not have happened then.

It is true that the RAF had suffered too, not only our own squadron aircraft, and the other squadrons of the northern States, but those based at Singapore. Early in the first week of war a squadron of Wildebeests had been virtually wiped out on their way to torpedo the Japanese invasion fleet. True, it was a suicidal mission that was destined for disaster. The wire and fabric Wildebeest bi-planes were practically World War I vintage, with a top speed in level flight, carrying a torpedo, of barely 100 m.p.h. There was no fighter cover for them, and with little chance of surprising the enemy, who were almost certainly tipped off by spies in Singapore before the planes had even taken off, the aircraft were intercepted long before they could approach targets in the Gulf of Siam. The planes themselves were no great loss, for progress in the air had passed them by; but the loss of the aircrews was not only saddening, it was also a severe blow to the morale of the Royal Air Force.

In the early hours of Monday 15 December we were roused from sleep and told that the camp was to be evacuated. The first task was to push the three Buffaloes and one Blenheim out of their hiding places beneath the trees on to the air-field. These were the last planes able to take to the air, and they would not have been passed as serviceable under normal circumstances. At first light they were to be flown down to Singapore. We were to follow on by road using whatever transport could be commandeered. Indeed, since the first bombs had fallen a week previously there had been plenty of lorries parked around the camps, both at Sungei and at Butterworth, abandoned in a hurry by the drivers of the building contractors. Anyone who could drive, and some who couldn't, just helped themselves. The one that I had got hold of was so clapped out that I didn't stand much chance of getting past the camp entrance, let alone to Singapore.

No longer did we have to bother about packing our gear, for no one had more than could be lifted easily with one hand; usually a side or back pack, or a small rucksack. As we gathered in the half light by the guardroom we were joined by Sergeant Cohen and his gang of five, who had been detailed the day before to return to Sungei Patani to ensure that neither of the two unserviceable planes that had been parked in the servicing bays could ever be flown again when the Japs moved in. When they had finally pulled out of Sungei, only an hour previously, they said the sound of gunfire was clearly audible to the north. It was a disquieting thought, and we felt no desire to dally too long as we boarded the small Dodge truck that had been allocated to nine of us, plus the driver. We had between us two rifles and a tommy gun, with an ample supply of ammunition, for it was very likely that the Jap fighters would be patrolling the main road to the south, strafing anything that offered an easy target. For this reason we would leave at five minute intervals, so as not to bunch up in convoy, and to travel as fast as possible. We were to rendezvous on the first night at the Army transit camp in Kuala Lumpur; then on the next day to Kallang, in Singapore.

As we turned right out of the gates, heading south, the sun was just peeping above the horizon and the mountains of Perak. It reminded us too much of the dreaded emblems on the fuselage of the Zeros to be a welcome sight.

61

Chapter 10

As we began to put the miles behind us our spirits began to rise a little. True, we might be thought to be running away; and I am sure that we were looked upon in that way by the soldiers in the lorries chugging their way slowly northwards, armed and camouflaged, and looking very solemn. They knew it was no picnic they were going on. The Japanese infantryman, moving swiftly through the rubber trees and jungle, clad lightly and with bayonet fixed, was already known to be a deadly opponent. It was said he needed no more than a handful of rice to keep him moving for twenty-four hours or more.

At one point, where there was a break in the trees, we spotted a Jap fighter heading straight towards us at just above tree-top height. He passed by too quickly to strafe us before we gained the comparative safety of the rubber trees again. In any case, I expect he was more interested in shooting up transport heading towards the fighting zone. Percy Prosser, whose turn it was at the time to hold the tommy gun, let fly a short burst, much too late to do any damage to the Zero, but he did succeed in annoying Brem, who was squatting down beside him and got showered with empty cartridge cases.

By 10 o'clock we were nearing Taiping, a small town which had grown to some importance through the development of rubber plantations and a tin mine nearby. Beyond Taiping the road climbed through a pass in a line of high hills and spectacular rocks before descending to Ipoh, the largest town between Penang and Kuala Lumpur.

We decided our stomachs needed some attention as we entered the main street of Taiping, where we were delighted to find the town untouched by Jap bombing. For the first time in a week, since the war had exploded in all its fury, we felt that we could relax and treat ourselves to a slap-up meal. Our sense of security was to be rudely shattered.

We turned the truck off the main street, just past a Chinese restaurant that looked inviting, and parked in an alley round the back. In our shabby shirts and shorts that we had slept and worked in for a week, we must have seemed a motley throng as the ten of us marched into the restaurant. Nevertheless, the proprietor was clearly pleased to see such an influx of white customers at a rather unlikely hour for a meal. He did not know then that it would be the last time he would serve on those premises.

Always a slow eater, I was just about to tackle an ice cream sundae when there was an urgent rumbling of shoes down the staircase as those who had been dining on the floor above decided it was time to evacuate the premises in a hurry; I don't suppose they had paid their bills either. I could hear the drone of aircraft engines but, being the supreme optimist, decided I was not going to leave my ice cream sundae just as I was nearing the jammy part at the bottom of the glass. By then the others had legged it out at the back of the building and I was alone on the ground floor of the restaurant as I detected the now all too familiar whistle of bombs approaching. Too late to run, I decided, so I dived under the table; only to realise it was made of glass! What a stupid idiot, I thought; I've done it again, and surely I can't expect to get away unscathed once more.

Then all hell broke loose. The door and windows at the front of the restaurant shattered as I felt the air wrenched out of my lungs. Glass showered across the room, but my glass table was sufficient to protect me from that, as well as the plaster that fell from the ceiling; luckily, the main structure held. I could hear a rumble of masonry the other side of the wall as the building next door collapsed.

Picking myself up I could not believe that I was not even bleeding. I stepped cautiously across the broken glass, through where the door had been, and surveyed the scene of death and destruction in the main street. The building to the left was still subsiding into the road, blocking the pathway. Next door to the right smoke and flames were beginning to billow out. There was not a soul moving. I seemed to be the only one still alive. Certainly there were some that weren't; they were sprawled in grotesque positions down the street.

As I stood there transfixed, trying to decide what to do next, I glanced down at the gutter near to my feet. As with most towns in Malaya, where water is rarely in short supply, streams are diverted to the gutters in built-up areas in order to wash them clean. As I looked down the water started to tinge with red, becoming rapidly brighter and brighter until the whole channel seemed to be filled with blood. I had heard about gutters flowing with blood during battles, but surely this could not be happening to me.

I retreated to make my way out through the back of the building, which I thought might lead me to where the lorry was parked. I was not the only one still alive, I discovered, as I picked my way through the kitchen; there under the sink, curled up like a woodlouse, was a terrified Chinaman, whimpering and shaking with fright as I told him, in the hope of stirring him up, to help. No chance; he was too petrified to act sensibly. The back room was shattered, but I could see that a gate the other side of a small yard was partly open. I pulled the gate back, to be confronted with a very dead body sprawled across the path. Half its head was missing and brains were spilled over the pavement.

There was nothing useful I could do there, so I stepped quickly across, managing to hang on to my ice cream sundae so recently consumed. There, a few yards away, was our lorry. There were a few holes where shrapnel had peppered it, but the tyres were still okay. In the back I could see smoke beginning to curl skywards. Christ! there was fifty gallons of petrol there, I remembered, not to mention a thousand or so rounds of ammunition and our personal pieces of kit. As I dashed across the tailboard, flames were just beginning to burn one corner of my own back-pack. The thought of losing the last of my precious belongings, including my Baby Brownie, and my writing pack, given to me as a twenty-first birthday present by my girlfriend in Blighty, was enough to make me forget about the considerable risk that the whole lot was likely to blow sky high any minute. A few seconds later and I am sure I would have been too late to beat out the flames.

Now to get the lorry moving and try and find my mates, and to get out of this town, which had now experienced its baptism of fire, as soon as possible before Jappo paid another visit.

Maurice, the MT driver, had no ignition key, having commandeered the vehicles, so it was just a question of rejoining the bare terminals under the dashboard and pressing the starter button. Dammit! not a flicker. I opened up the shrapnel-punctured bonnet. Sure enough the main lead from the battery had been completely severed. I was just surveying the scene ruefully when the first of the lads returned from where they had taken refuge in some woods nearby.

'F----- it,' said Corporal Cocks, in charge of our party of ten. 'That's a re-wiring job that could take bloody hours. We'll have to find another garry.' He paused to ponder. 'I know, we'll split up into three parties of three, one going to the left, one right and one down the hill, leaving Mo here to look after our gear. Scour the town for an abandoned vehicle or any that doesn't seem to have an owner in sight and report back here. We will wait an hour from now if we find anything; if anyone is not back by then we will assume they have hitched a lift to K.L. Don't forget to take your packs in case you do make your own way.' That sounded quite a good arrangement: Brem, Fruity and I formed one party and set off back down the main street the way we had come in. We did not know then that that was the last we would see of the others, with the exception of Percy Prosser, who crossed our paths again, several weeks later, like the proverbial bad penny.

As we picked our way along the rubble-strewn main street of Taiping the town was beginning to stir into life again. A truck with an improvised sign stating 'ARP – Ambulance' was pulled up while the crew of two lifted a corpse up into the back. We could hardly commandeer that. Turning the corner to the right, at the end of the main street, we had only walked a few yards when a 15-cwt truck pulled up beside us. The driver, an Englishman, or rather a Scot, as we found out later, leaned out and called us: 'Do you lads want any help?'

We explained our situation, telling him that we were expected in Kuala Lumpur by nightfall.

'If you care to jump in the back, and come with me back to my place, you can take this van; it belongs to the Company, but I am sure they will think it in a good cause under the circumstances.'

It seemed too good an opportunity to miss, so the three of us hopped aboard. If we were not back in Taiping within the hour, the others would not wait and we could easily make our own way to K.L. Anyway, there would not be enough room for the other seven in this little van. The idea of having our own little van to drive to Kuala Lumpur, or even Singapore, seemed rather appealing; we might even be able to pick up some Chinese jig-a-jig girls on the way!

The man at the wheel was about thirty-five, clean shaven, and wearing khaki shorts and shirt and an officer's peaked cap.

'By the way, my name's Mike, Mike Ferguson,' he disclosed as he changed up into top gear. 'I'm not a real army officer, so you don't need to salute me!' he continued after a rather self-conscious chuckle. 'I'm a rubber planter, been out here twelve years now. Brought my wife out here in '34; now there are two kids, a girl of six and a boy aged three.'

'Are your wife, and the children, still with you?' asked Brem, his educated Scottish intonations being rather similar to those of our new-found friend.

'She elected to stay with me when the trouble blew up. I was already interested in the local Malayan Defence Force and would be expected to stay in the country if war broke out. I'm beginning to think now I should not have let her stay; I'm told the spearhead of the Jap advance is less than fifty miles to the north and there's not a great deal in between to stop them.'

'How come you are here on your own just now?' I questioned.

'My bungalow is just five miles out of Taiping. My detachment had already fallen back towards Ipoh where HQ think we have a better chance of holding the Japs. There is the pass across the mountains to the east of Taiping and the rail and road bridges over the River Perak will be blown up if the Japs get that far.'

'What about your wife and family?' chipped in Fruity.

'I have special permission from my CO to collect them,' said Mike, 'and fix them up with friends in Ipoh before rejoining my unit. I was just calling into town at Taiping on the way in order to collect a few cans of petrol and one or two essentials for the journey. I will collect my own car from the bungalow and you can then have this.'

At that point, some three miles out of Taiping, we turned right off the main road on to an unmade road leading upwards towards the hills. I could not help feeling a little disconcerted that we were heading back the way we had come; I would have much preferred his bungalow to have been five miles to the south.

Perhaps Mike was reading my thoughts. 'Sheila should be waiting for us with the children, ready to move off straight away. You three can follow us, at least as far as Ipoh.'

'Is all this rubber part of the estate you manage?' I asked.

'Yes, in fact as far as the outskirts of Taiping,' said Mike. 'Over the top of the next rise you will be able to see the bungalow.'

As we neared the crest of the hillock we could see smoke rising ahead of us. 'Christ!' shouted Mike. 'That looks mighty near the bungalow.'

The road levelled off as we reached the clearing before the bungalow. We could see then that some building beyond the main dwelling had been burnt to the ground; and as we turned on the final approach up the gravel track a woman with auburn hair streaming behind, presumably Mrs Ferguson, and clearly in a distressed state, came running towards us.

'Mike, it's Rory, I think his arm is broken, and he may be injured internally. You must get him to Doctor McIntosh immediately.'

'Have you bound his arm?'

'Yes, but I can't be sure I've set it properly; besides, the poor little lad must be in great pain. He is trying to be brave like his dad, and not cry. Fiona is being a great comfort to her little brother, instead of the usual squabbling.' It seemed clear to us that Sheila Ferguson was a true Scottish lass, with a stiff upper lip for an emergency, who would not be seen cracking up in front of the servants, or anyone else for that matter.

'By the way, Mike, you will have to take the truck; the car was burnt out with the garage when the enemy fighter came over with its guns blazing; poor little Rory was on the roadway outside with his tricycle.'

Mike turned to us. 'I'm sorry, lads, it wasn't easy to introduce you. As you may have gathered, this is my wife, Sheila. Sheila, these three RAF lads are Ken, Brem and Fruity – those are the only names I know. They will explain to you how they come to be here while I run back to Angus McIntosh. Mind you, it may not be so easy to find him; I suppose you know the Japs have just bombed Taiping?'

'Yes, some of the men who were on top of the hill at the time could see it happening.'

'So it may not be too easy to get Angus to attend to Rory straight away,' said Mike. 'I expect he is being kept busy with the wounded at the Cottage Hospital.'

By this time we had reached the steps of the bungalow. 'Come on in, lads, while I fetch Rory,' said Mike. 'Wait, though; perhaps one of you could back the truck up to the door – it will save a few minutes.'

I did as he bade, and soon Mike came back again, holding his small son, wrapped in a blanket, gently to him. Rory had a mass of red curly hair, even more fiery than his mum's, and was trying hard not to cry. There was a flicker of a smile as he spotted us, for he did not often see young white visitors. Following father and son to the car out to the truck was a little fair-haired girl, whom we assumed was the six-year-old daughter Fiona, holding the hand of her mother, and a kindly looking Malayan nanny who got into the truck first and took Rory very gently on to her ample lap.

We three stayed up on the verandah while mother and daughter waved sadly as the truck pulled slowly away, trying to avoid bumping too much down the rough road. It was not the moment to voice our fears that if Mike did not get back with Rory and his nanny before sundown it might be too late to head off the invading army. For the time being, as Sheila Ferguson and Fiona walked slowly back up to the verandah, all was quiet; in the distance we could just make out the low rumble of traffic down on the main road, which we reckoned to be a mile or more away.

'Now, boys,' said Sheila, trying to be more cheerful, 'it's past midday, would you like some *tiffin*?'

'The truth is, Mrs Ferguson,' I volunteered, 'we gorged ourselves in the town just before the bombing started. What we would really like, if you don't mind too much, is to wash the sweat of several days' active service off our bodies while you have your *tiffin*; I am sure we would be much better company afterwards!'

'No trouble at all, we have a bath and two showers, so help yourselves. While you are about it, leave off your clothing and I will ask one of the boys to *dhoby* it; it should dry in an hour, before Mike is likely to be back.'

'Marvellous,' we chorused, 'if you don't mind seeing us wrapped in towels for a while. I'm afraid we had to leave our wardrobes in rather a hurry at Sungei Patani.'

None of us had enjoyed a soak in a bath since the salt water tubs aboard ship; so we tossed up for turns, allowing each other twenty minutes each in the bathroom. For the time being there was nothing to do but enjoy the luxury of cleaning ourselves up and then sitting around in our towels until our clothing dried.

By mid-afternoon the boys had returned our shorts and shirts, all neatly folded and pressed, and once again we were ready to face the world, having scraped several days' growth of beard from our chins. We felt that we ought to try and comfort Mrs Ferguson, but were half afraid that she might detect our fears for the future. Having seen the devastation the bombing had caused in Taiping we had reason to think that the doctor would be very hard pressed to attend to Rory in time for him and his dad to return before nightfall; and if the boy needed to have an anaesthetic it would be the next day before they could come home, by which time it might well be too late.

We walked into the lounge and rejoined Sheila Ferguson, who we believed was grateful for our company and our moral support.

She told us that she had heard the rumble of the bombs in the distance and was naturally worried that her husband might have been caught up in it, just as we were. In fact, he was a few miles short of Taiping, on the road from Ipoh, at the time of the bombing. Within minutes of the bombing there had been a sudden roar of an aircraft engine, flying just above the trees, then the rattle of cannon fire as the shells ripped across the ground, luckily missing the bungalow but tearing into the store houses and garage nearby.

'It was all over in two or three seconds.' Sheila recalled, 'and when I ran there was Rory in a pathetic little heap, screaming as he tried to pick himself off the ground. The shells had missed, but large splinters of timber had been flung from the garage door and one piece had felled him. You can imagine that I was beside myself with worry. I can't help feeling happier now, although I know we are by no means out of the wood yet.'

'If it is any consolation, Mrs Ferguson,' said Brem, 'we will stay here with you until your husband and son return. I hope you will let us squeeze in with you in the truck.'

'I know that you are now in a difficult position, boys,' said Sheila. 'Had it not been for us Fergusons you would now be well on your way to Kuala Lumpur.'

'You must not try to blame yourself, Mrs Ferguson,' Brem tried his best to convince her. 'It is just the fortunes of war.'

'If you want to have a look round about before it gets dark for a couple of hours or so, feel free to do so,' said Sheila. 'If Mike returns he will give a long blast on the horn. In any case, be back to the house by six o'clock and we will have a sundowner before dinner, even if Mike has not joined us. It may be the last meal we shall have in this home.'

We strolled out from the verandah, the three of us, first to inspect the damage caused by the lone raider. There was no doubt the car was unusable; it was just a blackened shell. The blackened timbers of the outbuilding and storehouse were still smouldering and overall was the repulsive stench of burnt rubber.

We started to follow a path downhill through the rubber trees, presumably made by the estate workers to reach their own huts or merely to get around to the collection points.

'If the worst came to the worst,' Brem expounded as we strolled down beneath the shade of the trees, 'and the Japs arrive here before Mike returns, we could retreat down this path and make our way to the sea.'

'What sea?' ejaculated Fruity, startled at the thought of having to hack his way through jungle, and the privations that he would suffer.

'The sea can't be more than ten miles to the west,' replied Brem, 'and we might well find a creek with a boat in it before then, just as we did at Sungei Patani.'

'It's funny that we forgot all about the boat that we had sweated for weeks to build,' I chimed in.

'I didn't forget about it,' said Brem, 'but it would have been desertion at the time. Anyway, the herd instinct prevailed with you lot, not like us individualistic Celts!'

'Sod off it,' was Fruity's response. 'You know very well you couldn't have paddled across to Sumatra on your own.'

By this time we had moved downhill along the path, almost out of sight of the bungalow, between the tree trunks, when we came across a low shed. Inside were rows of rubber sheeting, strung up on wires like clothes lines for drying the weekly wash. At each end were benches with large flat zinc trays on top where the raw latex was poured for setting. Above on shelves were the various tools required, large rollers, something like decorators use, and various cutting instruments.

'If the Japs take over the house,' said Brem, 'we could lie up down here. We might even slit a Jap throat or two if they followed us down.'

'I wouldn't fancy spending long in this God-forsaken place,' chimed in Fruity.

'Better than being machine-gunned on the steps of the verandah. By all account Jappo is not too well disposed towards Europeans who wave the white flag,' retorted Brem.

'Suppose we forget about all this for a while,' I cut in, 'and make our way back to the bungalow; it's nearly time for the promised sundowner.'

'Yeah,' agreed Fruity, 'I could just do with a stiff whisky after the doings of this day.'

As we made our way back up the hill to the bungalow came the realisation that there had been no sound of Mike's returning truck.

We mounted the steps up to the verandah on the west side of the bungalow, and before us were set out several large bamboo arm chairs, each with a plentiful supply of cushions and a small bamboo table at the side. Our hostess came out to greet us.

'I hope you have enjoyed your walk around, boys. Fiona has already had her meal and I have put her to bed to get a good sleep while she can,' Sheila announced. 'If Mike is not back by sunset we will have our dinner, as I feel sure he will have had something at the club whilst waiting to bring Rory back.'

'It must be wonderful, Mrs Ferguson, in more peaceful times to relax out here and watch the sun go down,' said Brem.

'Indeed it is; there are some of the finest sunsets to be seen across the Straits, comparable with any in the world. Let us sip a drink while we are watching, for it looks like being a good one tonight.' So saying, Sheila clapped her hands for the boy, and in he came with his tray of bottles and glasses at the ready.

'Mostly we drink whisky, probably because we are Scottish, but we do have other drinks if you prefer them,' continued Sheila.

'Whisky would be fine, Mrs Ferguson,' said Brem, 'I am Scottish too.' Fruity and I both murmured our approval rather than be awkward and ask for anything else.

'Cheers, then,' said Sheila, when all had been served to their liking. 'May the Japs be thrown back for the sharks in the South China Sea.'

We all felt silent; in our hearts we each knew that it wasn't going to happen for a long time.

It was Brem who broke the silence after a pause. 'Just supposing – I don't expect it is likely to happen – but just suppose that the Japs get here before Mike and Rory get back; what do you think we all should do?'

'Yes,' said Sheila after a pause. 'I had been wondering how I should face up to that situation without my man at my side. First of all, let me say that I would not expect you three to just hang around here to be captured. We have already been hearing ugly stories, which I only hope are not true, about what the Japs have been doing to captured British servicemen. For my part I would just tell them that I and my servants are unarmed and I would hope that they would leave us alone. Maybe Mike would be able to join us later.'

71

'In that case, Mrs Ferguson,' said Brem, 'it would probably be better if we withdrew from the bungalow out of sight if we got wind of an approaching posse of Japs. If the enemy do decide to leave you alone, we could always creep back to the house and then plan what to do next. It is no good trying to plan too far ahead.'

He did not go on to voice the thoughts that were in my mind, and of the others as well, I expect, that the future didn't really hold much in prospect for any of us.

We fell silent again as the sun touched the horizon across the Straits, and a golden halo spread out around the western sky. It was particularly beautiful on this night, with little smudges of brown and purple clouds etched on a back-cloth of brilliant blue and gold. It might be the last sunset we should see from here, or even in our shortened life span, should the morrow bring disaster; but the sun would go on setting day by day, and often looking just as beautiful.

Sheila broke the silence. 'Dinner is ready to be served, boys, let's go inside.' Although not a religious man I had learnt something of the bible at Highfield School in Muswell Hill. It must have been something like this at that last supper some nineteen hundred-odd years ago.

A genuine Indian curry was something new to me, with a line of serving boys, all wearing spotless white jackets buttoned to the collar, each holding a little dish in each hand which was proffered in turn to each guest to partake of what he fancied. The array of dishes seemed endless. The main course was followed by a vast selection of fruits, some of which we were familiar with but which had not been on sale in England for the past two years, and others we had not tried before, but all were equally delicious.

The meal finished we adjourned to the lounge and the large bamboo chairs with their comfortable kapok cushions. The boys brought in coffee and brandy and cigars. We felt at that moment that Sheila Ferguson must be desperately missing her husband, who every night they had lived here would have been relaxing in his favourite chair, idly watching the smoke from his cigar curling towards the *punkah* fans set in the ceiling, listening to the incessant high pitched note emitted by the insects of the jungle, and watching the movements of the fireflies beyond the verandah. This night especially she had no means of knowing whether Mike was safe and if little Rory had suffered greater injuries than she had thought. It was no good trying to phone the hospital in Taiping; all telephones had been out of order since the bombing.

If Sheila was thinking these things and worrying inwardly, her Scottish stoicism was strong enough to mask all outward signs.

'Mrs Ferguson,' began Fruity, 'you have really done us proud. It is many days since we have enjoyed such luxuries.'

'It has been a comfort having you boys around; I only wish Mike were here too.' She paused then continued. 'That is rather a silly thing to say, for if he were here none of us would be; that sounds a bit Irish, but you know what I mean.'

'We understand, Mrs Ferguson,' said Brem, 'and we won't leave you before Mike returns and then we hope to be coming with you – that sounds rather Irish too!'

'If you feel you want to push off while the going is good I would not wish to stop you. You could probably get a lift from where the plantation road meets the main road; it is less than two miles away.'

'At this time of night,' I said, 'we might find ourselves thumbing a Jap armoured car!'

The truth was that we were too tired, or at least I was, after a very long and wearing day and hardly any sleep the night before, to be able to walk even two miles. As I tried hard to keep awake in my armchair I felt I couldn't care less if the whole bloody Japanese army marched up the drive at that moment.

I was dimly conscious that Sheila was talking. 'If it does come to the crunch that the enemy arrive before Mike, please help yourselves to any of the things we have packed in boxes in the hall for our own evacuation. You may get a chance to grab something; there are various tins of food, and bottles of drink that may sustain you for a while if you are thinking of making a break across country.'

'Brem has some nutty idea,' replied Fruity, 'that we can borrow a sampan and row across to Sumatra. He was brought up near the North Sea and spent half his life in a coracle!'

'The truth is, Mrs Ferguson,' I chipped in, having roused myself to semi-consciousness, 'that neither Fruity nor I have any better ideas. If we do find ourselves behind enemy lines, and that seems very likely now, we might as well give it a whirl; we have nothing to lose but our lives, and we'll probably lose those anyway sooner or later.'

'Whenever you leave,' replied Sheila, 'and it will probably be tomorrow, one way or the other, I can only wish you all the luck you deserve. Perhaps we can meet up again sometime in England, when all this terrible business is just a memory.'

'In Scotland, please, Mrs Ferguson,' cut in Brem.

'In the United Kingdom then,' smiled Sheila; it was the first time we had seen her smile. 'Let's drink to that.'

When our glasses were drained Sheila continued: 'I know you are all very tired, in fact I can see you are. The boys have prepared three beds in the main guest room; it may be your last chance to sleep under mosquito nets for a while.'

We needed no second telling, and bade our hostess goodnight. In no time at all we were all fast asleep.

In my dreams I thought I could hear gunfire. At first, in my befuddled state, I felt I was re-living some of the traumatic moments of the past eight days. As I drifted more towards consciousness I knew it was real. The Japs were near at hand; the crunch could not be far away.

Chapter 11

It was still dark as I slipped out of bed; Fruity and Brem were still snoring. Beyond their snorts and snuffles I could also hear the deep throated rumble of tracked vehicles to the west, and spasmodically a burst of machine gun fire.

I had a quick shower and slipped into shirt and shorts. The splashing of water in the shower had woken the others when I got back into the bedroom.

'Christ Almighty, what's that?' exclaimed Fruity, obviously just made aware of those ominous noises in the distance.

'It's the bloody Japs, what do you expect?' chipped in Brem phlegmatically. 'I told you they would be here for breakfast.'

'I don't think I have much appetite for breakfast,' I contributed, as I gathered up my few bits and pieces into my pack. 'I'm going outside to see if there is any sign of life while you two wash the sleep out of your eyes.'

Out on the front verandah I heard Sheila Ferguson call out, 'Who's there?'

'It's only me, Ken, Mrs Ferguson; what time is it now, and when did you first hear gunfire?'

'It's just turned 4 o'clock. I think I first heard gunfire in the distance soon after midnight – I was finding it difficult to sleep for thinking of Mike and Rory.'

'Yes, I realise how it must be. I expect the advanced units of the Japanese army are now through Taiping on the road to Ipoh. I don't suppose even the Japs would harm the hospital.'

'I hope you are right; maybe when the Japs find this place they will let me go to the hospital. It cannot be possible for Mike to get back here now with Rory.'

At this point Brem and Fruity joined us. Just visible over the mountains of Perak there was a faint glimmer of light that heralded the dawn.

Fruity and I both looked instinctively towards Brem, the brain man of our trip, to plot our course of action.

'Mrs Ferguson,' said Brem, after a moment's pause, 'I think it best if we move out of the bungalow as soon as it is light enough and take up temporary residence in that hut we saw yesterday down the bottom of the hill. The Japs will probably send a patrol up your road, once they have secured Taiping, and it would be best if they did not find you sheltering British servicemen: best for us too; they might fire first and ask questions later.'

'Yes, that sounds sensible to me; don't forget to take what you want first from the stores in the hallway,' said Sheila.

'That's very good of you, Mrs Ferguson,' we chorused, moving towards the boxes of tinned foods, and medical supplies.

'You can be medical orderly, Brem,' I ventured. 'I will be navigator; at least I have a few pages of Pears Cyclopaedia maps of the world in my writing compact. Fruity, you had better be chief cook and bottle washer.'

'Thank you, chaps,' responded Fruity. 'I shall expect a bit of help with the drying up!'

'I think it is about light enough now, Mrs Ferguson, for us to think about taking our stroll down the hill,' said Brem.

'I can only wish you three the best of luck,' said Sheila, 'and only wish we had met in happier circumstances. As a small parting gift, and I hope a practical one, help yourselves to any of my husband's old hats on the pegs there. He uses them when he trudges through the rubber in the rain, and they may be necessary when you are on an open boat in the Straits.'

'You ought to say "if" to the open boat; we've got to find one first. But yes, that's very kind of you and please thank your husband when you see him. Fruity and I both mislaid our pith helmets on the first day of the war, but Brem managed to cling to his battered old topee.' In fact, Brem's greasy old sun helmet, with part of its pith missing, had become something of a fun object to his mates, but it didn't bother him at all.

So we made our way down the verandah steps, turning at the bottom to wave to Sheila Ferguson and Fiona who, clad in her nightie, had now joined her mother.

'Thanks again for everything, Mrs Ferguson,' we shouted. 'We shall hope to see what goes on from down in the rubber hut.'

In ten minutes' easy walking we reached the hut we had explored on the day before. We were now about a quarter of a mile nearer to the main road, but divided from it, as the crow would fly, by more than a mile of what looked like fairly impenetrable jungle. The sun was by now beginning to peep across the tops of the hills.

'The first thing we ought to do,' announced Brem,' is to plan our line of retreat from here in case the Japs come looking around.' The obvious direction was down beyond the hut where the drainage gully around the rubber plantation formed a boundary between the regimented rubber trees and the undergrowth on the edge of the uncleared jungle. The gully was quite deep on account of the large quantities of water it needed to carry during the frequent Malayan storms. About two feet down from the level ground there was a ledge of grassy soil, presumably lodged during flooding, beyond which was the stream a further two or three feet down.

'We can lay some strips of latex down there,' directed Brem. 'The tall grass will form a screen in front, and it would not be possible to see us from the other side without crossing the gully, which looks quite deep.'

'OK, boss then,' I responded. 'Let's do that; it could be quite cosy lying down there.'

'Not if you've got a Jap pointing a gun in your direction,' countered Brem, always the cheerful one.

The knives that had been left lying around made short work of cutting up conveniently sized strips of rubber latex that had been hanging up to dry. It was still very immature rubber, so we sprinkled a few handfuls of dust over our evacuation beds, in order to minimise the stickiness, as we laid them out down in the gully.

'That done, let's go back into the hut and enjoy a fag while we see what happens next,' said Fruity. 'I put a sealed tin of fifty Capstan in my bag.'

'We might as well hang on to these knives,' said Brem. 'There are enough to go round and we might be glad of them later, either to hack our way through jungle, cut up fruit, or slit Japanese throats. By the way, do you both feel you could nobble a Jap like cutting open a pawpaw?'

Fruity and I looked at one another unsmilingly. 'I suppose, if it was a last resort, one would do it instinctively,' was all I could blurt out, without much conviction. 'Anyway, Brem, you've made out a good enough case to keep our knives tucked in our belts; I will while away the time shaping three rubber balls to stick on the points of the knives in case we jab ourselves in the arse when we sit down.'

77

It was really quite comfortable as we sat puffing fags facing up the slope towards the bungalow. We had quite a good view, between the lines of trees, of the last part of the road leading to the bungalow. It would be virtually impossible for us to be seen from that distance, sitting as we were in the shadows inside the hut.

I don't think it had fully penetrated our heads that we were now behind enemy lines; we were potential prisoners of war – that was if we did not get shot in the act of giving ourselves up.

As if to voice the thoughts formulating in our minds Fruity piped up, 'I suppose you two have got your white handkerchiefs handy to wave at Jappo?'

'I only hope he knows what it means,' said Brem, adding with more bravado than conviction. 'Anyway we are not going to get taken.'

'Probably not . . . alive,' voiced Fruity. At that, silence fell again on our little trio. For the first time in my life I felt on my own, and I expect it was the same with the other two; we just had one another, no one to tell us what to do or where to go; we just had to use our own initiative to try to help one another. I dare say it was much the same for the Three Musketeers a century and a half or so before. With the optimism of youth the tremendous odds against us succeeding in keeping our freedom did not seem to matter. I suppose it was all just a great adventure, something that we, leading our rather drab little lives in the British Isles, never thought could happen to us.

There had been no further gunfire since dawn, although we could still hear the steady rumble of heavy traffic moving down the main road. We began to be lulled into a false sense of security; perhaps the Japs wouldn't bother to probe up the road to the bungalow; maybe we could live on here undisturbed. But it was all just a silly pipe dream.

As the sun reached its zenith in the sky above our leafy canopy we began to detect a low rumble of a vehicle that was more distinct than the drone of the traffic in the distance, and it was definitely becoming louder. Our blood began to freeze in our veins.

When the leading vehicle reached the top of the rise, about the point from where we had first seen, the day before, the smouldering ruins of the outbuildings, it began to slow to a walking pace, and came to a halt about a hundred yards short of the bungalow. Behind the front runner, which looked to be an armoured car, two other vehicles came into sight, both open trucks with about ten armed men in each. The trucks stopped too and men jumped over the side, one lot running through the rubber trees on each side of the bungalow, quickly forming a circle at a convenient range for tossing hand grenades.

For perhaps a minute all was quiet, no one moved; the platoon crouched in the rubber trees, guns at the ready. Then the officer in command stepped slowly out of the armoured car, a hand gun in one hand and in the other a loud-hailer. Even at a distance of a quarter of a mile the sound of his voice sent a chill down our spines: 'All outside, quickly.' Again the chilling silence. 'All outside, hands over heads, or we fire!'

From the door of the bungalow, keeping close together and unable to disguise their terror, came the three house boys, their hands held above their bowed heads. As they moved down the path from the steps they were each held by a Japanese soldier. Behind the three, her head held high, came Sheila, the sun glinting in her auburn hair as she moved slowly out of the shade of the verandah. As a small gesture of defiance both hands were down at her side; one held the hand of Fiona, and the other the lead of their Highland terrier.

The officer beckoned them forward, signalling two of the men from the armoured car to enter the house, presumably to ensure it was empty. We could not hear what instructions he was giving to Sheila. When the two men returned after a few minutes, presumably satisfied there were no Allied soldiers lurking there, the officer himself entered the bungalow.

After nearly half an hour had passed the officer returned and we could hear his staccato commands rattled out. The men surrounding the bungalow then 'fell in' on the concourse as he approached Sheila. What he said we could not hear, but we saw her escorted back into the bungalow, leaving Fiona to hold on to the little dog. We thought for a moment that perhaps they would let her remain; but our hopes were soon shattered. In a few minutes she returned carrying two small cases, no attempt being made by the guards to help her carry them. It now seemed certain that her captors were going to take her and Fiona away.

We watched through the trees as Sheila, her head still held high, with Fiona trailing just behind her, was led to one of the trucks by an armed escort of four. It was the last we were to see of Sheila as the truck turned around and disappeared over the hill. Although we had only met the day before I think we all missed her strength of character, and suddenly the realisation came over us that our last link with the past had been cut, we were quite alone and all around us was hostility.

It was Brem who broke the silence; 'I think we had better retreat now to our hideout in the ditch. It looks as if the Nips are going to set up some sort of command post in the bungalow, in which case they are sure to send scouts around the immediate area and are bound to come down the path that we took.'

It was by now early afternoon as we tidied up the hut to eliminate signs of our habitation and crawled down to the ditch, using the hut as cover from the bungalow.

'It should be safe to move back to the hut at dusk,' said Brem, 'and then we can make a start at first light on our jungle trek tomorrow.'

It was really quite cosy on our strips of rubber, partially shaded from the sun. It would have been ideal had not Fruity suddenly spotted the approach of an invasion force much nearer at hand. They were after our blood too: leeches. Along the banks of the stream from each direction they came, their backs humping up and down like little pistons as they raced towards us.

'We're going to be eaten alive,' exclaimed Fruity.

'Shut up, you silly bugger,' said Brem. 'You'll get a belly full of Japanese lead if you yell like that, long before any leeches can suck all your blood away. When each one has had its fill it will drop off; whatever you do, don't knock them off while they are feeding – if they leave their proboscises in a vein you can bleed quite profusely. The only sure way of getting them off, complete with their suckers, is to apply a burning cigarette end to their backsides. We can't risk lighting up here until after dark.'

'But that's four or five hours off,' moaned Fruity, 'by which time I will be bled white.'

'Don't be a stupid prick,' responded Brem. 'It would take about a couple of dozen of them to suck a pint of your blood in that time; don't forget you've got eight pints!'

It was not long before the activities of the leeches were of secondary consideration. Peeping through the clumps of grass we could just make out detachments of soldiers beginning to fan out from the bungalow, guns slung over their shoulders. Two were heading down the path towards our hut, which was some fifty feet away. Slowly they made their way down the path, looking to right and left. It was our first close contact with the Japanese infantry, and we did not wish it to be too close a meeting.

They were dressed in olive green singlets, which camouflaged well with the rubber tree leaves, below which were baggy green pantaloon-like trousers buckled at the tops of their boots. On their heads were green caps, something like those worn by engine drivers. They entered the hut, and we heard their strangely high-pitched sing-song voices as they foraged around. They did not seem in any hurry to clear off. Again we heard the sounds of Oriental discourse but this time in a higher and more excited tone. We could just see them follow one another out into the light, the first one holding something up between his fingers.

'Christ! it's one of our dog-ends!' I murmured. We froze as we tried to flatten ourselves into the ground. I could see the knuckles on Brem's hand whiten as he gripped harder on the rubber cutting knife that he held. We dared not try to look through the grass but we knew they would be looking in our direction, guns at the ready. For what seemed hours we held our breath.

Suddenly there was the crack of a twig from the vicinity of Fruity's foot that sounded to us as loud as a pistol shot. Then all hell was let loose. Unbeknown to us there had been an iguana sleeping in the long grass just a few yards downstream. Perhaps the tension that we were feeling had somehow alerted him too; certainly the cracking of the twig did. He started off at a rate of knots for the denser undergrowth, helped in his acceleration by bursts of automatic fire from the Jap soldiers. A Malayan iguana is quite harmless where humans are concerned, in spite of its size, some five or six feet on average from nose to tip of tail, and it looks quite fearsome. Its resemblance to the dragons we used to read about in fairy stories when young have given the iguana a sinister reputation it does not deserve. This one certainly deserved our ever-grateful thanks as it charged like a tank into the jungle. Had the Jap bullets been on target I doubt if they would have done more than sting it a little through its horny hide.

Although we still did not dare breathe we believed that the soldiers were satisfied that the cracking of the twig had been caused by the reptile. At that moment large spots of rain began to fall, and when that happens in Malaya it heralds the afternoon daily deluge. Our two little Japs decided it was time to make tracks back to the bungalow. Our immediate crisis was over as we crept back into the hut when the enemy was safely out of range.

The first task, having hung up our wet shirts and shorts to dry, was to light up fags and burn off the leeches, by now getting quite plump on our blood.

'This is really quite fun,' said Fruity, as the insects curled up and fell off one by one. 'I only hope they have not injected any disease into us.'

'Probably done a bit of good removing some of your piss-poor blood,' responded Brem. 'Don't forget that surgeons, even into the nineteenth century, were never without their cache of leeches when they went to visit a sick patient.'

As dusk began to gather, and it does not take long at latitude five north, we began to discuss our immediate plans of escape.

'It's clear we can't hang around here longer than this night,' I began, 'and Jap has set himself up in the bungalow, even if there was any sense in going back there.'

'I believe there are two roads and the railway line between us and the estuary,' said Brem. 'If we keep close to the stream we might be able to negotiate those hazards by using the culverts.'

'We shall need to watch our provisions,' I interposed. 'There's going to be nowhere to pop into a shop for a packet of Gold Flake. We've got about forty fags left in the tin; so it's one per person per day at sundown from now on, unless we have another leech emergency. We have a dozen tins of bully; so one tin between us every other day; the rest of the time we must try to live off the land or the sea. Fruity, you must be as good as your name by shinning up trees for coconuts whenever we can find them, or any other fruits we know to be edible.'

'There's one thing,' cut in Brem. 'We can always reckon to wring out our shirts each day for drinking water.'

'Right, lads,' I said. 'We had better get some sleep while we can, it may not be so comfortable for the next few nights; at least we have a roof over our heads here and the sheets of latex hanging up alongside us will help to keep the mossies off.'

'One of us had better keep awake all the time, just in case there are any sleep-walking Japs; so two hours on and two off. I'll take the first shift,' said Brem.

Chapter 12

At the first glimmer of light I roused the other two. We rolled up our rubber sheeting, which we secured with twine, of which there was plenty lying around, and, fastening the bundles on to our backpacks, we set off.

'I hope you've got a spare length of twine and a bent pin, Brem; we may need your fishing expertise if we survive the next day or two,' I said as we trudged along the edge of the rubber plantation, heading westwards.

'Sure thing,' responded Brem. 'I didn't mis-spend my youth in my coracle for nothing!'

As it became lighter it was apparent to us that we would have soon to forsake the comparatively easy progress alongside the rubber trees; for one thing we would be too exposed if any prowling patrols of Japs were around; also the stream was diverted towards the north-west. So we began the hacking through jungle routine, frequently finding ourselves sinking to crutch level in evil smelling mud. We began to sweat profusely in the hot and steamy atmosphere. Our shorts became saturated, either from the boggy water below or from the sweat running down our torsos. As we moved slowly forward we were conscious that the rumble of heavy traffic on the main road was getting closer.

Sometime after midday we reached a point, a hundred yards or so from the road, where a large tree had fallen across the stream. Climbing on top of its thick trunk we could see the traffic. Mostly it consisted of heavy lorries, some trailing guns, and tracked vehicles, heading slowly and remorselessly southward. There did not seem to be many gaps of more than two or three minutes between vehicles.

'We shall have to wait until after dark to get to the other side,' said Brem. 'In the meantime we can try to hack a passage through the undergrowth whenever there seems to be a worthwhile gap in the traffic; but don't take any chances of being seen.' By this method, with two moving forward cutting at the undergrowth whenever possible while the other one kept watch from on top of the tree trunk, before sundown we had cleared a passage to crawl through almost to the culvert under the road.

'Now it's just a question of waiting until the traffic thins out a bit after dark; there should be some light from the moon before midnight,' said Brem.

When the last vestiges of daylight faded in the west the mosquitoes came out in force. We had no protection for our faces, legs and arms, so the insects set about us and had a ball. It was some relief from the bites when we started eventually to crawl forward, very often on hands and knees. We had to be especially careful not to disturb any snakes; there would have been no chance of seeing whether they were the lethal variety or not, even if we could have told the difference.

We reached the gully that paralleled the road and lay down. We were sufficiently shielded there from headlights of vehicles.

'We'll draw sticks for who goes first through the culvert,' announced Brem. The short stick was picked by Fruity. He moved forward and into the mouth of the culvert, which was about four feet from roof to floor with two or three inches of water in the bottom. It was lucky for us that such large water passages were needed in order to cope with the frequent floods of rainwater.

Soon Fruity was back out again. 'Christ there's a pong in there; smells like several dead rats.'

'You can't be pernickity now,' I said. 'Take a deep breath and push on.'

Back in he went, only to shoot out again twice as fast this time. We couldn't see the pallor of his face but we knew his hand was shaking. 'There's a dead body in there,' Fruity blurted out. 'I kicked a skull.'

'Poor devil must have bought it when the Japs came down the road,' said Brem, 'and could only get as far as crawling into the culvert for protection before he snuffed it.'

'That could only have been a couple of nights ago,' said Fruity, still shaking.

'Doesn't take long in this climate to go off a bit,' said Brem unemotionally.

'Nothing is going to get me back in there, anyway,' said Fruity emphatically.

'Okay, then,' said Brem. 'It must be over the top, like in the First War trenches. Give a low whistle when you can find somewhere the other side

84

where we can take temporary refuge from headlights.'

At the speed most of the transport was moving we had about a minute from the time we could first see headlights approaching the bend to our right. As one truck passed us, with no more lights in sight, Fruity was up and across the tarmac like a hare. It seemed an age before we differentiated his low whistle from the insect noises that are ceaseless in jungles.

Soon we were both across and crouching in the opposite ditch. 'Where are you, you silly bugger?' I called out. A voice from several yards away in the undergrowth answered, 'Up here, there seems to be a clear path in the undergrowth where we can lie up.' We were soon all together again, one major obstacle having been overcome.

'It looks as if this must have been the lair of some animal,' said Brem. 'At least it's not here now; probably frightened away by the gunfire.'

'Let's hope it wasn't something large like a tiger, and wants to reclaim possession,' I chipped in.

'Right then,' said Brem. 'I took first guard duty last night, you two draw for who bats first tonight.'

The next day followed the same pattern as the previous one, and by mid-afternoon we had reached the single track of the Federated Malay States Railway. 'At least we are unlikely to be bothered by the Singapore-Penang express, or anything else for that matter,' announced Brem. 'The bridges will surely have been blown up.'

Wrong again. Just as we were about to make our crossing there was a low sort of metallic rumbling noise. Into sight round the bend came a hand-pump operated trolley. We fell flat on our faces in the scrub and prayed we hadn't been seen. As it passed by I am sure we would have burst out laughing had we not been so terrified. There at the rear of the trolley were two little Japs pumping up and down on the crank handles, whilst on the short bench in front, sitting rigidly upright, was a gold-braided Japanese officer, samurai sword dangling from his belt; beside him sat a sergeant, with his Japanese version of a tommy gun at the ready. The scene reminded us all of a clip from an old Buster Keaton comedy.

Once that had passed we crossed easily under the small bridge that carried the railway across 'our' stream, which had become much bigger by now. We pressed on through jungle until just before sunset when we came across a small clearing with some palm trees nearby. We decided to bed down for the night and explore around at dawn, for where there are palm trees there is usually some habitation near at hand.

The night passed uneventfully and by dawn we were moving again. Sure enough there were some native dwellings just beyond the palm trees which we crept by cautiously. There was no sign of life, either Malayan or, more importantly, Japanese; no doubt the occupants had fled at the sound of gunfire. We helped ourselves each to a young coconut, the milk of which made a welcome change from the rain or ditchwater we had been drinking.

Further on we came across a second road, presumably by-passing Taiping on the coastal side. It did not seem to be carrying much traffic, but we took the precaution of wading along the stream, which now showed signs of becoming tidal, and crossing under the bridge. Sure enough, about a mile past the road we came to the first of the mangrove trees. Mangroves spread up all tidal estuaries in the tropics and can extend for many miles on the larger rivers, even in Malaya. Ours was only a small stream, but joined a slightly larger river not far along. For the rest of that day we searched around on the verge of the mangroves in the hope that a sampan had been left unattended, in the same manner that we had found one on a Sunday afternoon at Sungei Patani. It had been barely a month previously, but seemed like a year.

We were out of luck, so decided to bed down for the night on a strip of dried-out mud. It would be reasonably comfortable; at least there was little threat from the enemy, for they did not seem to have penetrated into this back-water.

By around noon on the following day we struck lucky. We had progressed down-river until we could see, by climbing a tree and looking across the tops of the mangroves, that the river had widened into a creek. It was there that we came across a couple of sampans, moored to the roots of the mangroves in just the same way as those we had ventured upon near to camp at Sungei.

We could just make out a hut a short distance away, so decided to hang around quietly for an hour or two to see if there were any signs of life. Nothing stirred. The native Malays are a peace-loving race and usually rather timid. If they were indoors and knew we were there they made no move to approach us, probably thinking that we were armed soldiers.

About an hour before sunset, we decided not to hang around any longer, but to board the better-looking of the two boats and push off. We were very sorry for whoever owned the boat, but there was a war on and we did consider this to be an emergency. We paddled slowly and in silence, so as not to alert any residents there might have been nearby, and as darkness closed in upon us so did the mangroves so that we couldn't move any further. We were literally 'up the creek,' but we did have a paddle – two in fact – so there was nothing for it but to lie down as best we could in the boat and wait for daylight.

The dawn seemed a long time coming, and we were cold and stiff from trying to sleep stretched out on the rough boards with nothing but our narrow strips of latex beneath us, and not enough room for three to stretch out properly. The creeks in the mangroves had seemed like Hampton Court maze in the twilight of the previous day, but in broad daylight we soon found out where we had missed a gap in the mangroves, and within the hour we were paddling out into a wide estuary. Life seemed quite good once again, and we began to worry less about being behind enemy lines; or at least, I did.

Brem, ever the more cautious one, must have read my thoughts. 'We must not be lulled into a false sense of security, the Japs are still around us and if they come towards us in a gun-boat we've had it.'

The risk from aircraft was slight while we kept near to the mangroves; we had often heard planes passing overhead whilst we were in the jungle, conjecturing that they were probably Zeros or Mitsubishis based at Sungei Patani and Butterworth. 'I wonder if they have been able to use any of the tools we left behind,' said Brem.

'They wouldn't be able to do much with my tool box,' responded Fruity. 'I had lost anything that was any bloody use!'

With our two paddles we fell into a routine, each paddling for half an hour, so that we had fifteen minutes' rest every three-quarters of an hour. After paddling down the estuary for a couple of miles or so we espied a quay with a few buildings ahead of us on the left-hand bank. 'That must be Port Weld,' I volunteered. 'It is served by a branch line of the FMS from Taiping. Probably used in normal times to bring rubber and tin down to be loaded on to coastal cargo vessels.'

'Are there any Japs there, is what matters,' put in Fruity.

'I should think most likely there are,' said Brem. 'I dare say our friends on the plate-layers' inspection trolley were heading this way. The quay might be of some use if the Japs have any subs in the vicinity, although they are more likely to use Penang.'

'So we had better look out for periscopes then?' I cut in.

'Well, it's unlikely they have any surface warships around here just yet; at least we should still have control of shipping in the Malacca Straits,' contributed Brem.

"All things considered, I think we had better pull into the mangroves on the right-hand side and lie low until dark,' I advised. 'If we moved down abreast of the quay during daylight hours we would be sitting ducks for anyone with a telescope and a small gun.'

'I reckon that's about right,' said Brem. 'There is a nearly full moon tonight so we should be able to paddle past without detection, provided Fruity doesn't break out in song, in praise of the moon!'

So we nosed into the mangroves and lay up for the rest of the day. We were quite safe from approach on the northern side of the estuary as the swamps, covered by mangroves, seemed to stretch some way inland.

Again after sundown we ventured forth, paddling slowly and quietly, not daring to utter a word, for we could clearly hear voices across the water to our left. The moon was over the horizon as we left Port Weld behind us, which was just as well as the way out to the sea, marked by buoys, took a sharp turn to the right. We paddled gently on until nearly midnight, by which time we could feel a gentle swell and knew that we must be feeling the effects of the sea.

'I think we ought to call it a day until daylight,' said Brem. 'We can tie up to the last straggling outposts of mangrove branches and move off to sea at dawn.'

Personally, I felt apprehensive about many aspects of the projected row across to Sumatra, but kept my thoughts to myself as I could not think of a better idea of trying to get away, and the others seemed to be in favour; anyway there was always the chance that we might be picked up by Allied shipping going down the Straits. Frankly, I had not really expected we would get as far as we had, and now that we were actually on the brink of the long row in an open boat, without any protection against the elements or the enemy, I think I was beginning to develop cold feet, but didn't want to admit it.

'Don't you think, Brem,' I blurted out after a long pause, 'it would be better to get as far away from the coast as we can under cover of darkness. According to my reckoning it's more than a hundred miles to the nearest point of Sumatra from here, a dozen or more miles tonight would at least put us on our way.'

'Then we are going to be knackered in the morning and will need to rest up,' chorused Brem and Fruity. Brem carried on. 'The first day is going to be the greatest risk anyway, either from coastal patrol vessels the Japs may now have appropriated, or the odd strafing aircraft; we might as well tackle it when fresh after a few hours rest and move as fast as we can. We could do thirty or forty miles without another break.'

'Okay,' I said resignedly. 'You win. Let's tie up then.'

At first light we slipped our rope, thereby severing our connection with the mainland of Malaya, and headed due west. We had no compass so could only hope to maintain our direction by steering directly away from the main mass of mountains that formed the boundary between the States of Perah and Kelantan. If we were lucky enough to row out of sight of the Malay Peninsula we would have to rely entirely on the rising and setting sun, although Brem professed to know some of the main groups of stars if we were paddling at night.

We all felt a certain exhilaration at moving away from the country now occupied by the enemy, although I could not clear from my mind the thought that we were merely moving out of the frying pan into the fire. Our main threats at sea were threefold: we might be strafed from the air, captured by a hostile vessel, or wrecked by a violent tropical storm. Our little boat had scant defence against unfriendly elements, while it was only a matter of luck if we survived either of the other two hazards.

To say that we were all eager to ply our muscle power to the paddles was not quite true, for Fruity was starting to complain that he wasn't feeling very well. It was rather surprising that so far the three of us had remained fit in spite of drinking water out of ditches and being regularly bitten by mosquitoes. The chances were that Fruity was sickening for malaria. None of us had experienced malaria personally. We had accepted Sheila's offer of quinine, so that should keep the fever in check; beyond that it was a question of just lying down and sweating it out, which would probably take a day or two, and then leave Fruity too feeble to be much use with a paddle for the next couple of days or so. Although we felt sorry for Fruity, his illness would considerably reduce the chances of escape for all of us. Brem and I could not expect to keep paddling indefinitely, and it was not found to be practical for just one to paddle as it merely produced problems and we used up energy trying to keep the boat on a straight course. In purely mathematical terms it would take us half as long again to cover the distance, and would mean much stricter rationing of our dwindling supplies of food. Neither Fruity nor I put much score on Brem's ability to catch fish with a piece of twine and a bent pin!

As the sun approached its zenith and I was feeling weary of paddling in the heat, and with blisters forming on my hands, I was thinking more and more that we were not going to make it to Sumatra. Quite suddenly, the decision to voice my views was rendered unnecessary as fate took a dramatic hand.

During the morning we had seen a few aircraft passing by, usually at quite a distance. We assumed them all to be hostile, but we were too small and insignificant a target for them to waste ammunition on us. At least, that was what we had been thinking. By that time we were probably about ten miles out to sea and could just make out the mountain of Penang Island some forty miles to the north.

From the south, and heading straight towards us, we began to make out the shape of a single monoplane, flying barely a hundred feet above the sea: probably a Zero, we thought.

'If that bugger pulls his stick back as he goes overhead,' I said, 'get ready to jump before he can bank and line up the target; and don't bunch together or he might decide to aim for us.'

'What if he sinks the boat?' was Brem's reaction.

'Then we have either got a long swim ahead of us or it's curtains.'

'I'm not feeling well enough to swim,' moaned Fruity.

'Better to feel ill than stop a cannon shell,' I retorted unsympathetically.

By now the roar of the Zero's engine was rapidly becoming louder. As he shot by us, barely a hundred feet away, we could glimpse the pilot's helmeted head; we thought for a split second he was not going to bother about us. Suddenly the tail plane dipped and he roared upwards with full throttle.

I did not need to have shouted, 'Jump and scatter!' I had not considered myself a strong swimmer but in the time the aircraft took to climb to a sufficient height to bank round and head in for us I think I had covered nearly thirty yards and I didn't stop to look round as I heard the bullets hissing and furrowing at a tremendous pace across the surface of the sea. The terrifying sound was punctuated by a rending of splinters and I knew the boat had been hit.

I did not stop swimming away from the boat until the noise of the aircraft engine was dying away in the distance. No doubt the pilot was satisfied with his bit of target practice and didn't think us worth expending more fuel and ammunition.

As I swam back to the boat, rather more slowly than the outward thrash, I could see the sampan was beginning to settle in the water. As we three joined forces again the thought must have been in our minds that we could be stranded out here with just driftwood.

'What do we do now?' voiced Fruity, who was the last to home in on our sinking vessel. He was out of breath and clearly sickening for a fever; the involuntary swim would have done him no good at all. We eyed the damage. There were three gaping holes in a line diagonally amidships; luckily, our precious back packs and latex rolls, which we stowed fore and aft, had escaped damage, as had the paddles. Even Brem's battered pith helmet was unscathed.

Brem surveyed the rent timbers thoughtfully. 'Have you still got your latex cricket ball, Ken?'

I had taken a small chunk of raw latex from the plantation when we evacuated it as the Japs moved in to the Fergusons' bungalow. As we had lain in the ditch it was a sort of therapy for me to knead it into the shape of a cricket ball. It took me back nostalgically to summer weekends before the war when my greatest thrill was to be out on a cricket field giving my all for the club. Whilst the leeches were sucking their fill in the plantation ditch I had been gripping my newly shaped ball in the manner of bowling a leg-break out of the back of my hand, something that I had never carried out successfully on the field. It had helped then to calm my nerves when first confronted at close quarters by the enemy; now it was going to be sacrificed in a worthier cause to improvise plugs for the cannon shell holes.

For more than an hour we squeezed and kneaded the rubber into the rends in the woodwork, at the same time baling out with Brem's battered bonce cover.

'We shall just have to paddle back to the comparative safety of the

91

mangroves and then hold a council of war about what we do next.' I said at length.

Fruity, who by now was in no fit state to wield a paddle, kept the water level inside the boat in check. We all fell silent, our hopes at the dawn of the day now shattered. No one was feeling like discussing our dismal prospects as we nosed our way into the mangroves again until we found a mud bank where we could heave the boat mostly out of the water. By now it was almost dark and we were tired and dispirited. We unrolled our rubber strips and all fell into a deep sleep.

Chapter 13

The sun was well up next day before we were all fully conscious. It was our day of reckoning; what should we do next? During our slow, laborious paddle back to the mangrove swamps the tide had carried us out some three or four miles to the north. To the south we could see nothing but mangrove swamps; further north, at a distance of some four miles, we could make out a few small buildings and *atap* huts. We could only see those by climbing up as far as we dared in the mangrove trees. It was a depressing place to be, particularly in our depressed state; but at least we were thankful for the shade and cover from the aircraft which we could hear from time to time and which were almost certainly hostile. Indeed, our time in the Air Force had familiarised us with the sounds of British aero engines and those that came near to us now had a different ring from their pistons.

'Who's going to chair the meeting then?' I started when the eyes of the others were more or less open. Fruity did not seem to be in a condition to be particularly interested in anything.

'It's now a question of elimination,' responded Brem after a long pause. 'We can't stay here for long; we have no more than a few days' bully and biscuits left and there is no fruit within easy reach. While we still have a boat, surely we don't want to go inland where we are bound to be picked up in no time. We now know that the risks are too great to paddle straight across to Sumatra, particularly with only two of us to use the paddles while Fruity is sick, and in a leaky boat. We can only move in safety at night; so do we paddle south or north?'

'If we go south we don't know how far the Japs have advanced by now,' I said. 'We would be quite likely to put into the shore in the morning, to lay up for the day, and find ourselves surrounded by armed Japs. I don't fancy our chances of being able to paddle all the way to Singapore, and even Port Dickson must be a couple of hundred miles south, and that might even be captured before we got there. So it has to be north.'

'At least it is only about thirty miles to the southern part of Penang Island,' ruminated Brem. 'We could almost do that in one night, certainly in two.'

'Perhaps we might find some friends willing to help us,' I continued.

'Certainly there are many Chinks who are not exactly ardent fans of the Japs after what they have done in their homeland,' said Brem.

'I think I've got it,' as an idea lodged itself in my brain. 'How about Fruity's girl friend and her family?'

At the mention of his name Fruity became slightly less uninterested in the happenings of the world about him. As the idea penetrated his throbbing head maybe the thought of getting to know Wong Befung a little better, or even a lot better, appealed to him, although in his present state he was hardly likely to thrill her; but she might just like to mother him. 'OK,' croaked Fruity. 'What have we got to lose?'

'So we are all agreed then?' said Brem, and without waiting for any replies: 'We'll disentangle ourselves from these mangroves just before sundown and paddle ourselves northwards as far as we can. We shall have to find ourselves a safe haven to rest up for a day or two while we improve our repairs on the boat for the crucial final paddle to Penang, and to give Fruity a chance to get better; we can hardly expect him to charm his way into the Wong household in his present state.'

'Too right,' moaned Fruity.

We consumed our meagre ration of bully beef and biscuits, then lay down to rest before the night's toiling. Our rest was only interrupted by the usual daily downpour of rain. It had become a regular routine to take off our khaki shirts and lay them across the boat to soak up the rainwater while we had a shower bath. Sometimes we were able to wring two or three pints into empty bully tins, which in turn we poured safely into our aluminium service issue water bottles. We took care this time to cover Fruity over with the two spare rubber strips.

It was most unlikely that anyone would find us in our place of concealment, but we took the precaution of not pushing ourselves clear of the mangroves before sunset.

Brem and I took it steadily, taking a short rest every twenty minutes and perhaps covering no more than two miles an hour. It was the day of the winter solstice, so we had a clear twelve hours of darkness; for most of that time we had help from the moon, which at least gave sufficient light to keep us on course.

As the first light etched the mountains to the east we could begin to make out two tiny islands on the port side, about a mile out from the shore. They seemed little more than large rocks and, as is often the case in this part of the world, rose high out of the water: probably the remains of some volcano many milleniums ago. We decided to head for these little islands, which we could expect to be uninhabited, in the hopes of finding some small flat area where we could heave our boat out of the water and, if possible, out of sight.

The first island seemed to be sheer right the way round, but on the second, only a couple of hundred yards or so away, we could just make out a couple of palm trees on the seaward side, which probably meant there was some sand. We paddled as fast as we could towards it, hoping that we had not been sighted from the mainland as the sun began its journey across the heavens once again.

Luck was with us this time as we grounded on some pebbles. Beyond them we could see a tiny patch of sand over which our two palm trees drooped. Brem and I hopped out, scattering some sand crabs as we did so, and hauled the sampan clear of the water and under cover of the trees, with Fruity still dormant inside it.

'This should suit us,' said Brem, 'for as long as it takes Fruity to get on his feet again.'

'Almost like a setting for a holiday brochure,' I said, and added, 'Do you know what day it is? Christmas Eve.'

'I shall take more notice of New Year's Eve,' said Brem, 'if we last that long.'

'With luck we should be with the Wongs by then,' I said. 'I wonder if they will celebrate the start of the New Year?'

'Sure they will,' responded Brem, 'but their one doesn't start until the end of January. I think the next one is the Year of the Horse; we are still in the Year of the Snake.'

'Ain't education wonderful?' mumbled Fruity, whom we had rather forgotten about.

'Glad to hear you are beginning to take an interest in life again, Fruity,' I volunteered.

'Like ----- I am,' he said, and promptly subsided into slumber again.

95

For Brem and me the day passed quite pleasantly. We were able to knock down a few fresh coconuts, and even found some plantains growing in a crevice of the rock. They were rather green and hard so we laid them out in the sun in the hopes that they might ripen in time to eat for dessert at our special Christmas dinner planned for the next day. The remaining hours of daylight were mainly used to improve our repairs on the boat. At Brem's suggestion we also started to fashion ourselves three Chinese coolie-type conical hats, by plaiting the fronds of the palm trees. It was quite a useful piece of therapy, and might help to disguise us as we paddled inshore on Penang Island.

From where we were we could see, due westward, the southern-most tip of Penang Island. 'Do you think, Brem, we ought to paddle round the island to get near to where the Wongs live?' I said. 'According to Fruity their home is to the north of Georgetown quite near to the sea-shore, but to get there direct from here we would have to paddle through the narrow strip of water between Butterworth and the Victoria Pier on the island.'

'On the other hand,' replied Brem, 'we would have a long paddle to go right round the west side of the island, which we might not be able to do in one night, and there is as much chance of being spotted doing it as the shorter route. I think we stand the best chance if we try to shoot through the narrow part about four o'clock in the morning, when the ferries are unlikely to be running, and we should reach the shore near to the Wongs by dawn.'

'Okay,' I responded, 'we will then try to hide the boat, and ourselves, while Fruity does his stuff. So it's only a question now of waiting until Fruity is fit enough to perform.'

There were no stockings hanging up for Father Christmas next morning on what was the oddest, and would probably be the most memorable, Christmas Day of our lives. At least, we were enjoying comparative safety on our tiny island, and it was a day of rest. Fruity was showing signs that his fever was abating, but it would be a couple of days before he would be recovered enough for us to move off.

Our Christmas dinner consisted of a double ration of bully beef which we were able to heat up with driftwood ignited with one of our preciously guarded matches – most had been rendered useless when we were machine-gunned. Brem concocted a kind of vegetable with mashed up plantains and flesh from the coconuts. For afters, we opened the one tin of peaches which

Fruity had insisted on taking from the Ferguson bungalow. The whole meal was washed down with coconut milk, laced with a few drops of brandy from the small bottle of Martell that Sheila Ferguson had insisted we should take in case of emergency.

'Here's to the folks at home,' said Brem, raising his empty bully tin that served for a mug. 'I expect they are thinking of us now, or rather they will be in about six hours' time when they have their Christmas dinners.'

We all fell silent at the thought of our homes; dare we expect ever to be in the bosom of our families again?

Fruity was able to sit up and partake of some of the food and drink, plus an extra tot of brandy. We prescribed him a further forty-eight hours light duty. 'We've got to have you fit enough at least to stand up and walk when we beach on Penang; our lives depend on you being able to win over the Wongs.'

'Depend on me, lads,' said Fruity weakly. 'Just let me lie down again now.'

'Do I remember, Fruity, that you said Father Wong is a sea captain?' I said, before he dropped off to sleep again.

'Sure did,' replied Fruity. 'I don't know what sort of vessel it is or whether or not he owns it.'

'Whatever the case, there is a glimmer of hope there as a means of escape,' said Brem.

Boxing Day passed quietly for us, as Fruity's strength began to return. We saw quite a bit of military activity from our little eyrie. In the skies above we saw several planes, some of which appeared to be climbing from take-off at Butterworth airfield, which by now was sure to be in use by the Japs. There was no sign of any Allied planes. At sea we saw two motor vessels moving southwards close to the coast. We presumed they had been sequestered by the Japs in Penang harbour. Fruity swore that he had seen the periscope of a submarine; but we put it down to hallucinations.

We awoke the next morning for the last day on our little island. Having finished weaving our mock Chinese coolie hats we caused much merriment trying them all on in turn. However, we thought we would get by in them in a dim light. We packed up our bits and pieces and stowed everything in the boat, ready to push off at sundown. In the afternoon we relaxed on the little patch of sand to compose ourselves for the crucial night's work.

At six o'clock, when the sun dipped down behind Penang Island, we cast off from our friendly haven and headed north. We paddled slowly so as to make as little noise as possible, and spoke only when necessary in whispers. We had some help in navigating from the light of a quarter moon, but most assistance came from noises on the shore, and also from the glimmer of lights in dwellings, for the Japs clearly had not been able to enforce a strict black-out by the Malays and Chinese.

All of our senses were sharpened during that night. Smell was a big factor; as we approached the narrow strip of water between Butterworth and Georgetown docks the pungent aroma became stronger and stronger as the off-shore night breezes wafted it out to sea. It was difficult to describe other than to say it was Oriental in flavour.

Just before we reached the critical narrows, at around midnight, we heard to our right the clanking of goods waggons as we drew abreast of the railway jetty on the mainland where we had disembarked from the express from Singapore last May. Paddling very slowly and quietly, not daring to speak, we had reached the critical point, where the channel was less than a mile wide, rather sooner than we meant to. Instinctively we moved closer to the mainland shore where all seemed to be quiet, while we could hear voices across the water from the harbour on the island. Whether it was Chinese or Japanese being spoken we knew not, but at times the tones became excitable. It was probably Japanese soldiers belabouring a Chinese ferryman to take them across to Butterworth; we had done the same when we were the top dogs. The sounds of voices grew nearer with the splashing of oars on the water. With the humiliation of the vanquished we cowered flat in our sampan praying the ferry boat would not hit us and we would not be noticed in the inky blackness. They passed by much too close for our comfort; if the ferryman had noticed our boat he would not have dared to stop, but may have made a mental note to look out for a drifting sampan on the way back. We were not intending to hang around to find out.

Soon we were skirting round vessels in the harbour; there did not seem to be as many as there used to be. We just avoided a black mass of metal which we took to be a Japanese submarine, then we were beyond the main harbour area and we began to ease gently to port to try to make contact with the land near where Fruity had described the Wong house was situated. In the almost complete darkness, for the moon had set soon after midnight, we could not

98

be sure of anything except that we had now passed most of the lights that were showing from Georgetown: there was nothing to do but wait for sufficient daylight to see our way in to a suitable landing spot.

At the first light in the east we could see we were further off shore than we had thought, but we were clear of the shipping. The twilight period is very short near the equator, and we hoped we had not been spotted as we paddled furiously in to a small indentation in the coast and quickly pulled our boat into some convenient trees that overhung the water. We could make out the outline of a large house some distance back from the top of a low cliff; there did not seem to be any sign of life. Brem and I helped Fruity up the twenty feet or so to the top of the cliff where there was a narrow track leading upwards.

'We are going back now, Fruity,' I whispered, 'to hide under that overhang of vegetation near the boat; for Christ's sake don't forget where we are. And good luck.'

'This is your big moment,' chipped in Brem. 'Don't forget it's what we brought you here for.'

'I shan't let you down,' whispered Fruity, glad to feel well enough again to take centre stage. 'See you both again soon.'

There was nothing for Brem and me to do now but wait and pray.

Chapter 14

The minutes ticked by; the sun rose clear of the mountains across Perak. We could hear noises of humans up beyond the cliff as people began to go about their daily business. We could also hear traffic moving along a road not far away.

An hour went by; still no one came to look for us. I began to feel edgy and apprehensive; I am sure Brem felt the same. Still nobody came near us. We were beginning to despair.

Just as we were deciding we would have to make our own way into the town, and try to find someone who was friendly, we both saw a female form working her way slowly and carefully around the rocks near the shore, followed by a second figure who looked remarkably similar. Indeed, we learnt later they were twins.

As they came nearer we also noted that they were young and pretty, in an oriental way, with long black hair hanging down almost to their waists. The one in front gave a little gasp of surprise as we moved out of the shadow of the bushes.

'Are you Brem and Ken?' she said quietly in perfect English, intoned in that enchanting sing-song voice of the Chinese maidens. 'I am Tau Fong, and here is my twin sister Hang Fong,' and they clasped their hands together in front of them and each gave a little bow.

We seemed both awkward and clumsy as we blurted out how pleased we were to see them. For my part, I really was enchanted with their beauty and the gentle fragrance that emanated from the two girls who stood before us smiling sweetly.

'I am Ken, with the blonde hair, and this is Brem, with black hair, like both of you; indeed all of your race,' I added rather unnecessarily; but it made the girls giggle a bit, and helped break the ice. I wished I was a bit better at chatting up.

'You boys follow us,' said Tau Fong. 'Put on your hats that Fruity says you have made and try to look Chinese!'

We really did not need the invitation. Come to think of it, Brem did look a bit Chinese already with his black hair, sallow complexion and several days' growth of beard. For my part I was rather conscious of my Saxon blondness and florid complexion.

Once we had rounded the little headland beneath the large house we climbed up on to a pathway near to the water's edge and set off at a steady pace.

'Fruity is not very well,' said Hang Fong, breaking the silence. 'He has fever, so Befung is looking after him. He told us where to find you.'

'Fruity has been ill with malaria,' said Brem, 'but we are thankful, very thankful indeed, that he was able to find you and that you seem prepared to lead us to your house.'

The girls smiled sweetly. 'We are very happy, and honoured, to give you shelter,' said Tau Fong, and continued: 'We must keep quiet now and not speak any English, for we are passing near to houses soon and one does not know who is one's friend now.' We fell silent and followed on for another few minutes, passing some high walled houses, all painted white, before turning into a doorway let into a wall of some eight or nine feet in height. Hang Fong shut the door behind us. 'Now you are safe and we can all relax,' she announced.

The girls led us into a large room, with windows and a double door leading out on to a courtyard beyond, where we could see potted plants growing.

Fruity was already reclined on cushions in one corner, with another girl, in many ways similar to the twins, kneeling beside him.

'This is our sister Befung,' announced Tau Fong to Brem and me. 'She had told us about Fruity when they first met some months ago. She said he was a nice polite boy who behaved like a gentleman to her.' That had not always been our opinion of Fruity, but we were glad he had projected himself in that manner to Befung.

Befung clasped her hands in front of her, facing first Brem and then myself, bowing her head and bending her knees quickly in the approved Oriental greeting which we were finding quite enchanting, particularly when carried out by a pretty, smiling young girl.

101

'You boys must be very hungry,' announced Befung. 'I and my sisters will cook you a proper Chinese meal; you just sit down and relax.' So saying, the three of them glided out through a door to one side of the big room.

We did as bade and sank on to the soft cushions that were strewn around the room. For the first time in three weeks we were really able to relax and the tensions that had been with us all the while dropped from us, so much so that we all drifted into blissful sleep. How long we slept I know not, but I was brought back to consciousness by the most exquisite aroma of hot food and realised that the girls were busying themselves at low tables which they had placed near to us.

I had not experienced a proper Chinese meal before, and would not have known where to start had not Tau Fong knelt down beside to explain the dishes and ladle out something from each.

'You really ought to eat with chopsticks,' she said in her lilting voice, 'but we will teach you another time; for now you can use spoon or you will be all day at it.'

'You must eat with us,' I said, by way of trying to be polite.

'We want to see if you like first,' replied Tau Fong, 'then we have some.'

I would have said we could have eaten anything at that moment, but confined myself to commenting how delicious it was. When they were satisfied that we really did like it the girls selected a little for themselves and joined us eating. When all of us three were full to the point of bursting the girls served tea: China of course. I had never been particularly enamoured with China tea on the few occasions I had sampled it back home, but here, and in these surroundings, served with mint instead of milk, there was nothing could be more refreshing.

Brem broke the silence when all had finished eating: 'Do your parents live with you in this big house?'

'Our mother died a few years ago,' said Hang Fong sadly. 'We will tell you about it some day.'

'And your father?' I questioned.

'He is a merchant trader, he sails his own ship – a ketch, buying mostly cloth in places like Assam and Burma and selling it in ports in Malaya and Sumatra. Often he takes rubber from Malaya up to the north. When the war started he had gone to Mandalay and Rangoon with our two brothers, one older, and the younger one, aged fourteen, to act as crewmen. We are very

102

worried whether they have escaped the shooting and bombings; many houses nearer the centre of Georgetown here were flattened with the bombs and lots of people killed.'

'We know,' said Fruity. 'We saw much of it from the beach across the water at Butterworth; I was very anxious that you were not amongst those who suffered.'

'When father and the boys go away we look after the house and earn money from a shop we own in the town where father sells some of his wares,' said Befung.

'Do you have any husbands or boy friends?' enquired Brem.

The girls all giggled a little. 'Husbands, no,' said Befung, as eldest, acting as spokeswoman. 'Boy friends we have sometimes, but none seriously, or so my sisters say.'

'Does your father trust you all when he is away?' said Fruity.

'Of course,' replied Befung, a trifle indignantly. 'I am twenty and have been looking after the family since my mother was killed four years ago. We are good Chinese and respect our father.'

'I am sorry,' said Fruity. 'I did not intend to offend you. We are just uncouth Britishers.'

'How is it you all speak such excellent English?' I asked. 'It is almost better than Brem's and Fruity's, though come to think of it, they are not English either.'

'How do you mean?' questioned Tau Fong.

'Don't you remember at school in Shanghai,' cut in her elder sister, 'we had a teacher from Scotland, who was proud of being British but would disown the English and Welsh.'

'So that is why you know our language and customs so well,' said Brem. 'Do I understand that you attended an English missionary school in Shanghai?'

'Yes,' said Befung. 'We spent most of our formative years there until the Japanese invaded. We will tell you some time about the terrible things that made my father leave his native land. He was a fairly wealthy man, with a profitable business, plying his own ship up and down the Yangtse River. He has always liked the English, sorry, British, and did much of his business with them. He hates Japanese.'

'That may be just as well for us,' said Brem, 'We are learning to hate them too.'

103

'We are hearing terrible things that they are doing to Europeans who don't do as they are told,' said Hang Fong. 'People say that white men have been tied to trees and bayonetted.'

'But surely they would not do that sort of thing to prisoners of war?' said Brem. 'The Geneva Convention would not permit it.'

'Geneva is a very long way away,' said Befung. 'Maybe the Germans and Italians observe convention, but here in the East the Japanese Empire will be a law unto itself; you had best not try to find out at close quarters.'

'We certainly have no desire to give ourselves up easily,' said Brem, 'nor do we want to get killed. On the other hand we cannot stay here indefinitely, for we must be a risk to you and your family.'

'You are safe behind these walls, so long as no one who is not our friend saw you entering,' said Befung. 'Please do not go before our father returns, he will plan what should be done; we think he will help. Anyway, we don't want you to go.'

'Of course we do not want to go,' said Brem, 'but the war may go on for years, probably will; even if we stay in the house out of sight, someone sometime is sure to find out and will disclose his knowledge to the Japanese in exchange for favours.'

'For a while we think you are quite safe here,' continued Befung. 'We were searched by the Japanese within days of them taking control of the town. Penang was not heavily defended and there was no organised fighting in the streets. The Japs set up their local headquarters in the Town Hall and commenced rounding up all the Europeans on the island. Within two days the Elysée dance hall and the main cinema were full of refugees; although most were not military personnel they were going to be made to suffer. Most have now been moved across to the mainland, we know not where.'

'Have you seen many Japanese soldiers?' I asked.

'There are a lot billeted in the old barracks and the hospital is full of wounded,' said Hang Fong. 'There are some sailors too; we think they are from the submarine that arrived two days ago.'

'Why do you think they searched the house?' Brem asked. 'Surely they can't search all the houses in Georgetown.'

'I expect it's because this house is close to properties owned by Europeans who were taken prisoner,' said Befung. 'They thought that there might be some hiding here. Luckily the Japs did not try to rape us.'

104

'We will see they don't now,' said Fruity with bravado, although not in a fit state to overcome an enemy himself.

'When we have cleared away,' said Befung, 'we will show you to your rooms. This house has many rooms, some of which are used partly as store-rooms for the wares that father buys. There are many bales of cloth, some of which we make up into clothing to sell in town.'

The girls moved silently outside, taking away the evidence of our meal with them. In the meantime we were all trying to nod off to sleep again. The volume of food and drink that we had consumed, after a week of near starvation, had played its part in weighing down our eyelids.

In half an hour or so the girls returned from the kitchen, beckoning us to follow. The house extended much further than we had thought and beyond the courtyard there was a corridor with several doors on both sides.

Befung showed each one of us in turn into a room. 'Each room has a shower and a mattress, and we will stack the bales of cloth that are in them in such a way that you could conceal yourselves should the Japs come back again.'

'This is all beyond our wildest expectations,' I said to the girls when we had completed our conducted tour. 'I don't know how we can ever repay you.'

'You do not have to think about it,' said Befung. 'This is wartime, and we consider the Japanese to be as much our enemy as yours.

'Enough of the future,' she continued. 'Let us just live for the present now. Each time we have come into the room we have noticed your eyes have been closed, so we think you ought to throw yourselves on to your mattresses and sleep right through to tomorrow morning.'

We did not need a second telling; within minutes of bidding the girls goodnight we had crawled beneath our mosquito net and were fast asleep.

Chapter 15

I awoke next morning to find the sunlight streaming through a window in the opposite wall. I felt the days of growth around my chin and decided I didn't want to grow a beard just yet. I still had my Gillette with me and a stick of shaving soap, so I soon set about scraping it all off.

I was just about finishing when the door opened softly and Tau Fong entered, clad in a white kimono with a band of blue material loosely knotted round the waist; she was carrying a cup of tea.

'I thought I heard you moving around and expected you might like a cup of tea,' she said.

'I most certainly would,' I said as I took the cup from her and began to sip. Her sweet smile, beneath her large brown eyes, emboldened me to continue: 'I think you look very pretty,' I managed to stammer out, 'standing as you are in white and blue.'

She blushed a little and gently shut the door behind her. 'Will you let me wash your clothing, it must be very dirty after your days living rough.'

'Well, yes, it is,' I responded. 'That would be very good of you – my shirt is there on the mattress.'

She reached down and picked up the shirt, streaked as it was with salt deposits from immersion in the sea. 'And what about your shorts?'

'B-but I am wearing the only pair I have,' I stammered.

'Give them to me, then,' she commanded, and then paused as she realised my confusion. 'You are not ashamed of your body, are you?'

'No, of course I'm not,' I got out, my voice rising a pitch.

'I am not ashamed of mine: look!' So saying she quickly undid the waistband, wriggling her shoulders a little at the same time so that the kimono gently fell down around her ankles.

I think I must have presented quite a sight as my jaw fell open and I knew I must be blushing a deep shade of red.

She let out that tinkling laugh that I found so attractive. 'Why are you so shy, Ken, have you not seen a girl with no clothes on before?'

'To be truthful, not a fully grown one, or so near,' I had to tell her. True there had been the time when my four-year-old cousin had taken off her knickers to go paddling on a hot summer's day on the Essex coast, but that was hardly in the same league.

'I could be nearer,' said Tau Fong, casting her long lashes down as she moved slowly towards me with her arms extended to my waistband. Gently she undid my belt and buttons, and my grimy shorts fell to the ground. In tropic climes underpants were not usually worn.

As her arms moved up around my neck my shyness was overcome by emotion as our lips met, softly at first, then passionately. I don't remember how we subsided on to the mattress, I only know she was doing wondrous things with her hands and soon my whole world erupted with ecstacy.

Time was suspended as we lay there clasped tightly together. I became conscious that Tau Fong was whispering in my ear, 'Now, my big boy, you are no longer a virgin.'

'I just know that I feel on top of the world,' I exclaimed. 'I want to climb on to the roof and shout it for all the town to hear – I have had sexual intercourse!'

'If you do, you are not likely to be able to do it again; don't forget the Japs are still all around us,' reminded Tau Fong.

'Are you meaning you will let me do it again?'

'Maybe,' said Tau Fong coyly. 'Don't forget you are still a learner, but I think you will learn fast.' So saying, she slipped into her kimono and let herself quietly out of the room, taking my clothes with her for *dhobying*.

I was left wondering if the other two had been enjoying similar experiences. Fruity by his own account was no virgin; but Brem may well have been, for I cannot recall him ever having boasted about any conquests.

There was not much I could do, with propriety, about finding out how the others were faring as I had nothing to wear; even my towel was not big enough to stretch properly round my waist. So I took a long refreshing shower: there was no hurry; there was nowhere we had to go; indeed, nowhere we could go with safety.

I was just drying myself between the toes when Tau Fong came back in the room. Instinctively, I clutched the towel across my private parts; or to be more exact, parts that had been private until half an hour before. My actions caused Tau Fong to emit that little tinkling silvery laugh that I found so enchanting, sending little shivers up and down my spine every time I heard her do it.

'I have come to bring you a change of clothing. These are what we sell in the shop; what colour would you like?' she enquired.

'I think I would like the white shorts, they will remind me of when I played cricket as a small boy.'

'Cricket, what is cricket?' enquired Tau Fong, rolling the word round in her mouth, and flashing her pearly white teeth.

'Never mind,' I replied. 'Maybe I will be able to show you one day.'

I turned around, still feeling bashful, and slipped into the beautifully tailored and creased shorts, with shirt to match.

'Turn around now,' commanded Tau Fong, 'Yes, you look beautiful.'

'Boys are not beautiful,' I remonstrated.

'You are to me,' and she kissed me full on the lips, then put her forefinger across my mouth, for she must have seen my eyes kindle with desire. 'Not now, perhaps when it is dark. I go now to cook a meal,' and away she flitted again.

In an hour or so I heard the beating of a gong and made my way along the corridor to join the others. I could tell by the oblique glances cast by Brem and Fruity that they also had been sexually entertained. So it was all a conspiracy on the part of the girls; but who were we to complain?

Again we sat down to a sumptuous repast, but with several subtle variations of dishes, washed down with a wine distilled from rice.

'If you continue to feed us like this, girls,' said Fruity as he cleared up his plate, 'we will leave here looking like balloons.'

'But you were so skinny when you staggered in here yesterday,' responded Befung. 'We could see your ribs standing out. We like to see you eating well and enjoying the food we prepare. Do you not have Chinese meals in England?'

'I suppose you can,' I mused, 'in the Chinatown areas of cities like London and Liverpool.'

'Perhaps there is a fortune to be made in Chinese restaurants after the war,' exclaimed Fruity. 'Will you marry me, Befung and come to England? We could start up a chain of Chinese restaurants, helped as we get older, of course, by our family of Anglo-Chinese children!'

Everyone laughed at this suggestion but Befung seemed inclined to give consideration to the thought. 'If you are really serious I might just say yes to the idea. We could start by living over our first shop and selling meals to take away to be eaten at home.'

'That's an idea that could just catch on,' responded Fruity. 'I'll pop the question again if we both survive this war.'

We were suddenly jolted back to reality by this remark, to realise that our future was very far from secure.

Secretly, I could not wait for night time and wondered whether the other two were thinking the same. It must be like being on honeymoon, but with friends near at hand. The main difference was that there was a hard and hostile world the other side of the walls and one could get one's head blown off just peeping over the top.

Darkness came at last, as it always does, but just seemed to take longer this day. I think we all made some play of showing tiredness, like the half-stifled yawn now and again, as we talked about our respective countries and traditions.

Fruity was the first to make the move, using the excuse that he had not yet fully recovered from his fever. In fact, when I lay down in bed I really was tired and soon dropped off into a deep sleep. The unwinding of all the tensions since the fateful 8 December was not to be denied.

I don't know what time it was when I became conscious of the stirring of the mosquito net and the warm silky skin of Tau Fong's naked body sidled up to mine, sending electric shocks darting up and down my spine. She whispered in my ear, 'I have come for lesson two.'

'Just lesson number two?' I questioned sleepily. 'May we not have number three, or even four, and perhaps five? Then I might consider myself having passed my test, if you are in agreement, by tomorrow morning.'

'You might have passed out altogether by then, at that rate,' said Tau Fong, emitting her infectious little giggle.

'You must tell me sometime, my little sweetheart, how it is you are so knowledgeable in the ways of love and life at the age of seventeen,' I retorted in mock reproach, 'and me a clear four years older than you; but now it is not a time to start arguing.'

Slowly and tenderly we entwined together and joined in union; it was a night I shall always treasure till my dying day.

I don't know how long the sun had been shining when I awoke, nor did I care; we had nowhere to go. Indeed, where else should I want to go at that moment; I only wished it would last for ever. I glanced down at Tau Fong, still sleeping peacefully encircled by my left arm, her head on my chest; I cast my eyes downward over her honey-coloured body, her jet black tresses draped across her ribs, and before them the lissom curves that ended at her tiny feet. I knew then that I was falling in love. It was complete madness, of course, and I knew I should fight it but the will was weak; what would be, would be.

Tau Fong opened her eyes and gazed up into mine in a way that was irresistible; who was I to resist. At length we heard girlish voices calling in Chinese, amid much giggling. Tau Fong sat up with a start and blushed. 'I must not kiss you again before departing or we shall be here all day. It is me who is the novice now.' And so she threw on her kimono and hurried out of the room.

Our midday meal finished, rather later than on the previous two days, we three felt that we ought to be doing something, apart from making love to our hostesses, that might be appreciated by way of earning our keep.

It was Brem who enquired what we might do to help.

'We usually spend our spare time at home making garments for the shop,' replied Befung, 'but as the shutters have been up since before the bombing and we do not consider it safe to reopen, at least until father returns, there does not seem to be much point in us making more clothing; indeed we may never open up the shop again. I could not bear having to sell goods to Japanese, but we will do what our father bids us.'

'If you feel you need something to occupy your minds as well as your time,' cut in Hang Fong, 'may we not teach you some simple Chinese words and phrases. It would come in useful later on.'

We three looked at one another; I think that we all thought that it might be rather pleasant to have our respective girlfriends kneeling by our sides, even if we weren't able to grasp the lingo.

So that afternoon, and indeed every afternoon while we were in Penang, we passed the hours pleasantly in the big room with the three girls, trying to twist our tongues round the Chinese sounds amid much merriment, particularly amongst the girls, who would try to will their own special boyfriend to get it right and clapped their hands with glee at each little success. Fruity was the star pupil, perhaps because the Welsh spoken in his native valleys has something of the sing-song sounds of Chinese. Also, Fruity was less inhibited about making a fool of himself than Brem and I. Languages never had been my strong point.

That night I thought perhaps Tau Fong would not come again to visit me, and as dawn began to break I opened my eyes to find I was still alone. Had she not cared? Perhaps I was mistaken about the light in her eyes; maybe she had just been providing comforts for the troops. These thoughts and many others in similar vein were passing through my mind when the door opened softly and Tau Fong tiptoed in with my morning cup of tea. This time there was no pretence at covering herself in a kimono; she wore only the white hibiscus bloom in her hair where her long tresses were held back to reveal a delicate ear. I drank in her beauty as she stood there in the half-light holding out my cup of warm tea.

'Do you not want your tea this morning, my sweetness,' she whispered softly in her tinkling tones that sent shivers up and down my spine.

'Yes, my darling, of course I do, it's just that I want you more.'

She nestled down beside me as I gulped down my drink, eager to get it finished. 'I thought that you weren't coming to me this night, that perhaps you had not enjoyed the night before after all.'

By way of an answer she kissed me gently on the ear as I finished the last gulp of tea. 'I simply thought that you would want a good night's sleep – I did too, after the night before,' she said coyly.

'If you are not going to be here long let us make the most of our time while we can,' I said, forever practical, as I slipped my right arm around her slender waist and caressed her small but firm right breast with its hard little cherry of a nipple.

'You need not be in such a hurry,' responded Tau Fong, but not attempting to remove my caressing hand. 'We sisters have decided we will prepare a feast for tonight as it is New Year's Eve, and we will drink to the New Year afterwards. So we are not going to rise from bed until the sun comes out this afternoon after the daily rain.'

'That seems a marvellous idea,' I beamed. 'Do you mean your sisters are now telling Brem and Fruity the same thing?'

Tau Fong nodded.

'Lucky lads – and lucky me,' I sighed, as our lips met and we rolled

111

together as one.

I was conscious at one time that heavy rain was beating on the roof, but that did not seem to matter, except that after the rain would come the sunshine and our honeymoon might be over. The girls had told us already that their father and brothers were due back home by the end of the month. I did not expect that Tau Fong would be sleeping with me each night when her father was in residence. Each morning one or other of the girls had climbed up to the roof of a small tower at one corner of the building to see if they could sight their father's ship; from there the harbour was in clear view, as well as the sea to the north of Penang.

As the sun came out when the rain clouds rolled away inland we rose and showered together, letting a cool clear water stream down our bodies.

Dinner was planned for 9 o'clock, leaving it as late as possible in the hope that the rest of the family might have returned, but as darkness fell there was no sign of the Wongs' ship. The girls said they had seen from the tower another submarine ease its way into the harbour, but there were still no large surface Japanese naval vessels; this indicated that each end of the Malacca Straits was still under the control of Allied Naval forces, and only the submarines had been able to slip through.

For the first time we attempted to eat our meal using chop-sticks, much to the merriment of the girls, who spent most of their time demonstrating how it should be done, and placing morsels in our mouths like mother birds feeding their fledglings. The method of eating did not detract from the excellence of the meal, again washed down with the rice-based wine that we were now developing a taste for. A bottle was put aside to toast in the New Year.

'Do you always celebrate the Western New Year?' I asked the girls.

'Yes,' replied Befung. 'We enjoy the best of two hemispheres; our upbringing at the Christian Mission in Shanghai taught us many things about the ways of the Western world, but we save our main celebrations for the Chinese New Year at the end of January. This year, or rather next year in 1942, we shall be seeing out the Year of the Snake and welcoming in the Year of the Horse.'

For our part I think we all three felt thankful to have survived 1941 at all. 1942 promised very little; again we would be lucky to see the end of it.

In the meantime we were just living for the present as we relaxed on the

112

cushions after our banquet, each with our Wong daughter curled up alongside us. What could be more wonderful? Bugger tomorrow; and next year, come to that.

We listened in to Radio Singapore, which seemed to be continuing broadcasting as if the city were not imperiled. In a detached sort of way the announcer of the news stated that Allied forces had consolidated around Kuala Lumpur (Ipoh had fallen some days before) and were counter-attacking the Japanese.

At the stroke of midnight we lifted our glasses together in traditional fashion and drank to the New Year, following by kissing all round. The cushions were then pushed back in the corners and dancing commenced to the strains of Hawaiian music, so popular then in the dance halls of Singapore and Penang, carrying on well into the small hours of the morning. Just before dawn we led our respective partners to our rooms and paid little interest in what was happening in the rest of the world until the following afternoon.

Chapter 16

By now we were falling into a sort of routine, although we knew it could not last. So far we had avoided the humiliation of being taken as prisoners of war, but nonetheless we *were* imprisoned in the house of the Wongs; the difference was that it was of our own volition. Anyhow, who could wish for sweeter jailors?

Each day two of the girls would venture into the town by rickshaw to forage for provisions which became scarcer each day. Penang was no longer the island of plenty, and the Japanese authorities announced that they were introducing food rationing. Stories were being whispered that certain Chinese, who were known sympathisers of the British, were being beaten up. We were concerned that the girls were taking risks on our behalf; but they would not hear of it. In all conscience there was nothing we could do about it; we had given our word that we would not leave the house other than by the decree of father Wong.

That was something else that we were aware was causing concern to the girls, although they never spoke about it in English. For most of each day, during the first few days of the New Year, one or other had kept watch from the tower, but no sign was there of their father's ship. We could tell by their dejected expression each time the lookout came down from the tower that their concern for the safety of their father and brothers was mounting.

It was just as the sun was setting on the fifth day of January that we heard excited voices and the patter of sandalled feet running down the steps from the tower. Tau Fong ran over to me, her features animated with excitement, and looking prettier than I had ever seen her. 'It's our ship!' she exclaimed excitedly as she threw her arms round my neck and kissed me full on my half-open mouth, even before I could utter a word. 'It has just rounded the northern headland of the island and is moving slowly in towards the harbour. We expect father will anchor outside in the shipping road tonight and wait

114

for daylight tomorrow morning before berthing; he will then have to report to the harbour master.' So saying she led me by the hand towards the bedroom.

'I think this should be the last night of our honeymoon, my sweetest,' Tau Fong said softly. 'It is not that I am ashamed of having entered your room to sleep with you, indeed the opposite is so, I am proud of the fulfilment of our love; but I know it would embarrass you if we were brazenly to walk up to bed together when father is at home. It may take him time to adjust. He is a kindly man who loves all his children equally, and will soon know that I am deeply in love with you. I feel the same applies to my sisters.'

We closed the door and dispensed with our garments, nestling down beneath the netting, to all the world like an old married couple. If this was what marriage was always like then I was prepared to take the plunge.

I awoke soon after sunrise to realise that the water from the shower was splashing, and Tau Fong must be underneath it. I shot out from under the net to join her.

'Today, I and my sisters,' she said when we had kissed, 'must prepare for the homecoming of the rest of the family. It would be best if you and the other two boys keep in your rooms until we girls have had a chance to greet father and tell him about you.'

'I can see that makes sense,' I said. 'It would certainly be something of a shock if he were to walk in and see us lounging on the cushions sipping his drinks.'

'I will come up to fetch you as soon as we think it timely to do so,' said Tau Fong, and slipping into her kimono and kissing me swiftly on the forehead she quickly left the room.

Apart from bringing a meal on a tray I did not see Tau Fong again throughout the day; all seemed quiet downstairs except for girlish voices from time to time. It was not until nearly dusk that I heard the main door open and much excitement ensued, with deeper voices intermingling. As only Chinese was spoken I had no idea what was being said.

Brem and Fruity had joined me in my room by now. Not a word was spoken as we sat around, apprehension written on our faces. We could not have blamed Wong Ten if he had flown into a rage when told of our presence and ordered us out of the house. As the minutes ticked by there was no indication of voices being raised in anger, and so we began to feel a little more at ease. I am sure we three were all wondering how the girls would be breaking the news to their father.

What seemed like hours passed by before we heard the soft patter of feet approaching. The three girls entered smiling.

'We are sorry to leave you alone so long,' said Befung, 'but our father was tired when he reached home with the boys, and not a little irritable. It seems he had difficulty in explaining to our new masters in the harbour master's office that he lived in Penang and had merely been going about his lawful, peaceful business. They insisted on searching the ship, presumably expecting to find arms, or even European stowaways. The whole business has made him hate the Japanese even more than he did before.'

'So, have you told him about us?' I ventured apprehensively.

'Yes, when he settled down with a drink after his meal,' replied Befung.

'Is he going to chuck us out?' cut in Fruity.

'Of course he is not, you are our honoured guests and we have come to lead you down to meet him,' said Befung. 'I will lead with Fruity as they have already met briefly before.'

So saying, each girl took a hand and we made our way down to the main lounge. Wong Ten stood at the other end of the room with his sons on either side. He was a thick-set man, of medium height, with an air of authority about him, but a kindly twinkle in his eyes as he smiled in greeting when we entered the room.

The three girls introduced each of us in turn. 'Greetings and welcome to my humble abode,' he said as he bowed to us in turn. We also bowed in response as Fruity said how grateful we were to enjoy the shelter of his roof.

'I remember we met before, young man,' said our host, his English not quite so good as his daughters', with the traditional Chinese tendency to substitute 'r' for 'l'. 'I thought then you were an English gentleman who treated my eldest girl with respect.'

Fruity beamed with pleasure, and everyone else smiled as well: it was probably the first time Fruity had been referred to as a gentleman; he even let pass the 'English' adjective.

Glancing to his right and left Wong Ten motioned to his two sons. 'The bigger lad here is my eldest, and heir to the Wong household, Choy; and here is the baby of the family, Koo.' Again we each bowed to one another in turn.

'We are very conscious, sir,' I said, 'that we put the lives of you and your

116

family in danger by staying in your house; if you wish us to go tomorrow we will do so.'

'If you were to leave this house you would very soon be captured, for the Japanese soldiers are all around,' replied Ten and, after a pause: 'We do not like Japanese either; indeed, we have a very special reason for hating them. Somehow we will think of a way of getting you away from here and back to your own folk.'

'We are indeed grateful, sir, for your kindness and consideration,' said Brem.

'I have had a long and tiring day,' said Ten, 'arguing with stupid Japanese naval officers who now control the harbour. They make me do many things no honourable man would make another do. Soon I am going to my bed.' Turning to the twins he continued, 'Now, my blossoms, will you please fetch the wine casket and I will give you all a toast.'

The girls, whose names in English meant Peach Blossom and Cherry Blossom, did as they were bade and filled all our glasses.

'Now I give you the toast,' announced Ten, raising his glass. 'To the defeat of the Imperial Japanese Army, may they be driven from these shores and from the land of our fathers also.' So saying he drained his glass as we echoed his words and drank too.

'Tomorrow, when our minds are refreshed by sleep, we will talk again and make our plans.' So saying, he kissed each of his girls in turn and, bowing solemnly to the two boys, departed slowly from the room.

We talked together for a while with Choy and Koo. The elder was a serious faced man of some twenty-three years and very much in his father's stamp while the younger, Koo, in his early teens, was probably more like the mother who was taken from them. No one had yet mentioned how she came to die at a comparatively early age.

The next morning when I joined the others downstairs Wong Ten had already departed for the town, taking Choy with him. The girls said that he had much business to be done. In the evening we all joined together for the main meal of the day. We talked only of everyday matters and the latest rumours of atrocities committed by the Japanese. By now Kuala Lumpur was in danger of falling into the hands of the enemy, and the way would then be clear to advance to the Johore Straits. Nothing was said by Wong Ten about his plans for the future. It was the same the next day and the day after that.

On Saturday 10 January, Wong Ten returned to the house a little earlier than usual. When the evening meal had been cleared away he motioned us all to stay on our stools. He rose slowly to his feet, his features serious, but in a way more relaxed than we had seen him before.

'My children all,' he began, 'and by that I mean also our honoured guests from the British Isles. I have now made up my mind about our plans for the future. I feel there is no place for us to find happiness any longer in Malaya, and as we were driven from our homeland those years ago, the time has come now to move again. Things will only get worse from now on; the standards that were upheld under the British will decline as the war continues, for the Allied Forces will not give up their claim to this land, and as time goes by it will become more and more difficult to live in a civilised manner, in the way that my forefathers taught me to live. When food and money become scarce those whom one thought to be one's friend will turn against us; just one word whispered in the ears of our new masters by someone we had thought to be a friend would be enough to bring our family to destruction.' Wong Ten took a sip of his drink and looked around at each of our faces in turn before continuing.

'I have decided that we should sail in the *Hang Tau* to Palembang, where our cousins live. Maybe the Japanese will not bother to invade Sumatra, for it is mostly jungle and swamp, and there are no ports to compare with Singapore and Penang. Surely they will take Singapore, for they have set their mind to it for many a year and have planned exactly how they will go about it; the great guns around the harbour will be of no use at all.

'I still have some business to attend to in the next few days; we should be ready to sail by next Thursday, 17 January, when the tide and the moon will be right to leave after sunset, for I think we should get as far as we can from the island of Penang under cover of darkness. The authorities, after some persuasion, have given their permission that I may go about my business of trading between the coastal ports, but it is entirely at my own risk and they cannot guarantee any protection, particularly if we try to go near to Singapore.' Wong Ten paused. 'Do any of you wish to say anything?'

It was Fruity who spoke up first. 'We are not presuming that you wish to take us with you, but may we please be signed on as crew on your ship?'

'Of course, we would not think of setting sail without you,' replied Ten. 'As to how you can make your way undetected to the quay, I shall have to

118

leave you to think about it.'

'We graciously accept your offer of a passage to Palembang, sir,' said Brem, 'and I am sure we will think of a way to get aboard without arousing the suspicion of the Japanese.'

Wong Ten retired from the lounge to his room, leaving us and the Wong brothers and sisters to our own devices. Choy told us that they had reached Rangoon when they had heard of the Japanese invasion, and the bombing of Pearl Harbour. Wong Ten decided it would be too risky to sail up the Irrawaddy to Mandalay, as he had intended, in order to pick up a consignment of cloth and ivory; instead they sailed on up the Bay of Bengal to Dacca which was much less vulnerable to the advancing Japanese Army. It was because of this change of plan that they were several days late returning to Penang. The journey southward had been uneventful as they had kept well clear of the coastline until near to home.

We gathered together again the next morning to discuss ideas about getting safely aboard the *Hang Tau* on the following Saturday.

'We girls will cut off some of our hair to make pigtails for you,' said Befung. 'They can be fixed on under your Chinese hats.'

'That might certainly be a help,' I said, 'but can we not paddle back in the catamaran to the harbour?'

'That would be too risky,' said Hang Fong. 'You were very lucky to get here in the first place. Besides, Koo says the boat you came in has already disappeared.'

'Can we not ride in a closed van down to the quay side?' said Fruity.

'Father says that the Japanese guards at the dock gates have been searching all vehicles going to the quay if they are not familiar to them,' said Befung. 'It would be the same if you were in rickshaws.'

'I am afraid that you do not even walk like Chinamen,' said Tau Fong, with a little giggle.

'No, there's not much we can do about that,' said Fruity.

We sat silent for a while waiting for the next suggestion. An idea was beginning to crystallise at the back of my mind.

'I've got it, I think,' I burst out suddenly, startling the others as the solution took shape in my head. 'Father Brown and the Case of the Thingumibob!'

'What the hell are you prattling about?' said Brem.

'Don't you remember the story where the detective had been watching the only entrance to a building all the morning, as it was thought there would be an attempt to kill the occupant; but he was stabbed to death all the same, although the detective swore to Father Brown that no one had entered the doorway during the morning, and he had been watching all the time. When pressed again by Father Brown he said that there had only been the postman go in with his sack over his back. That's it, said Father Brown, the killer was disguised as a postman.'

'Does all this clap-trap mean we walk through the dock gates disguised as Malayan postmen?' said Fruity. 'Surely the guards are not going to believe that three postmen would be delivering all at once?'

'No, you big nit,' I rebuked him, 'but there are rickshaw coolies constantly taking fares down to the harbour. We will go as rickshaw men, then the guards won't give us a second look there between the shafts, they will only think of examining the passengers.'

'That might just work,' conceded Brem. 'What's more, we wouldn't have to walk; we would be running!'

'Do you know of three rickshaw men,' I enquired, turning to the girls, 'who would let their rickshaws out on hire for one day?'

'Yes,' said Tau Fong. 'We nearly always used the same rickshaws to go to the shop; I expect they have been missing our trade lately.'

'I expect they have been missing a lot of trade lately,' cut in Hang Fong.

'So, if we pay them what they would earn in a good day, plus a little bit,' I reasoned, 'they should be quite happy.'

'They need to be more than just happy,' interjected Fruity. 'We don't want them blabbing about what they are going to be used for.'

'They need not know until after we are all safely on board the ship,' said Befung. 'We will simply ask the men to leave their rickshaws outside our door in the morning, and then pick them up again at the dockside after we are aboard.'

'Sounds simple enough,' said Brem, 'but won't the dockside guards not think it odd if they see three coolie men leave their rickshaws and go on board a ship, then three others appear and take away the rickshaws.'

Koo was the one to come up with a solution. 'The three rickshaw men must be smuggled on board earlier in the day, it will be quite easy while we are loading up, and then they will stay concealed below decks until Ken,

Brem and Fruity come aboard in the evening, in the pretence of loading on bags. The coolie men can then go off and collect their rickshaws; the guard won't notice the difference. It will be dark by then anyway.'

'Bravo, Koo,' chorused the girls, echoed by us. 'I do think that solves the problem,' said Befung, 'and you boys will have the rickshaws during the day to practise with around the courtyard.'

Wong Ten, when he returned home later in the day, was happy that we had come up with the answer. 'We shall not be able to take much with us from here in the house, only as much as we can carry easily in a suitcase on each rickshaw. Anyway we must not take too much weight for the boys to pull.'

'Don't mind about that, sir,' I said. 'We are strong enough after all the food and rest we have had in your house; we are looking forward to going outside and getting some exercise.'

'It is not so easy as you may think to pull a rickshaw,' said Choy. 'It's mostly a question of balance and not going too fast downhill, or you will tip us all into the harbour!'

'There is one more thing,' said Ten. 'I want you all to conceal some gold coins about your person; it will be easily converted into guilders when we get to Palembang, and if anything happens to us, or to the ship, whoever survives will need money.' So saying he opened up a lacquered casket that stood on his writing table and asked each in turn to come to him.

'We have done nothing to earn this,' I said, when my turn came to receive a handful of gold coins. 'Indeed we are indebted for what you have given us and done for us already.'

'But I want you to take it,' said Ten. 'You may perhaps like to think of it as payment in advance for acting as crew on the ship.' There was no more to be said but to thank our host and place the coins in the money belts we had all bought when we first came to Malaya.

Chapter 17

With our plans of escape now drawn up the days began to drag somewhat, although for my part it was always pleasant to be in the company of Tau Fong, and I am sure the others felt the same way about her sisters. We had now been confined behind the walls of the Wong house for more than two weeks and were becoming impatient to move on, although we were aware there were likely to be many dangers in facing the outside world.

By the middle of the week we heard that the Japanese forces had taken Kuala Lumpur and were moving further south. We began to think that we might be too late to join up again with any Allied forces anywhere in the Far East, for Wong Ten had convinced us that Singapore should no longer be considered impregnable. He told us that the 'soft under-belly' of Singapore Island was the Johore Straits; it was almost possible to wade across in places at low tide.

Wednesday 14 January 1942 was my twenty-second birthday – rather different from the previous year when I got stuck in snow drifts on the Cotswolds, trying to hitch a lift home from Cheltenham. I suppose I had mentioned it to Fruity and Brem at some time, and they in turn had told the Wongs.

That evening, when we entered the dining room, the best silver was laid out and the room illuminated with little Chinese lanterns. I was given the seat of honour at one end of the table, where Choy usually sat, opposite his father, and in front of me was a cake that the girls had made and decorated with twenty-two candles. It was an understatement to say that I was overwhelmed. Although this was meant as a joyous occasion for me, I could not help thinking back on other birthdays at home, and I thought how much my parents must be worrying about me; but there was nothing at all I could do about it so I might as well eat and be merry.

I probably did swallow too many of the Wong's potent Chinese drinks, for I remember nothing about how I got up to bed when the party finally broke up. What I do remember was being woken up just before dawn, in the pleasantest way possible, by Tau Fong kissing me tenderly. I became conscious of her tantalising perfume and reached out to clasp her naked body close to mine.

'I did not know in time that it was your birthday, Ken, so I have brought you the only present that I can – me!' whispered Tau Fong.

'What more could I wish for?' I replied softly, as our bodies locked together and passion took over.

When I next awoke it was broad daylight and I thought at first I had merely dreamt that Tau Fong had entered in the night; but her perfume had lingered on and the memory of that night will stay with me for all of my days.

It was now only two days to D (for departure) day, and the final packing was being done. For us three airmen it was only a ten-minute job, but for the Wong family it must have been heartrending to have to leave so much behind. Some things had been taken down to the ship in small amounts throughout the week: Wong Ten did not want to arouse suspicion that he was leaving Penang for good, or at least until the Japanese were driven out again. He had merely let his friends and neighbours know that he and his family were going to visit relatives in Palembang. He had, of course, said nothing about our presence. So anything of any size or weight had to be left behind.

When Saturday morning arrived we were up and about early, the adrenalin beginning to flow as an air of excitement gripped us. Could we carry our masquerade through? If we were detected before we reached the ship the whole Wong family would undoubtedly suffer too; it would take more than gold to persuade the Japanese authorities that they had not been harbouring their enemies. For us it would mean incarceration and quite likely torture. I was not at all sure that I would not break down and tell anything my tormentors wanted to know.

The rickshaws had duly been left outside the door, and the men who earned their livelihood from plying them had made their way down to the quay separately, to be less likely to raise suspicion when boarding the ship. Choy and Koo fetched the vehicles into the courtyard. We found it easy

123

enough to trot around the four sides of the courtyard, but realised it might well be a different matter when it came to negotiating the couple of miles of undulating road to the harbour, pulling two people with their baggage. There was going to be no second chance if we made a mistake.

Towards sunset we partook of our last meal in Penang. There was little conversation across the table; for the Wongs it was a sad occasion, as was reflected in their faces, to be leaving the house where the children had spent their most formative years, to move on to somewhere where they must try to settle in all over again. For my part, and I expect for Brem and Fruity also, there was suppressed excitement of being on the move again, and the hope that we just might not fall into the hands of the Japanese. However, it seemed too much to hope that we might be reunited with our mates again somewhere, somehow.

The meal finished, the girls set about perfecting our disguises as rickshawmen. Our rather tatty khaki shorts and shirts were all right; so were the *chapplies* on our feet. With our genuine Chinese conical hats on and the pigtails that the girls had woven from their own hair hanging down the back of our necks, we quite looked the part. For me, with my fair skin, Tau Fong had prepared a sort of brown oil solution which she proceeded to massage on my parts that showed. That was really rather satisfying, to the point of eroticism, and at another time and place would have lead to other developments. This was not the time, nor the place, and the stuff was pretty evil-smelling anyway.

We left at intervals of a couple of minutes, so as not to attract too much attention from neighbours or passers-by. Brem, who had been elected unanimously as the one most resembling a rickshaw coolie, led the way pulling Hang Fong and Koo. Fruity followed up with Befung and Choy. I waited until Wong Ten locked the door of his house for the last time and we set off down the road with Tau Fong beside her father.

I could not help feeling joy at moving in the open again, after three weeks incarcerated in the Wong villa; also I felt I was being of some use to the family.

The first mile was easy enough; there were not many people around on this Saturday evening as darkness fell, and the road was not too steep to make pulling difficult; in fact it was really rather pleasant. The first test came as we approached the old army barracks, now being used, we were told, as a sort of rest camp for Japanese soldiers who had done their stint in active service, or who were recuperating from illness. At the gateway were two sentries watching the traffic and people passing by. I don't suppose there was any real danger that we would be apprehended at this point, but it was difficult not to feel nervous. I could just see Fruity in front trotting past at a steady rate, so Brem must have made it okay. My confidence flowed back into me as we left the barracks behind us unchallenged and headed down through the main streets of Georgetown towards the harbour.

Wong Ten had instructed Brem and Fruity to pull up within sight of the gateway that guarded the entrance to the harbour; we would then lead the procession as Ten had the necessary documents giving us permission to board the ship and leave the harbour. Now was going to be the real test as I trotted at a slowing rate past the others and down the last hundred yards towards the gates. I could see the two Japanese soldiers, rifles slung over shoulders, move smartly out from either side of the gates as we approached. It was difficult to stop my knees from knocking as I passed between them, within inches of their rifle muzzles, and drew to a halt. But they were looking only at the occupants of the rickshaw. I was conscious that Brem and Fruity had drawn up close behind as a third Japanese, whom I took to be the officer in charge, came out to inspect the documents that Ten had handed to the guards. I could not understand what was said as all the conversation was in Cantonese, which the Japanese officer clearly understood well. I could see Wong Ten indicate that the two rickshaws close behind contained his family.

The officer walked slowly back to the hut, clasping the papers in his hand. I could see through the guardroom window as he lifted the telephone, and heard muffled sounds of Japanese intonations. My legs went to jelly and my throat felt like sandpaper.

It seemed like an hour, but was probably only five minutes before he returned at the same measured pace, and without a word handed the documents back to Wong Ten and waved us on. I had a hard job to resist breaking into a run as we started up the short distance to the point where we would need to traverse duck-board planking down to the ship. The other two 'coolie Brits' grounded their shafts behind me and we proceeded to carry bags down the plankway, trying to resist the urge to break into a run.

Once on board we went straight below decks, where the real rickshaw men had concealed themselves for most of the day. I saw Ten slip them each a gold coin as they moved towards the gang planks smiling and mumbling their thanks. Choy came below after a while to report that the rickshaw men had collected their vehicles and trotted out through the harbour gates without being stopped. Maybe they would talk about the day's work when they reached home, and it might get to the wrong ears that there had been some sort of conspiracy; by then we would hope to be well out to sea.

We were removing our conical hats and pigtail when the three girls came down the companionway laughing merrily as we handed them their hairpieces back again, hugging and kissing each in turn, just for the plain relief of having overcome another hurdle. In truth I think we all felt that our real troubles were only just about to begin; but tomorrow was another day.

'Father has told us to keep below decks while he and the boys cast off and move the boat clear of the harbour,' said Befung.

'That suits us,' said Fruity, gripping Befung more tightly round the waist, causing her to let out a mocked cry of pain.

'I hope you are going to get off this foul brown stuff you smeared over me,' I said to Tau Fong.

'I might consider it,' giggled Tau Fong shyly. 'There are two salt water showers at the front of the ship.'

So saying she led me away, amid guffaws from Brem and Fruity.

Around ten o'clock that evening Choy called us up on deck. We could see by the bright light of the moon the mass of Penang's mountain to the south, as we turned due westwards, past the northern shore of the island of Penang. We were leaving the island behind for the last time, and my thoughts, and I am sure those of the others too, were tinged with sadness, for we had enjoyed many happy hours there.

When the island had dropped away into the blackness of the night we went below to our bunks in the cabin we three friends had been given.

The next morning, with the sun streaming through the porthole, we made our way on to the deck. Judging from the position of the rising sun we were now heading almost due south, which I reckoned would take us obliquely away from the mainland towards Sumatra. There was no land in sight, nor was there any shipping, or more importantly, any aircraft within view.

Ten and Koo were together in the wheelhouse when we greeted them and enquired what we might do to help.

'Perhaps you would like to take watches in turn at the wheel throughout the day,' said Ten. 'Choy and I will go below to get some rest; call us if you see any other vessel, or aircraft that might be taking an interest in us. I will go down now and Choy will tell you something about the ship.' So saying he took himself down the companionway.

'This vessel is not a junk, as you might expect,' explained Chow. 'She is a ketch of some sixty feet long, from which the bowsprit at the front protrudes a further sixteen feet, supporting three jig sails which angle up to the main mast; as you can see there are two masts, the rear one, the mizzen mast, being slightly shorter. Both masts have a mainsail and a topsail. At present, in the middle of the Straits at this time of the day, the breeze is quite light and we have full canvas rigged; I will show you later how we go about altering.'

'So what do we need to know while you are sleeping?' I asked.

'Just keep her on the same course,' said Chow. 'Koo knows how to read the capstan and will explain to you. He slept last night as you did.' Choy went below to catch a few hours sleep.

Throughout the day we took turns in watches of two hours manning the helm, and the day passed uneventfully. Choy and Ten came on duty again at six o'clock in the evening to navigate through the night. The same pattern was followed the next day. The girls, who were mostly below decks tending to the galley, came up to the wheelhouse from time to time to chat to us. We were beginning to get the hang of raising and lowering the sails. By sunset, at the end of the second day out from Penang, Wong Ten told us we were nearing the coastline of Sumatra. There was little enough to see, for the mangrove swamps stretch inland for miles on the east coast of the island, then it is a hundred miles or more to the foothills that rise up to the main mountain range, with the highest peak more than ten thousand feet above sea level, that forms the backbone of Sumatra. At this point we were some two hundred miles from the nearest point of Malaya. For a while we were likely to be clear of enemy aircraft and shipping whilst we kept as close as possible to the Sumatran shoreline; as we progressed further south-eastwards the Malaccan Straits narrowed towards Singapore.

'In three days time we shall be near to Rupot Island and the small port of Dumai,' said Ten. 'We shall put in there to buy fuel oil for the engine. Although we normally use the sails, we need to use the engine for rivers, or to get us out of trouble. We were unable to buy any fuel from the Japanese at Penang. It should be easier to buy from the Dutch.'

127

For the next two days we progressed as close in to the mangrove trees as we dared. The coastline was a monotonous expanse of mangrove swamps as far as the eye could see, while to the east was just sea. On the morning of 23 January we were obliged by the contour of the coastline to veer due east, and reached a point only fifty or so miles from the Malayan coast before we were able to turn south-easterly again. We saw some aircraft flying low over towards the mainland, but they took no notice of us even if they could see us.

Towards sunset we reached the channel between Sumatra and the small island of Rupot on the port side. Wong Ten decided to drop anchor for the night and proceed through the narrowing channel towards Dumai by daylight the following morning.

The three girls came up from below, and Fruity, Brem and I sat together with our respective girlfriends watching the sun sink below the horizon in a blaze of crimson. I daresay the other two were thinking the same as I, that a closer relationship would be desirable in such a romantic setting, but in the confines of the ship we would not wish to incur the displeasure of Wong Ten by presuming we could make fast and loose with his daughters. In truth we did not know what the girls had said to their father about us, whether or not they had even hinted at the feelings we held for one another. I feel sure that Ten would not have pressed his daughters on such a delicate matter; it was not in his nature to do so, but I suspect that he was well aware, if only by watching the eyes of his loved ones, that there existed a depth of feeling that might not be denied for long. Once again we went our separate ways to our cabins when darkness descended upon us.

By 10 o'clock the following morning we had negotiated the narrow channel for the last few miles to Dumai. The town was no more than a few huts and small buildings, like an oasis in the interminable mangroves, through which the one road from inland reached the sea. There were fuel storage tanks by the tiny jetty and we were able to fill two 55-gallon drums to ensure that we would be able at least to negotiate the length of the Palembang river if necessary.

Wong Ten decided it would be better to await the high tide for the eastern passage out of Dumai which skirted the southern part of Rupot Island; therefore we would set sail soon after dawn the next day. This gave us a few hours in which to straighten our legs on land, not that there was anything to see in Dumai.

Ten and Koo stayed on board to look after the ship while the rest of us made our way along the dusty street towards the one hotel, which would not have looked out of place in a film of the American West at the turn of the century. For the hotelier, who appeared to be half Dutch and half Malaysian, it was quite an event for seven people to sit down for a meal.

We three airmen were feeling in good spirits, for we were, in theory, back on Allied territory; at least there were no signs of any visitations from the Japs. The innkeeper said they had seen one or two aircraft flying high and could not tell if they were Japanese or Allied planes.

If it was in the mind of any one of us to jump ship here and try to join up with any Allied forces that might be on Sumatra, no-one wanted to broach the subject. For my part, and I believe for the other two as well, the attraction of staying with our respective girlfriends was stronger than the dubious alternative of trying to make our own way from this God-forsaken place. In fact, our minds were made up for us rather unexpectedly.

A large Dutchman, whom we had seen earlier when we were purchasing the fuel oil, sat down at the table next to us. As with most Dutchmen he spoke excellent English.

'I am Willem,' he boomed, by way of introduction. 'Where do you come from?'

'We have sailed from Penang,' said Brem, 'which is now occupied by the Japanese. We have the Wong family; Befung, Hang Fong and Tau Fong here with their younger brother Koo, to thank for giving us a passage on their father's ship.'

'Are you British servicemen, then?' said Willem. 'Let me shake your hands; we are Allies in trying to stop the pestilent Japanese.'

'We are RAF trying to escape to join up with any forces there may be in Sumatra. We lost nearly all our planes, then got separated from our mates on the way to Kuala Lumpur. Is there an airfield near here?'

'The nearest is at Padang, which is nearly three hundred miles west, over a very rough road and across the mountains,' said Willem. 'What is more, the forces at Padang expect the Japanese to invade there, when they have finished with Singapore, for the port has easy access to the Bay of Bengal.'

'So you think Singapore will fall, then?' I questioned.

'No doubt about it, the Japs have been planning it for years,' said Willem.

'What will you do then?' asked Brem.

'I have a fast motor launch here and will try to reach Batavia in Java; maybe a stand can be made there.'

'So it's no good for us to stay here, even if we wanted to,' said Brem.

'You would do best to go with your friends to Palembang, which is the capital of Sumatra; there is an airport there, and I hear there is a second military airfield that has been constructed in the jungle some twenty or thirty miles to the south of the town, near to the big American and Dutch oilfields. At least if the Japs reach Palembang, you will have a chance to get to Batavia; there is a railway that links the town and the oil fields with a ferry across the Straits to Java.'

'So that's it,' said Fruity, turning to the girls. 'You are stuck with us to Palembang; not that we were going to do anything else.'

We bade our Dutch friend goodbye and wished him luck. 'You will need much too,' he replied, 'just getting to Palembang, for you have to pass close to Singapore to reach there.'

On this sobering thought we made our way slowly back to the ship.

Chapter 18

Next morning we cast off from the quay on the flood tide and headed due east. At first progress was slow as we nosed our way along the channel between the endless mangroves, on the port side Rupot Island, and to starboard Sumatra. By midday the channel began to open out as we reached the Straits of Malacca. Once again we were converging gradually towards the mainland of Malaya and must pass close to where the spearhead of the Japanese army was advancing towards the Straits of Johore, which separated Singapore Island from the mainland of Malaya. With each nautical mile our dangers would increase and we would only be comparatively safe at night.

During the first night out from Dumai we reached a position where we were able to steer almost due south for a while and for the next day we remained almost stationary, with sails furled, in an indentation of the Sumatra coastline.

This procedure was followed on the next day, 27 January. That night as we headed out eastward into the Malaccan Strait we could see flashes on the horizon, which at first we took to be lightning. But it was all coming from around one spot and just above sea level. We began to hear muffled noises across the water. 'It's bloody gunfire,' exclaimed Fruity, and we knew that he was right. Involuntarily I felt a shiver down my spine and Tau Fong, who was holding my hand, gripped a little tighter.

The bombardment continued throughout the night as we watched, fascinated but afraid. We thought of the poor devils manning the guns, particularly the British, most of them newly arrived in Singapore, unused to the humid heat, the mosquitoes and being under fire. As always with an army on the retreat morale was low, the will to fight back lacking.

As dawn broke we could still hear the muffled thuds of the artillery but the sounds were now to our rear and growing fainter. As the light grew stronger we could make out on the horizon the shapes of ships, silhouetted by the light of the rising sun.

'My God,' exclaimed Fruity. 'I do believe the big one is a troopship; she looks like one of the P & O liners in our convoy last year; the other two vessels must be Naval escorts.'

'Poor bastards,' said Brem. 'If they reach Empire Dock they'll be just in time to swell the ranks of the prisoners of war.'

For us, creeping along as close as we could to Sumatra, it was a lucky distraction for Allied shipping to be in the vicinity, for it created a diversion for the Japanese Air Force. We could see aerial activity towards Singapore, but could not distinguish the types of planes.

The seas to the south of Singapore abound with islands of all shapes and sizes, some of them little more than rocks, while others tower hundreds of feet above the sea; they are probably the remains of volcanoes of some millions of years ago. Wong Ten decided it would be safest for us to anchor in the lee of a small island during daylight, moving on after dark, with the moon to help. This ploy served us well for the next two days and nights, by which time we had reached a position some hundred miles south of Singapore and only a few miles north of the equator.

At dawn on 30 January we could see no land to the south: there was nothing for it but to run the gauntlet. During the morning we saw aircraft approaching from the south; three, four, five in no particular formation, flying low and on a course to pass close to us.

Wong Ten called to Choy to start the auxiliary engine, for it was his plan to try to change course quickly in the event of aerial attack, and the additional use of the screw added considerably to our manoeuvrability. As the planes drew nearer we all placed ourselves in positions where we could gain some protection – bulkheads or gear on the deck, in the event of dive bombing or strafing. No one was keen on going below decks and not knowing what was going on, or, if the worst came to the worst, being trapped below if the vessel was destined for the bed of the sea.

As the first aircraft came near, Fruity was the first to shout, 'I believe they are ours!'

'Famous last words!' cut in Brem.

'I think they are American Bostons,' said Fruity, with some conviction. As the first three aircraft roared by, ignoring our little craft, we could make out the white US stars on their fuselages and the large bulbous perspex noses that distinguished the twin-engined Boston, one of the American workhorse planes, that basically was a light bomber, but possessed useful fire power from its gun turrets.

There was no denying the boost to our morale and we all cheered spontaneously.

'What are those two kites over there then?' I enquired of Fruity. 'They are not Bostons, and are certainly not Blenheims – perhaps they are German Junkers,' I continued with a note of sarcasm.

Choy was looking at them through binoculars. 'They have large yellow triangular markings on them.'

'That must be the Dutch markings,' said Brem, 'in which case they could be Junkers, for the Netherlands Air Force bought some of its planes from Germany before the war.'

'Whatever they are,' I rejoined, 'they seem to be leaving us alone, which is what matters most at this moment.'

Following along behind and above the light bombers of the US and Dutch Air Forces were two pairs of aircraft that were presumably intended to provided fighter cover.

'I do believe those are Hurricanes,'shouted Fruity, barely able to contain his excitement.

'Right again,' said Brem. 'How the hell did they get here?' There was no denying our spirits were high as we set about eating our *tiffin*. Perhaps we were going to save Singapore after all, and we could once again play a useful part in keeping our planes in the air.

By mid-afternoon we could again see aircraft approaching, this time from the north. As a precaution Choy started up the engine once more, then trained his binoculars on the planes as they drew nearer on our port beam.

'They have their wheels down, and are bi-planes,' Choy announced.

'That sounds awfully like the Stuka type Jap planes that pestered us at Sungei and Butterworth,' exclaimed Brem.

'I can now see the red circle markings on their fuselages!' cried Choy.

'I think this must be it,' said Brem, as the two planes began to circle round us. We could see Ten, through the glass front of the wheelhouse, twirling the capstan round, his face set with a grim expression as the first of the Jap planes dived in towards us, its engine working up to a high scream as it levelled out just above us. I caught a glimpse of the two bombs as they screeched downwards. The first struck the water a few yards from the port bow as we wheeled sharply around, while the second hit the water just beyond it, sending a shower upwards and drenching us with spray.

There was no respite as the second aircraft came in at us from the opposite side. Again came the screech of aircraft and bombs. The first landed far too close for comfort in the sea close to our starboard beam, at the same time as a rending of timber and canvas, as the second bomb went through the rigging of the mizzen mast, but luckily did not explode until hitting the water.

It was great good fortune that no-one was hurt as spars crashed on to the deck and splinters flew; the mizzen mast sails with their ropes fell in a heap around us. The planes, having used up their bombs, and probably deciding their job had been done, circled round once more before heading north. We were left in peace to clear up as best we could.

'We must pray to God for our deliverance,' said Ten as he left the wheel to Choy to come and see how we had fared. He knelt down, his hands clasped and mumbled words of thanksgiving as we bowed our heads in cognisance.

'There is a group of small islands ahead of us now,' continued Ten. 'We must hope we can reach them before sundown so we can find shelter to drop anchor while tomorrow we carry out repairs.'

As we moved slowly southwards, hampered by the loss of sail power, we began to make out some four or five small islands, and beyond them were two much larger islands, according to the chart both bigger than Penang, called Lingga and Singkep. We headed for the largest of the island group, which rose some two hundred or more feet above the sea, and bared a sheer cliff towards us on the western side. As the sun touched down on the horizon Wong Ten edged in as close as he dared to the cliff and dropped anchor.

The tension ebbed away from us as we gathered in the evening beneath the acetylene lamp in the dining room for our meal.

'Tomorrow,' began Befung, 'our father says we girls may swim to the shore to see if we can find some fresh fruit while he and our brothers set about the repairs. You three boys can come with us if you like.'

'That sounds like a good idea,' said Fruity, as Brem and I echoed our approval too. 'Here's to tomorrow then,' continued Fruity, raising his mug. 'May it be more peaceful than today.'

134

The next morning, soon after sunrise, we three made our way up to the deck to find the three girls already there, chattering away in Chinese, laughing and giggling. 'Good morning, boys,' said Hang Fong and Tau Fong simultaneously, 'Are you ready for your swim? We are going to split up into three groups and explore round the island for palm trees and any other fruit trees that we can find. Befung and Fruity will go to the left of the cliff face, Hang Fong and Brem, to the right and we will swim right round to the other side.'

'Fine,' we all said, warming to the idea. I don't think I had faced the prospect of swimming quite so far before, but if Tau Fong could make it I was sure I could too.

'Here we go then,' Befung signalled; so saying they all three slipped out of their kimonos and dived head first over the side in quick succession, causing barely a ripple in the sea, but ribald cheers from their two brothers.

As they rose to the surface and shook the water from their heads, Befung called out, 'Come on boys, what's keeping you?' For my part I was beginning to feel not a little shy, being somewhat unaccustomed to exhibitionism.

'Well, lads,' piped up Fruity, 'What are we waiting for? When in the China Sea do as the Chinese do!' With that slightly inaccurate geographical comment he unclasped his belt and stepped out of his shorts as they hit the deck, amid cheers from the Wong boys and shrieks of laughter from the girls below treading water; even Ten's drooping moustache twitched a little. Not to be called 'chicken' Brem and I followed suit and were quickly over the side behind Fruity. Ours was hardly an elegant entry into the water; bottoms first, holding our noses with one hand and everything flying in all directions, culminating in three great splashes that must have frightened the fishes for miles around.

As if by magic we had soon paired up with our respective girlfriends and started to strike out in the pre-determined directions. The water was clear and refreshing, and the mere experience of swimming in the nude exhilarating, especially with a beautiful girl, similarly unclad, swimming alongside. After a while we headed around a rocky prominence and could see that the island sloped down to the sea less steeply on the eastern side, and was possibly half a mile across, by less than a mile the other way.

'Look over there,' said Tau Fong, as she changed from a crawl to a steady breast stroke. 'There are two or three coconut palms, which probably means

135

there is sand nearby.' As she moved ahead of me towards the trees I could see she was right in her surmise; there was a small strip of sand in front of the trees. It was difficult not to feel a certain stirring of the loins as Tau Fong ran up out of the water towards the sand, the sun glistening on the rivulets of water trickling down her beautifully lissom body. She threw herself face downward, panting from the exertion, as soon as she reached the sand beneath the shade of the palm trees. I quickly followed suit beside her.

No word passed between us, but she must have sensed that I was looking at her from the corner of my eye; indeed, what else should I be doing? Any other red-blooded male would not resist the temptation. She raised her head, resting the upper part of her body on her elbows, her back arching in a delightful curve down to her delicate buttocks: I could just glimpse under her arms as tiny glistening grains of sand trickled down from her shoulder to her ivory coloured breasts, returning to the beach from her pert little nipples. It was all too much for me to bear; this she must have seen in my eyes as she slowly turned her face towards mine, and I could see the desire that must have been in my eyes reflected in hers. Our arms slowly entwined, our lips met, at first in a tender kiss, then more passionately as we became united in love with just the sea, birds and the sand crabs as witnesses.

The rest of the world became of little consequence for I knew not how long; but the sun and time move relentlessly on, and in the equatorial climes the mid morning rays from the source of all energy, striking through a gap in the palm leaves onto a tender portion of my anatomy not normally exposed to the elements, was enough to return me back to the land of reality, and a sitting up position on the sand. Tau Fong following suit when freed of my perspiring frame.

For a while we just sat watching the waves gently breaking on the tiny beach, the sea beyond it sparkling in the bright sunlight, with flying fish flickering across the water every now and then on their brief airborne excursions. All was quiet.

'It does not seem possible that a war is being waged around us when all is so peaceful,' I observed. 'I wonder if it was like this in the garden of Eden? Did you learn about the Book of Genesis at your school in Shanghai?'

'Of course, we were instructed from the bible by the missionaries. Did not Eve tempt Adam with an apple?'

'You don't need an apple to tempt me; not that you would find an apple in

136

this part of the world.'

'Perhaps a coconut?' said Tau Fong, coyly tilted her head to one side and eyeing me mischievously.

'Okay, then, you find me a coconut; after all that *is* what we were supposed to have come for.'

'Here goes, then,' and so she skipped across the sand to the nearest palm tree. The tree was not a tall one, and the nuts were clustered some twelve feet above the ground, where the fronds splaying outwards formed a large bole. Clasping her hands around the trunk of the tree, then gripping the ringed ridges of the trunk with the soles of her feet, she moved steadily upwards.

With fascination and admiration, and it must be confessed, with growing excitement I watched as she reached the growing fruit above my head. Straddling her legs across the nuts to secure her feet at the base of the fronds on either side she leant forward, grasping another frond with one hand whilst trying to prise loose the nuts with her remaining hand. Clearly the nuts were not eager to surrender.

In fact, all this had been too much for me; I was going to get up that tree somehow. I recalled the song that Phil Harris used to sing entitled 'Woodman spare that tree'. In his case it was a slippery elm that nobody else could climb, and he could do it only when his wife was after him. In this instance the situation was in reverse; my 'wife' was already up the tree providing one heck of an incentive to get up there too.

My ascent was by no means graceful and I barked my shins a few times without really noticing. In the position Tau Fong was standing she had no real defence, even if she had wanted to have. One little scream of surprise, followed by that seductively tinkling laugh as she hung on for dear life while I had my way.

Had a casual observer been nearby he would have puzzled that just one tree in a group appeared to have been hit by a hurricane, whilst all the rest were still as statues. I wondered whether our primeval ancestors had ever ventured out of their caves on a fine summer's day for a little light relief to make love up a tree. I am sure that had there been any of our primate cousins around they would have looked on approvingly!

Love and games over, and still up the tree, we did succeed in gathering quite a harvest of coconuts during the next couple of hours. These we then carried down to the water's edge, forming a pile on a large slab of rock.

'How are we going to get them back to the ship from here?' I queried.

'The boys are going to row round the island in the dinghy before sunset.'

'That sounds a good arrangement to me; now you can see about tempting me with a coconut.' She gave a little laugh and, grasping one of the nuts, gave the husk a sharp rap on a handy rock. Stripping off the husk, I found the nut was young and soft within and not difficult to knock a hole in in order to drink the milk. We sat on the sand slaking our thirst and eating mangoes and plantains that we had found growing nearby.

'A penny for your thoughts,' said Tau Fong, as we sat there side by side. 'I remember my English teacher asking me that when I was sitting staring into space, just as you were then.'

'I suppose I was thinking of home, wondering what my mother would think of me could she see now.'

'I expect she must be very worried, not knowing what has happened to you,' said Tau Fong.

'It has only just occurred to me that I will have been reported missing by now, which in some ways is worse than "killed in action" which is just one shattering blow to near and dear ones. It can mean weeks or months of torment when just missing; but it's no good worrying about it. I only wish I could tell them at home how good life is at this moment.'

'What would your mother think if she knew you were nude on a beach eating fruit with an equally naked girl?'

'My mother was brought up in Victorian England, in a rather straight-laced fashion, so I must confess she would probably be a little shocked at first; but when she got to know you, and to realise how much I care for you, I am sure she would come round to my way of thinking.'

By way of an answer Tau Fong turned towards me and kissed me lightly on the cheek. 'I wish my mother were alive so that I could tell her how much I love you.' It was my turn to demonstrate my affection, and in no time we were rolling together on the warm sand locked in one another's arms, oblivious to the world.

At length we fell apart and lay on the sand facing each other. 'I remember on the first day we met, which seems years ago now, you said you would tell me one day what happened to your mother.'

As Tau Fong cast her eyes down, and her face became solemn, I wished I had not raised the subject, and told her so.

'No, it is right you should know, for it helps to explain why my father hates the Japanese. I have said that we lived near to Shanghai where my father was in business and well respected as a good man who loved his family. Because of his business he was often away long distances from home, leaving mama with us three girls and Koo, who was then about nine years old.

'Like Hitler in Europe, the Japanese began their Empire-building in the early thirties, moving first into Korea and then Manchuria by the middle of the decade. There were many rumours that the Japanese army would sweep south through China, but rather like you in Malaya we did not really think it would happen. As happened to our family in Penang last month, so the big push south through our part of China came when father was on a journey in his ship in the South China Seas.

'It all seemed to happen so quickly, the orderly life we had been used to suddenly collapsed and we retreated behind our barricaded doors.

'After the city surrendered the Japanese soldiers moved around the suburbs and their officers did little to stop them pillaging and raping women. One day there were five men came to our house, and when my mother would not let them in they broke down the door. Everything of value had been hidden where they would be unlikely to find it; thwarted in the attempt at robbery they turned on my sisters and me. One soldier tied mama and Koo to chairs and the rest set about us, stripping off our clothes and having their way with us while the others laughed. We all were virgins then: Hang Fong and I were only thirteen. You can imagine that we were in a state of distress, while mama was distraught and kept screaming at the men, telling them that my father and Choy would be back soon.

'After what seemed hours three of the soldiers went away, leaving just two who must have thought they would then have some sport with my mother, threatening her with a gun and making her undress too, then carrying out unspeakable things with the gun. It was at that point my father and Choy burst into the room. The soldier with the gun held it to mama's head and indicated he would fire if my father approached any nearer.

'Father was so incensed that his desire to kill the man for the indignities to mama overcame all reason. He had a knife in his hand and rushed forward with a yell of rage. The knife plunged deep into his chest, but not before the soldier had pressed the trigger and mama slumped to the floor. Mad with

139

grief and overcome with the desire for revenge, father then turned on the other soldier, whom Choy had grabbed as the shot rang out, and father sank his knife through his heart also; then sank to the floor sobbing uncontrollably.'

I had listened in silence while Tau Fong had poured out her sad story, which clearly had required an effort to relate. She was in tears as she ended and I was near to weeping myself as she clung to me, her wet cheeks resting on my shoulder.

'Thank you for telling me, I realise what an effort it must be to relate such a tragedy in your life: but how did you escape the wrath of the Japanese?'

'My father knew he must act quickly to keep his family together; for the sake of his children he overcame his grief and we prepared to leave. We were wealthy enough then to own a car into which we packed what valuables we could and the body of mama laid reverently in a trunk. The two Japanese soldiers were hidden in the cellar, and by dusk we joined the hundreds of refugees who were fleeing the city. By bribing our way we got aboard father's ship and set sail down the Yangtse River and eventually to Penang. My mother's body was committed to the depths of the South China Sea a few days later.'

'I can see that your father must be a marked man in the books of the Japanese hierarchy and thought he and his family were out of their reach living in Penang.'

While Tau Fong had been telling me her story the sun had dipped low down across the sea. We heard the splash of oars being plied just around the headland, and soon the dinghy came into sight rowed by Choy and Koo.

We ran together down into the water, near to our pile of coconuts and plantains, waving and calling to the boys. It seemed a little less immodest to be submerged to the waist as they paddled their way in towards us.

'Have you had a good day?' said Choy with a smirk. 'Father says we shall need more time to get the ketch properly seaworthy, so you can stay here until tomorrow evening if you wish.'

Tau Fong looked at me coyly: I was trying to suppress the joyous leap of my heart and to reply in a matter of fact sort of way to the boys. Yes, it would be best if we kept out of the way until the repairs were finished; besides, we should be able to gather some more fruit by tomorrow night. By the broad smiles on the boys' faces I knew I was not convincing; but Tau Fong was squeezing my hand beneath the surface of the water so I did not care about

140

anything else.

We quickly loaded the fruit onto the dinghy and waved to the boys as they rowed out of sight again round the rocks. Hand in hand we walked back up the beach as darkness descended.

Chapter 19

It was still dark when I was awoken by a blinding flash and simultaneous crash of thunder, and to the realisation that it had started raining. Tau Fong let out a little cry of alarm, instinctively gripping me tightly. I rolled over on to her as another crash of thunder echoed from the rock face above us.

'I can't think of a pleasanter way of keeping you dry,' I whispered in her ear.

'You are just using the storm as an excuse,' Tau Fong chided.

'I did not think I needed an excuse,' I replied as our lips met. I don't know which was the more erotically stimulating, the hailstones that now beat upon my back or Tau Fong's fingernails as they dug ecstatically into my buttocks. Whichever, the storm receded into oblivion.

When I released Tau Fong from the weight of my body the centre of the storm had moved away, although it was still raining lightly as the first streak of daylight appeared in the east. Tau Fong gave a little shiver involuntarily, for although we were almost exactly on the equator the night rain was quite cool.

Tau Fong jumped up, clasping one of my hands with both of hers, trying to pull me up. 'Come with me; we will go for a swim; it will be warmer in the sea.' So saying we raced down the beach and plunged beneath the phosphorescent ripples. Holding our breaths as long as we could we moved around below the surface marvelling at the wondrous colours and shapes of the fish that abounded in the clear green water. There were many strange creatures that I had never seen in my life before; but in my estimation none was as beautiful as Tau Fong as her lissom shape glided around the submarine rocks, her long hair streaming out behind her reaching almost to the exquisitely rounded shape of her buttocks.

When, at length, we had tired of swimming, the sun was up as we walked slowly up the beach, hand in hand.

'Why don't we try to climb to the top of the cliff before it gets too hot.' I always had possessed the desire to reach the highest point in the near vicinity to wherever I happened to be.

'Okay, I'm game if you can help me,' said Tau Fong.

So we began to move up from the beach towards a narrow gully between two masses of rock face. The warmth of the sun soon dried the sea water on our bodies, but it was not long before we were wet again, this time from perspiration as we toiled in the rising temperature. It was my first rock climb in the nude, which was not surprising, and there were certain disadvantages; it was often rather painful on the toes, as one sought footholds, and undergrowth could sometimes be painful when digging into a tender spot. On the other hand there was no problem about getting clothing snarled on rocks or branches.

It took us most of the morning to reach the summit; over the more perpendicular parts when one had got a secure foothold it was necessary to reach down for the other, pulling at first, then pushing upwards to gain another foothold further up. We seemed to spend quite a lot of time gazing up one another's rear quarters.

It was hardly surprising that when we reached the top, panting and perspiring, we flopped down in close embrace on a handy stretch of grass. It did nothing for our panting and perspiring but a great deal for our feeling of well being. As we returned once again to reality we became conscious of the drone of aircraft engines in the distance. We had been too absorbed with one another when we reached the summit, some two or three hundred feet above the level of the sea, to look around. As we stood up, scanning the horizon to the north, we could make out four or five vessels, one of which from its shape looked like an aircraft carrier. Almost certainly they were Japanese. The drone of engines emanated from three planes, only specks in the sky at first, but soon we could see they were heading our way.

'Should we hide out of sight if they come near?' enquired Tau Fong anxiously.

'We must just hope they don't spot the *Hang Tau* moored beneath the cliff.' After a pause whilst the planes drew nearer, we could make out the shapes of bi-planes, like those that had dive bombed us two days earlier. 'Perhaps if you stood on that rock over there, arms and legs akimbo, it might

143

render the pilots so goggle-eyed that they will spatter themselves on the cliff face!'

'I think I will settle for the less adventurous way,' replied Tau Fong, 'and lie with you beneath that bush over there. Perhaps you will make love to me again!' and she tried to look coy as she broke into her infectious giggle.

'The mind is willing,' I responded, 'even if the body may not be!'

From the cover beneath the bush we caught a glance of the underside of the three planes as they wheeled around, apparently satisfied that our island was uninhabited, and then made off in the direction of the much larger island of Lingga.

The immediate danger past we moved across to the southern edge of the cliff from where we could look down on the *Hang Tau*. Our shouts brought waves of acknowledgement from Wong Ten and the two boys who were busy securing the repaired mizzen mast.

'I can see no sign of the others,' said Tau Fong. 'Perhaps Brem and Fruity are not mountaineering types.'

'I don't suppose they've got round to climbing any higher than the depth of their partners' bodies off the ground!'

Before descending we strained our eyesight looking northward towards Singapore, some two hundred miles away; we could still see the menacing shapes of the warships of the Japanese, waiting, it seemed to us, like vultures to descend upon Singapore once the big naval guns that guarded the harbour approaches had been spiked by the hordes of Japanese infantrymen surging southward down the peninsula; and even now, on this first day of February, poised to cross the narrow Johore Straits for the final assault on the citadel. After that, what next? Surely it must be Sumatra and Java, only sparsely defended by the Dutch and their Allies, that would suffer the same fate. Our chances of avoiding capture and returning to service in the RAF seemed remote in the extreme. For the time being here I was, in a tiny oasis insulated from the war, with a beautiful naked girl beside me in a similar state of undress and the rest of the day to ourselves. I recalled an opera that I had listened to on the radio some years before, the title of which eluded me, but the two young people in love, and at the mercy of a tyrant, chose to have just one day on their own together, followed by torture and death, rather than be parted for ever.

We picked our way slowly and carefully down the rocky cliff to our private little beach that would hold a very special place in my memories for the rest of my life. We collected more fruit from around us and sat down under the shade of the palm leaves to eat and drink our fill.

I turned towards Tau Fong and put to her a question that had been in my mind since the previous evening as the boys rowed away back to the ship: 'Why has your father seemingly encouraged his daughters to stay out and sleep with their boyfriends?'

Tau Fong cast her eyes downwards, pausing for a moment before replying: 'We have each of us confessed to our father of our love for our partners; he knows that he cannot deny us our desires, so this is his way of proving whether our love is reciprocated. If you had elected to go back in the dinghy last night it would have meant to him that you thought more of your comforts than of me. After all, the prospects of a cold night, with no clothing or shelter, or any real food, might well have been daunting for some.'

'Good lord!' I responded. 'I had not really thought of that, for I would not have considered any action that took me away from your side, if there was any possible alternative. That is not very well put, I know, but it does mean quite simply that I love you too.' So saying I bent down and kissed her upturned lips. 'I wonder whether Brem and Fruity have passed the Wong test?'

'Does this now mean,' I continued, 'that your father would consent to a union between us?'

'If you wished it to be so,' she replied demurely, her eyes cast down.

'You know that I do – will you consent to be my wife?'

Tau Fong slowly looked up into my eyes, her own big dark eyes answering my question without the need of the whispered 'yes'. It was impossible to resist, even if we had wanted to, the fulfilment again of our desires. I believe we both felt that it could not last; certainly we could not spend the rest of our days on a tiny island, with no clothing or shelter, and only fruit to eat.

'How can we start to plan a life together,' I said at length, 'placed as we are in the middle of a war that seemingly has no end?'

'Could you not live with us in Sumatra until better days return?' said Tau Fong wistfully.

'The idea is very tempting, but I am still a member of the Allied forces; if we reach Palembang before the Japs, I, and the other two, must do our best to rejoin our Air Force unit, otherwise we will be considered deserters.'

145

'How will they know you have not been killed, or drowned in the sea?'

'Maybe they would not find out, but we would still have our consciences to overcome.'

'I understand,' said Tau Fong, sadness in her voice, 'and I will wait for you for as long as it takes for you to win your war.'

I kissed her tenderly and tears trickled down her cheeks; I knew not whether they were hers or mine.

As the sun sank towards the horizon we strolled slowly, hand in hand, down the little beach that had been our very own for two heavenly days. The gently lapping waves cooled our lower limbs, after the heat of the sun, as the water level gradually covered us. As it reached up to my waist, and Tau Fong's breasts she stopped moving forward, clasping my hand tighter. I felt her give a little shudder.

'Are you feeling cold, my dearest?'

'No, just afraid. I cannot help feeling that we may not be alone together again.'

'What, never!'

'That is what my intuition tells me, perhaps it is wrong. Make love to me just once more.' She clasped her hands behind my neck and brought up her feet into the small of my back as our lips met.

Only the fishes were witnesses to our ardours.

Chapter 20

As we swam slowly round the headland into the sunset Choy and Koo came upon us rowing the dinghy. We clambered aboard, drying ourselves with the towels the boys had brought with them together with Tau Fong's kimono and my shorts. For some strange reason I felt self conscious about appearing before the others in the nude, although it hadn't bothered me for the past two days, and quickly covered my confusion.

Soon we were all gathered again on the *Hang Tau*, laughing and joking, whilst sails were set and the anchor hoisted. Wong Ten was too busy getting the vessel under way to join us and for my part I felt that I did not yet want to precipitate the question of my intended relationship with his daughter. We had all had little sleep the night before, for one reason or another, and were pleased to seek the comfort of our bunks when darkness had enveloped the sky. Again, I suppose in deference to our host, we segregated the sexes, leaving the girls to chatter away in peace in their own quarters.

The next morning Fruity was the first to awaken, bringing Brem and me a mug of char in our bunks.

'I am going to stay in Palembang with Befung,' he announced. 'We will get married as soon as we can.'

I was somewhat taken aback and I reckon Brem was also, judging by the look on his face; but on reflection it was not too surprising.

'Well, congratulations, then,' we both echoed. 'Are you going to turn Buddhist then?' I continued.

'It wouldn't worry me,' replied Fruity, 'although Befung was taught about Christianity in the mission in Shanghai. Perhaps we can have two ceremonies; anyway, we intend to be man and wife officially, just as we were yesterday unofficially.'

'How do you reckon to keep your wife in Palembang?' said Brem. 'Assuming the Japs take Sumatra they are unlikely to be helpful to a European, even if they don't find out he is a member of the armed forces.'

'If we are already married they may leave me alone: there's a risk in everything. About earning a living – well, I can sing and I can cook a little.'

'I suppose you realise you will be considered a deserter if the Allied forces are still functioning in Palembang when we reach there,' I said, 'or rather *if* we reach there.'

'On that score,' said Fruity, 'Wong Ten does not think the Japanese are going to bother too much about Sumatra.'

'That's cobblers,' said Brem. 'One of the largest oil fields in production is near Palembang, and the Japs badly need oil for their armed forces. We would be better off going to Java; but it's not our ship.'

'Didn't you two fix anything up with the twins?' said Fruity, turning to Brem and me. 'Perhaps you didn't hit it off,' he goaded.

'We would hardly have stayed out starkers under the stars if we hadn't,' I retorted. 'Did Befung tell you about the Wong Ten test?'

'Sure she did and I reckon we passed with flying colours – grade one!'

'You haven't said much about your romantic entanglement, Brem; did Hang Fong resist your advances, or did you not make any?' I taunted.

'Mind you own ----- business; we Scots are more canny; we play our cards close to our sporrans!'

'So you are not settling in Sumatra, or Java, or anywhere east of Suez?'

'We will wait until this business is all over and then maybe we shall think about settling down in bonnie Scotland.'

'I wonder what Wong Ten thinks about it all; he seemed quite benign when we returned to the ship last night. I expect the girls have told him all about it by now, leaving out the lurid details of course.'

'I reckon we ought to think about going up on deck and giving a hand,' I said. 'Don't forget to put your shirts on, we are no longer on Love Island!'

It was only as we moved up the companionway that we realised that the ship was no longer moving, and we could see the jungle foliage of an island on the port bow as we stepped on to the deck.

'That land over there is the southern tip of Singkep Island,' said Choy as we bade him greetings for the new day. 'Father decided it would be safer if we anchor close to the land during the day and move south again tonight; we don't want to risk having another mast knocked down; it may be worse next time. We have already seen aircraft flying in the distance to the west.'

We all three bowed our greetings to Wong Ten, who smiled at us in return, which seemed to convey his knowledge of our love for his daughters; but we all three kept our peace on that subject, deciding the time was not right to confess all.

'We go below now for sleep,' said Ten. 'Wake us quickly if aeroplanes come near.' So saying, he and Choy started down the companionway.

Soon the three girls and Koo came up to join us, bringing with them fruit and bread made from rice. Our repast finished, we set about the usual maritime chores, swabbing down the deck and generally putting things ship-shape. To cool off after our work in the heat of the morning sun we plunged in for a swim. There could be no repeat of our sojourn on 'Love Island' because the coastline, as far as we could see on either side of the ship, was simply mangrove swamps which would be very difficult to penetrate in order to reach dry land. Nevertheless, it was enjoyable just to dally with the ones we loved in the shade of the mangrove leaves. Crocodiles were always a hazard in the swamp lands but they tended to keep clear of a group of humans.

On our return to the ship we drifted apart in pairs whilst Koo kept a look out from the wheel-house for hostile aircraft. Again we sighted some in the distance but could not identify them.

When Tau Fong and I were alone, sitting aft in the shade of the dinghy, I asked whether she had spoken to her father of our intentions.

'Yes, of course, how could I keep it from him?'

'Was he pleased or angry?'

'He was pleased that I am happy and my sisters too; he told us that our happiness is his also.'

'Is he worried about the mixing of our races, our different religions, not that I am very religious, and our differing ways of life?'

'He says if we really care for one another love will conquer all.'

'You are very lucky to have such an understanding father, and I to have a prospective partner in life prepared to risk all for love.'

That night we continued sailing southwards, reaching a headland on the coast of Sumatra by dawn, when again we laid up for the day. For the next two days and nights we did the same until we reached the estuary of the Palembang River by the evening of Thursday 5 February. We could not attempt to cross the bar at the mouth of the river during the night, so there

149

was nothing for it but to drop anchor and await the dawn.

As we went on deck at first light we could see the murkiness of the water as the reddish-brown mud swept down by the Palembang River intermingled with the green sea water. As the sun peeped above the horizon we espied a motor boat heading out from the shore towards us. Wong Ten knew the river pilots from his previous visits, and also knew the river well, so he was prepared to make his own way the hundred miles upstream to the town of Palembang.

When the pilot, also a Chinaman, climbed aboard he greeted Ten with a smile, clasping his outstretched hand. They spoke in Chinese so we could not understand what was said, but we could tell from the serious expression on the face of the pilot that his news was not good.

When the pilot left for the shore Wong Ten came over to us, his expression grave. 'We have news that the Japanese have landed across the Johore Straits on to Singapore Island. The bridgeheads are being contained, but my friend does not think the Allied army can hold out for many days beneath the continuous bombardment.'

We had heard news on our radio of the advance of the Japs, but always we were led to believe that Singapore would hold out. If what the pilot said was true, and he would be in a very good position to know, talking regularly to the captains of the ships that had sailed from Singapore harbour, the fate of the 'Key to the East' was sealed, and surrender could only be days away. We thought of the poor devils in the British infantry, most of them probably young recruits with no experience of active service, many straight from the cold climes of the northern hemisphere into the sweat box that was Singapore; it would not be surprising if morale was low. We thought also of our mates on the squadron. They should have reached Singapore weeks ago; would any of them be able to escape the hell-hole that Singapore was sure to become in its death throes?

Wong Ten told us also that small formations of Japanese aircraft had been seen flying up the Palembang River but several had been engaged by Allied planes that were still operating from a secret airfield in the jungle outside Palembang. Nevertheless, we would be in danger all the time we were sailing the one hundred miles upstream, which we would have to carry out in daylight. There would probably be little room to manoeuvre the ship if we came under attack.

We set course into the wide estuary of the Palembang River, using the engine to keep us moving against the strong currents and swirling waters that had begun their journey towards the Java Sea from the high rain forests on the eastern slopes of the Peg Barisan mountain range close to the western coast of Sumatra, some three hundred miles away. Our progress was only averaging about 4 knots, so we would take a full two days to reach the town of Palembang, during which time we would be particularly vulnerable to attack from the air if the Japanese were now turning their attentions to Sumatra, having got Singapore almost sewn up.

All through the day we chugged slowly on, keeping as close as we dared to the northern bank of the river; with our shallow draught of some six feet we could keep closer to the bank, without much risk of running on to mud banks, than the larger steamers that plied the trade route to Palembang. During the day two Dutch merchant vessels passed us on the port side, their anti-aircraft guns prominent fore and aft. For many miles there was no proper river bank, but just a mangrove swamp, straggly branches and roots encroaching into the murky river water gradually becoming denser inland. For as far as the eye could see in any direction the terrain was flat and dreary.

Throughout the day the few aircraft we saw were American Bostons, and this gave us heart and hope. In the morning they were heading out to sea in loose formation and later in the day straggling back in ones and twos; there did not seem to be so many on the return flight. We also saw two Hurricanes heading inland, and the sight cheered us greatly, just to see a plane that we had learnt to love and respect. We knew not where they could have come from, but it would seem they were in retreat from Singapore. It was not until later that we learnt that a squadron of Hurricanes had been flown off an aircraft carrier in the Indian Ocean, loaded up with an auxiliary fuel tank under each wing, to try to defend the skies above Singapore. Once the planes had lifted off the deck of the carrier there was no going back, for the Hurricane was not equipped with landing arresting gear, and it was not considered possible to put a Hurricane down on the deck of a carrier. In fact, this 'impossible' feat *was* accomplished by a brave pilot who really had no choice than to try it when his engine failed soon after take off.

Alas, the Hurricanes that reached Singapore were too late and too few, and those we saw heading dejectedly into Sumatra were probably the last of the Mohicans in the Far East.

151

We covered some fifty miles upstream before darkness descended upon us and it became too dangerous to proceed further without risking grounding on a sandbank.

We started upstream again as soon as we were able on what should be our last full day on board the faithful *Hang Tau*. During the morning we again saw a motley collection of Allied aircraft, even including a B29 Flying Fortress, going we knew not where. More ominously, in the afternoon we espied a full wing of twenty-seven Mitsubishi bombers heading relentlessly inland in perfect V formation. They passed directly overhead at some ten thousand feet taking no notice of us, for clearly they had more important things to do than to bother about a little sailing craft on the river. The sight struck terror into our hearts, not merely because of the nearness of the enemy but because it now became certain that Japan intended to conquer Sumatra in the same manner as all the other Allied strongholds and colonial possessions in the eastern hemisphere. Hong Kong had gone; the Philippines and Malaya were in their death throes: soon it would be the turn of Sumatra, Borneo and Java, and any of the smaller isles of the East Indies that the Japs thought worth their while to subdue.

Throughout the rest of the day our luck held and we were not molested. As dusk fell we dropped anchor just a few miles downstream from Palembang.

That night, when all was quiet apart from the heavy breathing of my mates nearby, I was conscious of a warm and fragrant body nestling in beside mine. Tau Fong did not exude her usual joy and vivaciousness as we entwined in each other's arms. We were both aware that soon we must be parted; maybe too she possessed some deeper premonition of what was to happen.

We made love sincerely and passionately, not a word passing between us; it had all been said before. We did not need to tell one another how deep was our love.

Before dawn she had gone. I gained consciousness as the eastern sky heralded the dawn, a curious feeling of foreboding and emptiness gripping my heart, just as if the ending of a chapter of my life was at hand.

As the sun peeped above the trees on the eastern bank we weighed anchor and started to nose upstream again. By around eleven o'clock we could make out a few buildings on the river bank a mile or two to the north.

Wong Ten approached Brem and myself, holding out in his right hand the lead weight and cord for depth sounding. He asked if we would position ourselves on the bowsprit to take soundings as we edged in towards the town. He and Choy would be in the wheelhouse to receive our shouted measurements, while the others would be aft getting the dinghy ready to launch when we had progressed as far as we could in the ship. Ten would then need to go ashore to arrange about berthing.

As Brem and I set about our task up front we were conscious that there were aircraft around, but we were paying close attention to our task rather than watching the skies, as were the others who were going about their allotted jobs at the rear end of the vessel.

Suddenly I saw Brem stop in his tracks as he was about to cast the line; a sudden look of fear crossed his face as both he and I recognised in that instant a fearsome sound that had become all too familiar since that fateful day early in December when the Japanese Empire had set itself irrevocably at war with the Allies. It was the sound of a dive bomber banking to attack, and there was no doubt about what was to be the target.

We both yelled a warning to the others as we flung ourselves into the water on the landward side. Either our voices were drowned by the engine noises or they did not realise the danger in time. In the space of a few brief seconds it was all over; this was the occasion when our good luck had run its course.

As Brem and I flailed our way shorewards the bomber's engine reached a screaming pitch; we heard the terrifying whoosh of the bomb released on course as the plane pulled up and away above the masts of the doomed *Hang Tau*. There was a great roar behind us as the bomb struck, somewhere between the wheelhouse and the rudder beam. Splinters of wood and pieces of metal plopped into the water around us. In our panic we had swum like two Johnny Weismullers, and were some fifty yards from the ship before turning and treading water to survey the destruction.

The Japanese dive bomber had now reached the top of its 'pull-out' and was heading away, no doubt its pilot elated that he had scored a direct hit. My whole frame was shivering, not with cold or with fear now the immediate danger was passed, but with the terrible realisation that my beautiful Tau Fong, whom I loved so much, and all the Wong family, together with Fruity, who had been such close and loyal friends, were being swept into oblivion. I hardly dared lower my eyes to survey the scene of destruction.

153

The *Hang Tau* had keeled over and was fast settling by the stern, her bows, that we had left only seconds before, rising up towards the sky. Within a couple of minutes she had slipped down out of sight to rest for ever on the bed of the Palembang River. Around the eddies that marked the spot were floating pieces of flotsam and jetsam, but there was no sign of life; nothing moved against the strong current that was sweeping all towards the sea and oblivion. I thought I caught a glimpse of a sarong floating away amongst the eddies. I felt so helpless and empty, for there was nothing either of us could do.

I would gladly have let myself float away in the current to join my dead loved one, but somehow an animal sense of survival took hold of me and I turned slowly towards the river bank. Brem was by my side, feeling, I am sure, just as I did, but not a word passed between us, we were just too choked to speak.

We dragged ourselves up on to a deserted mud bank and just sat there, the water trickling off our bodies mingling with the tears that could not be held back.

Chapter 21

How long we sat like that I do not know. Time meant nothing. Life itself meant nothing to me any more. What was the point in trying to go on? It was difficult to get things into perspective. Some guardian angel must have been looking after Brem and myself these last two months, during which time we had both loved and lost.

In theory we had escaped from imprisonment, but in fact we were only just one jump ahead of the enemy; he was still breathing uncomfortably close to our necks and our chances of getting clean away seemed as remote as at any time in the past eight weeks, but the faint chance was all we had to live for.

The sun was burning into our shoulders and necks, for we had no clothing other than our muddy shorts held up by our money belts. We slithered and scrambled along the bank of the river until we came to huts on the outskirts of Palembang. There was no sign of life as we reached the dock area; no doubt the Japanese aircraft had persuaded people to move away inland. We did the same, and came eventually to the main streets, where most of the shops were boarded up; but some were opening up again in the hopes of doing business.

Our first priority was to buy footwear. We came across a cobbler plying the small hammer of his trade, his lips gripping several brads as he busied himself on repairs.

Brem, who was a better bargain haggler than me, produced one of Wong Ten's 'pieces of eight' and approached the wizened old man. 'We want two pairs of strong *chapplies*, and change in guilders from this,' and he handed the old man the gold coin. The old man held the coin up to the light, bit it, then tested the weight on his forefinger; then the haggling commenced. The man had very little command of English, but he knew full well that gold was going to be a useful thing to have if the Japanese overran the country. We got our two pairs of sandals and more change in guilders than I would have expected, although I dare say we were still robbed.

When we had bought ourselves a couple of tunic shirts apiece, a loose canvas hat each, towels and shaving gear, not to mention cigarettes, we began to feel a little more civilised. As we stepped out into the main street from the bazaar we saw a service truck heading down the road. Sitting beside the driver, whom we could not see clearly in the shade of the hood, was a man with a large nose and sergeant's stripes whom I thought I recognised. Suddenly there was a shout from the back of the truck, 'Ken, Brem, what the ----- hell are you doing here?'

There was not mistaking the loud Lancashire expletives of Geoff Titherington. 'It's a long story, Geoff,' I answered. 'Maybe we'll tell you all about it some time.'

'We haven't seen you since we pulled out of Butterworth; quite thought you had both bought it. By the way, you both look as if you have just seen a ghost.'

'Maybe we have,' said Brem. 'We were very nearly in the haunting business ourselves. If you saw that ship being sunk in the river, then you are now looking at the sole survivors.'

'Christ! is that so?'

We now identified the NCO with the big nose as Sergeant Levy of 27 Squadron 'A' flight, and the ruddy faced driver of the truck as the down-to-earth Geordie Smith, an engine fitter from 'B' flight.

'Jump up on the back, lads,' invited Sergeant Levy. 'You can give us a hand; Geoff will tell you all about it.'

It was impossible to feel depressed for long in the presence of the irrepressible Geoff Titherington, one of the human race's natural comedians.

'We're on our way from P2 to P1 to collect a Hurricane airscrew from a kite that bought it on the ground in yesterday's raid.'

'That figures,' I said. 'We saw Jappo heading this way as we came up the river. But what's all this bloody P2 and P1 business?'

'That's easy, P1 is the old civilian airport of Palembang, which we will reach in a few minutes, while P2 is a clearing in the jungle some twenty miles south of here, near to the oilfields. Jappo knows all about P1, but he has not yet been able to find P2, and it must be making him very angry, for he knows there are Allied kites still operating near here as they have been making things very uncomfortable for his ships heading for the Palembang River. Every time a kite lands at P2 we push it into the jungle under cover of the big trees, and so far Jappo's recce planes haven't been able to spot them from twenty thousand odd feet. We had a bit of a twitter on one day last week when a B29 Flying Fortress dropped in for tea and got stuck axle deep in the ground. It took a chain of fifty men passing hundreds of four-gallon cans of petrol from the fuel dump in the jungle out to the big bird in the middle of the clearing to get it refuelled. Then every man jack on the camp pushing and pulling through the night got it clear and airborne next morning before Jappo's recce plane spotted anything.'

By this time we were driving into the main entrance to P1. The guard hut was still standing, but apart from a scarred control tower not much else in the way of brick buildings. The Malaysian guard checked Sergeant Levy's papers and waved us through. We drove through to the improvised cookhouse to get a meal.

'The Dutch Services food is pretty ghastly,' said Geoff. 'When we first came to Palembang, a month ago, we just couldn't stomach the grub they served up; for days we lived on pineapples, the acid from which started sores inside our mouths.'

'How did all you 27 Squadron bods come to be here in the first place?' questioned Brem.

'When we reached Singapore we only had four serviceable Blenheims left, so most of our time was spent filling sandbags. By Christmas things were beginning to hot up at Kallang. Even our Christmas dinner was interrupted between courses by an air raid. We were certainly glad of the sandbags we had filled. Jappo took to coming over at night, when the moon was full, and dropping the odd stick of bombs around the 'drome. By the first week in January we had filled all the available sandbags, which was beginning to pall a bit anyway, so when thirty fitters were asked to volunteer to help the Dutch in Sumatra we stepped smartly forward.'

'Bloody good move, I would think, by the way things are going in Singy at the moment,' I chipped in.

'You wouldn't ----- it,' continued Geoff, as we lined up with our irons at the cook's tent. 'We pulled out from Empire Dock, picking our way through the minefields in a Dutch tramp steamer, just as a P & O troopship was unloading its human cargo. There were the poor sods shuffling down the

157

gangplank, in their solar topees and moon-men shorts, staggering beneath their kit-bags and looking as happy as the guard of honour at a funeral.'

'So where are the others that came with you?'

'We split up when we docked at Palembang. About a dozen are still here at P1, while the rest are up at P2, doing any job that needs doing quickly, without much equipment, on any plane that happens to drop in.'

While we ate our corned beef fritters and rice pudding some of the other men from 27 Squadron came over to join us, and Brem and I told them briefly what had befallen us since Butterworth. Neither of us could bring ourselves to speak about our affairs with the Wong girls; the memories were too fresh in our minds, and the sincerity of our love would not be believed by the others.

'Corporal Boyle here has a theory that the Japs are going to try to take this airfield with parachutists,' Geordie Smith announced. 'I think it's a load of balls, whoever heard of Japanese parachutists? They would lose their spectacles on the way down!'

'I and my boys will make sure they lose more than their spectacles,' retorted Jack Boyle. We remembered Jack Boyle as an Orderly Room Corporal in 27 Squadron; like me he had been conscripted from civvy street where he had earned his crust as an auditor. With his rifle slung over his shoulder he was now bent on selling his life dearly if it came to the crunch.

'Don't listen to these silly buggers,' said Jack, his cultured voice contrasting with Geordie's raucous banter. 'Jappo needs the oil up road and this airfield is his quick way in. The river is a dicey and slow way to get here; by all accounts he had already had some of his ships battered by the Bostons from P2, which he must be mad about not being able to find. He can't just fly in here not knowing what he is going to find; what's more, his recce planes, which come over every day, will have noted the airfield potholed from his own bombers, so it would be very dodgy to try and land transporters. The obvious answer is parachutists to pave the way; they know that Hitler did it successfully in Crete; we can only hope the Japs are not as good at jumping as the Jerries.'

'You certainly seem to have a point,' said Brem.

'What's more,' continued Jack, 'It's going to happen soon – probably tomorrow morning,'

'It would be just our sodding luck if it did,' responded Brem.

158

'Have no fear, my men would be ready for them. I've got thirty-odd men, all volunteers, who have reasons for disliking the Nips, armed with rifles and tommy guns provided by the Dutch. We have dug a series of slit trenches strategically around the control tower, which any airborne force would need to capture; I reckon we could overcome a far larger force of men armed similarly.'

'We wish you luck, Jack,' I said. 'It would be a great morale booster to see one put across the all-conquering Japs, even if we get caught up in it.'

After our meal Sergeant Levy rounded us up. 'Come on, lads, we'll take a look at this Hurricane we have come for.'

As Geordie drove slowly round the perimeter of the airfield a sorry sight met our eyes. Planes of all sorts of makes and sizes were dotted around the field, all of them unserviceable, some gutted by fire and almost unrecognisable. Most bore the large red triangle of the Dutch Air Force, but there were also two with the US Navy White star, and in the furthest corner of the field we could just make out the shape of a lone Hurricane, its red, white and blue roundels no longer visible on the fabric-covered fuselage which had been burnt off in the last raid; the tail section was just a tangle of warped metal.

On reaching the battered plane we could see that the airscrew, with its shiny black nose-cap, was unscathed; even the engine looked serviceable, but we did not have the facilities for lifting it out, even if we had wanted to.

'Right, lads,' commanded Sergeant Levy. 'We shan't have time before sunset to get it off and loaded onto the truck before sunset, so we'll just shift off the holding nuts while the light holds, and lift off, load and away first thing in the morning.'

We had only one tool box and, working from the back of the truck under the nose cap, only one man could use the spanner, so it took a full hour to get the prop free for lift off. By this time it was nearly dark and we did not want to risk using the headlights of the truck for fear of attracting any marauding Jap planes that may have been around. So we made our way back to the tented area near to the canteen and drew out mattresses apiece to kip down for the night.

'OK, lads', said the sergeant, who had joined us for a drink in the canteen. 'Your time's your own until one hour before dawn, but no spending the night in a knocking shop, you've got to have strength in the morning to lift off that airscrew.'

'That's quite an idea,' said Geoff Titherington, when out of earshot of the sergeant. 'The Dutch are much more open about the running of brothels. I know of one on the edge of the town; we'll probably collect a dose of the clap, but who's to worry. I don't suppose we shall live long enough to have to worry about it.'

'Anyone would think you had only just thought of it, Geoff,' said Geordie. 'I'm game for a quick bang while we've got the chance; are you two Chink lovers coming?'

The comment stung sharply, but I let it pass for the sake of comradeship, as did Brem, who could not hide the scowl on his brow. Brem and I had no intention of indulging in the attractions of the brothel, particularly as the memories of the Wong twins were still so fresh in our minds; it was only last night, but seemed like weeks ago, that they had visited our bunks, and the memory of Tau Fong's warm body close to mine was locked tenderly in my mind for ever. Rather than seem like queers, and perhaps a little out of curiosity, we accompanied the others to a long low wooden building alongside a stream.

There seemed to be no charge for entry to a long corridor, reminding me somewhat of the monkey house at the London Zoo; but instead of the waft of urine-soaked straw there was the pungent aroma of perfume; instead of monkeys in wire cages there were oriental girls lying on beds, visible through the heavily bead-hung doorways to each small compartment. I assume that there were curtains to be drawn if one made one's choice. Most of the girls seemed to be passing their spare time working at embroidery. I was rather glad that the scene did not stir any desires within me as I felt very sorry for the girls.

Geordie and Geoff seemed to possess no such qualms, having been out in the jungle for several weeks, and soon made their selections. They took the precaution of handing their money belts to Brem and me outside; I don't know what other precautions, if any, they took. It would not be long, I mused as we waited outside, before the girls would be lying passively in wait for Japanese soldiers and airmen. I suppose that to them one man was much like another.

I don't know what time it was when we located our tent, but it seemed a very short while before being dug in the ribs by the toe-cap of Sergeant Levy's shoe and ordered outside onto the truck. In my dreams I was still in

160

the Wongs' house in Penang being caressed by Tau Fong; I was beginning to wish we hadn't attempted to return to the fold, but told myself it would be far worse in a Japanese prisoner of war camp, where many of my mates were probably incarcerated by now.

It was still dark as we stumbled outside the tent, rubbing the sleep from our eyes. 'Wait while I have a pee, Sarge,' groaned Geordie.

'Put it away quick then,' ordered Sergeant Levy. 'No time now for anything more, we want to get shot of this place before Jappo pays another visit.'

As we moved past the shrapnel-scarred control tower Jack Boyle was beginning to marshal his men into their trenches. He waved to us cheerily as we passed by in the gloom. 'If they come today we'll be ready for them.'

Geordie drove slowly in second gear around the airfield perimeter without attempting to use the headlights in case there were any enemy planes in the vicinity. As we reached the stricken Hurricane, in the furthest corner of the aerodrome, he backed as close as possible to the propeller blade.

'Right, then,' commanded Sergeant Levy. 'One of you up on top to steady the upright blade, while we get the blocks ready on the truck – Geoff, you're always acting the monkey, get up there.'

Geoff Titherington jumped up on the trailing edge of a wing and then eased his legs astride the top engine cowling; alas, the Merlin would roar no more. Brem and I gripped one of the lower airscrew blades, while Geordie and the sergeant took the other, as we gently eased the hub off the spline. Within five minutes we took the strain as it came free and lowered the weight slowly on to the truck. During this time we had been totally absorbed in our task.

Geoff was the first to be relieved from his allotted task and eased himself back along the top of the engine to the main planes, looking up and across the airfield as he did so.

'Christ Almighty, look there!' he yelled. Startled by his cry we all turned to look in the direction of his outstretched arm.

There, just above the eastern horizon, glinting in the early rays of the sun that we could not yet see, were the sinister black outlines of many large aircraft. It was like that terrible first morning of the war all over again. As we watched transfixed we began to hear the menacing drone of twin-engined transporters as they moved relentlessly towards us.

'Do we run for it, Sarge, and scatter in the jungle?'

'That wouldn't be any use. If they are airborne troops they are just as likely to land around wherever we could get to in the few minutes left. Stay here together; if the worst comes to the worst we will wave a white rag, pray to God, and hope Jack Boyle and his lads do their stuff.'

By now the first of the large lumbering planes was almost overhead as they came towards us in line astern formation. We watched helplessly as the first plane unloaded its human cargo, reminiscent of a fish disgorging its eggs into the water, as the men followed one another out of the cargo door forming a line in the slipstream. As their parachutes opened out they seemed just to hang in the sky. There seemed to be about thirty men in each plane and we had counted eight planes altogether. Maybe the armada had already been decimated by the Allied planes operating from P2.

As the canopies all opened out it was a fearsome sight as the Japanese soldiers drifted down towards us. Now was to be Jack Boyle's big moment. We heard the chatter of machine guns from across the airfield. With the first burst of fire the invaders knew they did not possess the element of surprise; the defenders were ready for them and had the great advantage of being well concealed in prepared positions.

The seconds ticked by and seemed like hours. The small arms fire became more and more intense as parachutists came within range and we could hear yells of pain from above as several were hit. It became evident too that the pilots had misjudged the strength of the wind which was blowing up river quite strongly: many of the parachutes were drifting well past the airfield and would become entangled in the jungle trees to the south and east of the aerodrome. If the men were not injured landing in the trees they still had to disentangle themselves and then try to wade through the swamps and undergrowth before they could be effective in the attack.

Our immediate concerns were the three who looked like landing within yards of us. Above the furore of rifle and machine gun fire we could hear the moans of the Jap landing nearest to us as he clutched his stricken leg. As he touched the ground we saw him crumple in a heap. By now Sergeant Levy, who had seen there was no escape for us, had torn the white shirt off Brem's back and waved it aloft. It was spotted by one of the parachutists who had landed some fifty yards away between us and the control tower. As he raised his sub-machine gun and raced towards us I felt that this must be my last moment; it was a case of third time unlucky. In the first close encounter with

Japanese soldiers in the ditch of the rubber plantation at Taiping, we had been saved fortuitously by an iguana. On the second occasion we had succeeded in conning the guards that we were coolies, as we moved through the harbour gates at Penang. This time there could be no way out, we were completely at the mercy of the enemy.

Chapter 22

J ust why that Japanese officer, who had us five completely at his mercy, did not press his trigger I will never know for sure. I don't think it was because he was an officer and a gentleman, whose conscience would not allow him to contravene the Geneva Convention; I think it more likely that he thought we might be persuaded, once the airfield was under their control, to disclose the whereabouts of P2. He may well not have spared us if he had not a ready-made guard at hand; for clearly the man with one useless leg was not going to be any good at running across the airfield.

The officer could speak some English. 'Lie down, face on floor,' he commanded us. 'Hands, arms stretch out.' We all did just that, and very swiftly, only too thankful to still be allowed to live.

The officer rattled a few words to the injured man who propped himself on an upturned wheel chock, some ten yards away, and trained his automatic on us. Shouting further commands to other parachutists as they ran in from their landing points the officer led the men, at the double, across the airfield towards the control tower. Green uniformed men came running from all quarters converging on the tower, shouting and yelling at each other, firing quick bursts of automatic fire.

Although outnumbered, Jack Boyle and his men had one very clear advantage; they showed hardly any of themselves as they crouched in their sandbagged slit trenches, well camouflaged by undergrowth, whilst the enemy were extremely visible in the early morning light as they ran towards them. We prayed hard that Jack and the boys would keep their nerve, for it should not be long before the small Dutch garrison in the town came to their assistance. For the Japs it was imperative that the defence force was silenced quickly, and the airfield made ready in short time for transporter planes with heavy equipment and reinforcements to land.

We could hear the machine gun fire building up to a crescendo, and out of

164

the corner of my eye I saw several Japs cut down by crossfire as they dashed across the field. Our cheers as each Jap bit the dust were unsettling our guard who grunted what was probably meant as a warning to us. The man was obviously in great pain from his gashed leg and we could see the growing stain of blood on his trousers. Geoff reached one hand into the pocket of his shorts and fished out a packet of cigarettes which he held up for the guard to see, indicating that he was offering him one. At first the Jap seemed to suspect a trap, and raised up his gun as if to fire. Undeterred, Geoff tossed the packet at his feet.

The ice had been broken, and the soldier bent down to retrieve the packet; slipping a fag into his mouth he lit it from a lighter he carried, and drew in deep gasps of smoke, which probably did something towards deadening the pain he must be been suffering. For us, humiliated into grovelling in the dust, the suspense was almost unbearable. Thoughts of being herded behind barbed wire, perhaps for years, in the hands of an enemy who was unlikely to show much compassion, if any, was to say the least daunting. I was beginning to think it might have been better if our captor had pulled the trigger.

It seemed like an hour, but was probably much less, when we became aware that the arms fire had become less intense, and soon was reduced to intermittent short bursts. From our worm's eye view we could not really see what was going on over the other side of the field, but we had heard the roar of lorry engines as they neared the camp, and we hoped fervently it heralded the approach of a relief force. Parachutists who had landed in the jungle behind were still appearing over the perimeter fence in ones and twos and running across the field towards the action. We began to feel confident that Jack Boyle and his men, if they had not been overwhelmed in the initial action, could pick off the trickle of advancing enemy as they came into their sights. We could tell by the look in the eyes of our guard that all was not going well from his point of view; by now the airborne division should have been in control of the airfield and have signalled the transporter planes that it was safe to land.

The sun was high above the horizon when we heard the sound of vehicles approaching round the perimeter. I raised myself on to my elbows. Sure enough it was a Dutch armoured car, followed by a 30-cwt lorry, both moving very slowly forward with guns trained outwards on both sides. We saw our guard drop his gun as the armoured car came within range. There was nothing he could do but surrender, other than commit hara-kiri! but he did not seem to be the suicidal type.

A large Dutchman climbed out of the armoured car, his revolver drawn and trained on our erstwhile guard. He kicked the soldier's gun towards us and motioned him into the lorry, which already contained several Jap prisoners, most of whom appeared to be wounded.

The Dutch officer came towards us beaming, his right hand held out to shake ours, and spoke in impeccable English. 'You fellows must have had a pretty worrying time. Better stay here for a while while we try to flush out the stragglers; we are still several Japs short on the total that were reported to have been dropped. We will call back again with an empty lorry when we consider it safe to do so.'

'Okay, sir,' responded Sergeant Levy. 'We're only too glad not to be facing the wrong end of a gun barrel.'

'Here's a few bottles of beer,' said the Dutchman, reaching into the vehicle. 'It will have to serve as food as well for the time being.' So saying, they started off again on their task. We adjourned to the shade of the wings of the stricken Hurricane and began to swig our bottles of beer.

For the next two or three hours we could hear sporadic bursts of machine gun fire in the jungle behind us, but these became less and less frequent, and further away. We began to feel our confidence returning; indeed, a certain exhilaration at no longer being prisoners of war. True, it might only be temporary, but for the time being we were still on active service.

'I'm feeling bloody hungry,' exclaimed Geoff, for it was now about midday and we hadn't eaten anything since getting up. 'How about it, Sarge, can't we make our way across the field to see if there is any grub around? I expect that jolly Dutchman has forgotten all about us.'

Sergeant Levy, who was probably feeling hungry too, pondered for a moment. 'I daresay it would be quite safe if we marched across; Jack's boys are hardly likely to mistake us for Japs.'

'I can't think of five blokes around these parts who look less like Nippos,' responded Geoff.

'Right, get fell in,' commanded Sergeant Levy. We shuffled into two pairs, chortling at the comedy of the situation.

'No laughing in the ranks,' shouted the sergeant, maintaining a straight face. 'Forward march: left, right, left.'

As we approached the other side of the airfield we could see Japanese corpses still lying around and beyond them the occasional glint of steel from behind sandbags. It was not surprising that the parachutists were massacred in large numbers as they ran in, for we were on top of the defenders before we could see them; and *we* knew they were there. In the half light of dawn the attacking force was at a distinct disadvantage.

'Hello there!' we heard Jack Boyle shout. 'We thought you lot had bought it when we saw the parachutists landing all around where you were.'

'We did too,' said Geoff. 'It was just as well we had Brem's white shirt and that the Jappo who landed nearest to us was an officer and knew the rules.'

'We winged a few on their way down,' said Jack in a matter of fact sort of way, as if he had been out shooting grouse.

'The truth is, Jack,' said Sergeant Levy, 'we are bloody grateful for what you and your boys did, and everyone in Palembang should be grateful too.'

'I don't think they'll try that lark again, anyway,' said Jack Boyle, 'but I'm afraid it will all be in vain in the end. The Japs are determined to take Palembang, and unlock the key to the oilfields; at best we have delayed them for a few days.'

'Let's hope that gives us time to get shot of the place, then,' said Geoff.

We all echoed his hopes, but the way seemed by no means clear how we would expect to stay one jump ahead of the enemy and to reach comparative safety. What today's escapade had done was to remind us that the enemy was still breathing down our necks.

'Do you need any help, Jack?' said Sergeant Levy. 'The lads and I will give a helping hand – short of gathering up the stiffs, that might take our appetites away.'

'It's not much good having an appetite at the moment,' said Jack; 'I'm afraid the cookhouse tent got burnt down in the mêlée. Might be an idea if you and your boys could see what can be rustled up in the way of grub; we've had nothing all day.'

It was a couple of hours before we got anything to eat – the inevitable corned beef in a sort of batter; at least it subdued the pangs of hunger.

'I don't think we are going to be able to reach P2 with the prop before dark now,' said Levy. 'Might as well get it secured on the truck ready to move tomorrow morning. I think we all can do with a shower and a good night's rest after today's ordeal.'

For me, and no doubt Brem as well, the night time meant being alone with one's thoughts. It was only yesterday morning that the girls we had come to love so deeply and dearly were full of life and looking forward to sharing their lives with us one day. The only unhappiness was the prospect of being parted in Palembang. Now we were parted for ever: for them oblivion; for us, the tender memories of nights and days on Love Island, and in Penang; of soft skins and warm bodies nestled in our arms.

Dawn came at last, and with it new hope. Yesterday had been a victory, albeit a tiny one which would hardly feature in the war news of the world; but for us it was significant – the Japanese were not invincible, as it had seemed for the past two months; they could be overcome, and one day it would be our turn to hit back.

We had already secured the Hurricane propeller on to our truck the previous evening, and so it was just a matter of bidding farewell to our friends at P1 and setting out on the road to P2 before Jappo paid another visit. As we passed through the town of Palembang for the last time there was very little sign of life; shops were shuttered up and a general air of gloom hung over the place; there was the expectation that it would not be many days before the Japanese arrived in force, and there was very little hope of holding out.

As we rumbled across the girder bridge over the Palembang river I could scarcely bring myself to look down into those swirling chocolate brown waters that had swept away downstream, only two days previously, the great love of my life. I felt the saltiness of tears as they trickled down my cheeks. I could only hope that the light of Tau Fong's life was extinguished the instant the bomb struck, and that she did not suffer the agonies of drowning in those dirty brown waters.

168

Chapter 23

As we moved southwards along the road to the oilfields the country began to take on a little more character; the monotonous flatness of the river valley gave way gradually to gently undulating terrain, with many large and strange trees, interspersed here and there with native dwellings, each with its *atap* roof and a patch of ground nearby where vegetables and fruit were growing.

The camp of P2 was like no other aerodrome we had visited before. There was no formal guardroom or indeed an entrance gate; just a gravel road through a gap in the undergrowth. Sergeant Levy jumped out of the truck as we approached a hut, beckoning to Brem and me to follow him. He simply told the Dutch sergeant that we were from 27 Squadron and had joined him in Palembang.

'Okay, lads, welcome to P2,' said the Dutchman. 'We've got no clothing here, and very little equipment, but the sleeping quarters are down the road there – see if you can find room to bed down; the mattresses are stacked in the shed behind here.'

We duly collected our mattresses and continued down the potholed gravel road to the billets. There were no beds inside, just a long shelf arrangement, six feet deep, stretching the whole length of the hut on either side of a centre gangway. Geoff and Geordie made a space for Brem and me between their mattresses. We had no kit to worry about, apart from the bare essentials we had bought in Palembang market.

Having fixed our sleeping accommodation the first job was to find the place where the crippled Hurricane was dispersed in the jungle. The airfield itself consisted of no more than a grassed area, of no particular shape, but seemed to stretch for miles in the jungle that was all around us. Although it was situated along the top of a ridge, the heavy planes that had landed there after rain had created furrows in the soil; it wasn't surprising that our

Hurricane had fallen foul of a wheel track as it taxied in, finishing up on its nose with a very bent airscrew. This had already been removed, so it was just a question of the five of us reversing the procedure carried out at P1.

'There's no panic about getting the plane airworthy,' announced Sergeant Levy. 'The pilot went sick with suspected malaria soon after he landed.'

'He'd better hurry up and get well again,' said Geoff, 'or all our efforts will have been in vain, and we'll just have to bust it up to prevent Jappo making use of it.'

'Rather than do that I'd have a go at flying myself,' volunteered Geordie.

'Don't come the bullshit, Geordie, you wouldn't have the guts.'

'I would, you know,' said Geordie with bravado. 'I reckon I could get it off the deck and aim it at Java, and if I couldn't land it there I would use the chute.'

'All sounds easy,' said Sergeant Levy, 'I just hope the pilot gets well again soon.'

We all set about carrying out an inspection of the aeroplane; for Brem and me it was the first time in two months that we had worked on an aircraft.

'She seems OK as far as the airframe is concerned,' I reported.

'She needs coolant,' said Geoff who was perched on the mainplane peering into the engine. 'Must have lost most of it when she was tipped up on her nose.'

'That's one thing we don't have here,' said Sergeant Levy.

'Then we'll piss in the tank,' the rest of us chorused. We had all been told at training school that if you run out of coolant, which is just an anti-freeze mixture, you can use urine in an emergency; it would need to be pretty cold for that to freeze. It doesn't do a great deal of good to the circulatory system because of the acid in the urine, but corrosion was not likely to be much of a problem – this plane was unlikely to have many flying days left.

'I've sweated so much I can't strain a drip at the moment,' said Geoff, who always believed in using basic English.

'There's no great hurry,' said Brem. 'We'll take an empty four-gallon petrol can back to the billet and have a piss up, literally that is, tonight.'

'That's an idea,' said Geordie. 'We have a standing invitation to visit some friends we got to know down at the oilfield last week; one of them comes from my part of Blighty.'

'That's his ----- bad luck then,' said Brem, 'can't blame him for coming out here!'

'Are you coming along for the piss-up, Sarge?' enquired Geoff.

'Not me,' said Sergeant Levy, who probably thought his presence might dampen the proceedings, 'but you can use the truck if you want; for Christ's sake, though, one of you keep sober to drive it back.'

The four of us drew straws to settle that point, and Brem lost. Just before sundown we set off down the road; only a short distance away we came to the oilfield. I think I had expected to see drilling masts like trees all around, but in fact there were only one or two where new drilling was being carried out. For the most part the wells could only be discerned by a pipe plunging at right angles straight into the ground. No doubt there were pumping stations around which we did not have time to see.

Geordie Smith directed us to a neat wooden bungalow, not far from what looked like the oil company's offices. At the sound of our truck drawing up two men emerged, one a giant of a man with a large belly and balding on top, making him look older than his age, which we learnt later to be thirty. The other man was small by comparison, with a slim, rather dapper figure and high cheek bones setting off a ruddy complexion. They were clearly very pleased to see us.

'Come in, lads,' said the smaller man, in a Northumbrian accent. 'You couldn't have timed it better. We've just been told we have two days to get the whole place ready to blow up, so we might as well finish what booze we have left, and we shall need some help.'

'Glad to hear it,' said Geordie, matching accent for accent. 'Let me introduce two old squadron mates who weren't with us last visit: the one with fair hair and a sizeable konk is Ken, who comes from the Smoke; the one with the mop of black hair is Brem who hails from the top end of the UK, where they keep sheep for company and sit watching the northern lights.' Turning to us, 'Ken, Brem, this bloke here who talks proper, like me, is Fred and comes from Gateshead; the man mountain is Hans and hails from somewhere amid the windmills.'

Introductions over, we stepped across the threshold into the flat the two men shared. It was quite neat and tidy, probably because they had a servant to look after them.

Spotting the empty petrol tin that Geoff had brought in, Fred burst out.

171

'What the hell's that for? Are you reckoning on spewing your guts up?'

'Not exactly, we just want you to all pee for Britain.' Our hosts obviously thought it a joke and the room echoed to the booming belly laugh of the Dutchman. Geoff explained the reason.

'Right,' said Fred, 'so we are both doing one another a good turn; you by putting our booze to good use and after we've got sloshed it will help keep your Hurricane in the air,'

The evening got merrier as time went by; the bottles of scotch and gin became dead men, and the petrol can, set up in the centre of the room, filled up steadily. Great was the cheering each time someone unbuttoned his flies and let rip in the tin can.

'So you oil men look like being unemployed too,' said Brem, who must have been beginning to feel a bit out of things as we had restricted him to two small scotches.

'We were told today the bloody Japs have reached the mouth of the river and are heading this way. At least they are not likely to bomb this place, they need what we've got too badly. It's up to us to make sure it's not easy for them after we pull out.'

'Where do you reckon you will go?' I asked.

'Java first stop, then Aussy I reckon, if we can make it. You had best try to do the same.'

I don't remember much about the journey back or how I found myself on a mattress, still in my shorts and shirt, next morning. As I staggered out to the water tap, to immerse my head, I passed the petrol tin, half filled with urine, standing outside the hut entrance. Come to think of it, it was unlikely anyone would want to nick it.

The thing I recall most vividly about that day was seeing a ring of men, some dozen or so, around a clump of soil, on top of which was the biggest spider I had ever seen; the size of a man's fist, with six fat hairy legs and little red beady eyes glinting as it moved slowly forward. Some idiot hurled a clod of earth at it and it just disappeared. Having a phobia about spiders I suffered nightmares about that mighty insect for weeks afterwards, waking up in a cold sweat in the middle of the night thinking that I could feel it in my shorts.

The following day, 12 February, two Blenheims limped in and touched down on the far side of the field. To our amazement they were the last of the

27 Squadron planes, covered in so many red doped patches over bullet holes that they were hardly recognisable; indeed, it was a wonder they were able to fly at all. There were still more holes to be patched over, for the aircrews told us that they had been fired at by small arms fire as they tried to gain height beyond the perimeter fence of Kallang airport. They said that Allied resistance in the doomed city of Singapore was virtually at an end, and it could only be a matter of two or three days before the garrison surrendered.

That night I was conscious of a great noise nearby, but it took more than that to arouse me from a deep sleep. The next morning we saw just how near we had been to being annihilated by one of our own aircraft. An American Boston had landed short of the airfield and carved a swathe through the jungle only a few feet from our billet. I never did find out whether the aircrew had survived.

In the afternoon the pilot of the Hurricane turned up to see if his plane was serviceable. He was a young sergeant, not long out of flying training school, still pale from his bout of malaria. He had been lucky to survive so long, and his chances of living much longer seemed pretty remote. He told us that he had been ordered to stand by for take off to Java at first light the next day.

'There's room for one of you to stow down the fuselage behind the wireless operator's inspection panel; sorry I can't fit you both in.'

As Brem and I trudged back to the billet we discussed the prospect and decided we would stick together and take our chance overland. Maybe our luck would hold just a little longer. Anyhow, there was no guarantee that the Hurricane would reach Java safely, especially with our urine in its coolant tank.

At dawn on the 14th we made our way to the airfield for the last time, pushing the Hurricane clear of the trees that screened it as the young pilot walked over to us, already in his flying gear.

'Who's for a day trip then?' he said, trying to put a brave face on things. I think he felt lonely, just one inexperienced pilot left from a whole squadron that had taken off from the carrier in the Bay of Bengal. I felt rather mean telling him we had decided to stay together.

He taxied the plane out clear of the trees, and with the roar of full boost was soon airborne and lifting clear of the surrounding jungle. We watched for as long as it took the lonely Hurricane to diminish to a speck over the southern horizon and then we turned to make our way to the galley. I often

173

wonder what happened to that particular young man.

As Brem and I approached the hut we were accosted by a corporal. 'Grab what you need and can carry in one hand and report to the admin hut; the camp is being evacuated.'

We did not need telling twice; it could only mean that Jappo was just down the road and would be snapping at our heels again. Any thoughts of finding some food to eat disappeared with our appetites. We grabbed our side bags and headed smartly for the admin hut; there were ominously few bods around.

A friendly Dutch Air Force sergeant greeted us inside the hut. 'It's every man for himself now; try to make your way to Java. If you are quick there is a truck round the back ready to leave; they may be able to squeeze two more in. Grab a tin of bully beef each from over there and fill your water bottles from the tap outside. Good luck, chaps.'

In the clearing at the rear of the hut stood an open contractor's lorry, its engine already ticking over. It was going to be standing room only all the way, but that was better than walking. We recognised one or two mates including Geoff Titherington and Geordie Smith who helped us find a few square inches of floor space; Sergeant Levy was one of two NCOs sitting in the cab with the driver. As soon as we were aboard the driver let in the clutch and we chugged out towards the road leading to the oilfields.

Once again we were on the run, heading south and hoping.

Chapter 24

The first few miles were down the road we had taken a couple of nights previously to visit our friends at the oilfield. As we neared the area we could hear explosions at intervals, and saw columns of black smoke billowing skywards. No doubt Hans and Fred were busy detonating the charges they had laid.

Beyond the oilfield the tarmacadamed road deteriorated into a dirt track, and we began to pass through virgin jungle. Frequently the lorry stuck deep in mud, weighed down by the excessive human load it was trying to carry. Each time this happened everyone had to jump down and manhandle the vehicle on to firmer ground. We could only hope that it was not going to be any easier for the Japanese advance guard. However, the occupation of the oilfield, their main goal in the capture of Sumatra, would be sure to delay them for some while; our straggling rabble would be of no great consequence to them.

There was an awesome majesty about the great trees of the jungle, each of which seemed to have its resident primate, who whooped and screamed, apparently with delight, every time we got stuck in the mud.

By mid-afternoon, as we were beginning to think the jungle to be endless, the trees thinned out as we ran down a slope towards a collection of dwellings. The driver told us the village was named Baturaja, and it was the place where the road crossed the railway from Palembang to Telukbetung, near to the southernmost tip of Sumatra. With luck there might still be a train moving south.

Our luck was in, there *was* a train stationary on the track, steam hissing from its boilers while men were filling the tank with water. The odd assortment of coaches and trucks behind the engine were already crammed with refugees; men were on the carriage roofs, and sitting on the buffer mounts. We were told it would be at least an hour before the line ahead was

175

clear and the train ready to go on. If we cared to hitch on an old carriage that was standing on a siding to the rear of the train, we were free to do so. Willing hands set about manhandling the ancient coach along the track to the end of the train.

Brem and I were able to find room to sit down on the hard wooden seats and devour our bully beef, together with some local bread and fruit we were able to buy in the village nearby.

By now we were used to sleeping under primitive and uncomfortable conditions, so the upright wooden seats were no great deterrent to slumber, and I recall practically nothing of that journey through the night as we chugged steadily southwards, the locomotive driven by two Royal Navy petty officers, presumably ship's engineers who had volunteered to drive the train out of Palembang. We never found out how the Royal Navy came to be in Palembang; we were only thankful that they were. We were beyond asking how anyone was where they were, and no one enquired about our adventures. It was enough that we all had a common enemy who was uncomfortably close and likely to get closer if we did not keep moving.

As dawn broke on the fateful 15 February I was conscious the train was no longer moving; steam could be heard gently hissing from the locomotive up front. Out of the window could only be seen palm and plantain trees; as I stepped out of the coach onto the sidings I could see a track leading to a jetty; beyond that must be the Straits that divided Sumatra from Java. Indeed, as the light grew stronger, I could just make out land beyond the sea. If there was a town of Telukbetung, it was not evident, apart from a few dwellings scattered amongst the trees.

There was nothing we could do that morning but wait hopefully for a boat to take us across to Java. We were simply refugees, just like the other couple of hundred or so, cast by fate on to this remote jetty, still just beyond the grasp of the enemy. No longer were we under the motherly care of the Royal Air Force; once again we were on our own, with just a few mates, not knowing where we were going or what we were going to find if we got there. It would all have been a great adventure in peacetime.

As we stood around in the tropical heat, gazing out to sea for the promised ship, hunger and thirst began to take hold of us. Our water bottles had long since been emptied and we could find no water tap nearby. We pondered on whether to slake our thirsts from a ditch running alongside the sidings but considered that to be a surefire way of contracting cholera or some such unpleasant tropical disease.

So far Brem and I had been lucky to avoid any illness on our travels. We both knew it was essential to try to keep fit; we had heard of mates who had fallen by the wayside with malaria or dysentery or some such disease. At Palembang there was one idiot who thought he might find a safe berth in hospital by shooting off one of his toes. He and the other sufferers would by now be behind barbed wire, if still alive.

The answer to our immediate problem seemed to be to unscrew the drainage cock beneath the locomotive's boiler; at least the water had been boiled! It tasted foul; but it washed down our parched throats some plantains we had scrounged from a tree nearby. It was the very last service that the faithful locomotive was able to perform, for the RN artificers were preparing charges to blow it up. To me, who had always had a soft spot for steam engines, it seemed like shooting one's pet dog.

Late in the afternoon we saw the long awaited ferry boat closing in on the shore. It was a happy sight for us; but not so happy was the news the crew shouted across to the jetty as they tied up: the garrison commander of Singapore had officially surrendered to the Japanese that day. Palembang also had been occupied. Now there was only Java, and the city of Batavia, to provide any real opposition to the Japs in that part of the world. We must all have wondered if we were going to reach there before the enemy.

The defence of the ferry boat was entrusted to one soldier manning a rather ancient Oerlikon machine gun; luckily it did not need to be put to the test during the hour or so that it took to cross the Straits to Java. In darkness we shuffled along the jetty and on to a waiting train.

This time there was no seat for Brem and me, we simply wedged our bodies in the gangway between the seats of a first class carriage. Some Dutch civilians, presumably fleeing from Palembang, with much baggage and several children, took pity on us and handed out some of their food. We were grateful for anything after two days with practically nothing in our stomachs.

Once again I was lulled into fitful sleep by the monotonous clackety clack of the train as it rumbled through the night towards Batavia. We were still just one jump ahead of the enemy, having travelled some twelve hundred miles, I reckoned, by road, on foot through the jungle, by rowing boat, sailing boat, ferry boat, and by train. Now we must be nearing the end of the retreat;

there was little further we could go in maintaining our freedom without the help of a large ocean-going liner: where was that going to come from?

Anyhow, I was past worrying by then; fate would take its course, I mused, as I dropped into unconsciousness.

Chapter 25

I t was still dark as the train ground to a halt in the central station at
Batavia. We rubbed our eyes and stretched stiff limbs as we stumbled
out on to the platform; instinctively we formed into little groups as we
waited around: the casual observer would have been hard put to distinguish
one serviceman from another. Many, like Brem and myself, were simply
wearing civilian shirts and shorts, by now very grubby and bedraggled.
Some still bore regimental RAF flashes on sun hats that had seen better days;
we looked what we were, the battered remnants of a defeated army.

Slowly the civilians from the train melted away. We knew not where;
maybe many had friends in Batavia willing to help them. For what seemed
hours we waited around for someone to tell us what to do and where to go.

As we waited I began to feel pains developing in my inner regions. At first
I thought it might just be wind; after all, I had been uncrowned farting
champion of 27 Squadron. At one time Brem had aspired to the same
heights, until he messed himself one night and was disqualified. But this was
no mere bout of wind – more like giving childbirth I would have thought but
that seemed rather unlikely.

I looked across at Brem, and could tell by the pallor of his face and pained
expression, that he was similarly afflicted.

'Are you feeling crook, cobber?' I enquired: the close proximity of a group
of Aussies was beginning to affect our jargon.

'Bloody dysentery, I reckon,' said Brem. 'It's the shits anyway,' he
continued, as he dashed off to try and find a cubicle.

At length a small convoy of lorries pulled into the station forecourt.
Sergeant Levy reappeared from somewhere. 'Jump on lads, we're going to
be taken to a school that's now being used as a gathering place for escaped
servicemen.'

As we drove through Batavia I was surprised firstly by the size of the city,

179

and secondly by the fact that everything seemed to be going on like in peacetime. We saw no signs of bombing, so I suppose the citizens didn't really know what was in store for them. Shops were all still open and seemed to be well stocked; taxis were honking their way round crowded streets; and cycling rickshaw men tinkled their bells in and out of pedestrians thronging the street markets. Batavia was indeed a big and wealthy bastion of the westernised world, just ripe for plucking by the avaricious and all-conquering Japanese.

At length the lorries turned into a gateway and approached a large red brick building, built around the beginning of the century, and bearing in large gilt lettering across the portals the title 'King Edward's School'. I could not recall the Dutch ever being ruled by a King Edward; perhaps for some obscure reason it was in honour of our own King's grandfather; at least the erection of the building was probably carried out in his reign.

We were shown in groups into classrooms from which all furniture had been removed. Each one of us was handed a roll of rush matting: that was to be our bed wherever we could find a space six feet by two to roll it out.

The first thought of most of us was to try to contact our homes by cable while there was still time to do so. Brem and I, with a couple of others, hired a taxi from the school gate to take us to the main post office. We had been handed a few guilders each by the Dutch authorities on arrival at the school. We queued for nearly two hours in the post office to reach the cable counter; both Brem and I had to leave our places in the queue during that time in order to vomit in the gutter outside. I began to feel weaker and weaker.

The cost per word to send that cable seemed exorbitant: I merely said, 'SAFE – WELL – LOVE KEN'. That was lies anyway; I was neither safe nor well. I would probably be captured or killed, if I did not die first from dysentery or beri-beri, or something. It was several months later before I learnt that my cable had given great comfort to those at home in battered London who had quite given me up for lost.

From the Post Office Brem and I followed the others to a restaurant. We had not had a proper meal for a long time, but now we were too ill to care.

Before sundown we dragged our way back to the King Edward School and collapsed onto our thin rolls of rush matting. The stone floor was hard and cold, but we were used to roughing it by now: I was getting beyond caring anyway.

180

For four or five days we lay most of the time on the floor caring little about anything. From time to time we would stagger outside to fill our water bottles and to relieve ourselves. It was pointless to report sick for most of the men in King Edward's School seemed to be suffering from one ailment or another. A long queue of dejected men stretched for yards each morning to the door of the medical officer's room. The mere effort of queueing was more than I could cope with; in any case I kept losing my place in the queue in order to attend to nature. By now only water was passing through my body.

The mere business of using one's bowels was daunting. The normal plumbing arrangements for the school were completely inadequate for such an influx of men. To provide some semblance of hygiene the authorities had hastily erected a bamboo walkway extending from the bank of a river nearby some fifty feet out towards the middle of the stream. The bamboo planks, separated by a six-inch gap in the middle, were some thirty feet above the water level. It wasn't a pretty sight to see a row of bare bottoms as the men crouched down to do the necessary, clutching with one hand the rather frail looking handrail, clasping in the other hand a precious piece of old newspaper. While all that was going on a group of *dhobi* women were busily beating their laundry on half-submerged stones a short distance downstream. I'm glad I wasn't having any *dhobi* done.

In fact, to wash our shirt and shorts meant wearing just a skimpy towel until they dried. During those days, prostrate on the schoolroom floor, our clothes just had to cake with sweat and stink.

Most of the others in the school were in the same condition. Many had been fished out of the water when vessels that they were on were sunk between Singapore and Java. There were two men we got to know who had spent twelve hours swimming before being picked up completely naked, a state that they had to endure until reaching Batavia, when they were handed a pair of white overalls each. They were the lucky ones who had survived, suffering no more than badly sunburnt foreheads and noses. Most of the men gave up the struggle before help came.

On the fifth day my bowels seemed to have dried up, and I could keep water down. Both Brem and I were desperately weak, but thought we ought to try to eat something; so I ventured towards the kitchens to see what I could find. On the way back, tottering with two mugfuls of a sort of stew, I was accosted by a sergeant.

181

'We need every fit man to go up country to Bandung in order to man and defend the airfield there: collect any kit you have and fall in outside in the courtyard,' he commanded.

I continued back to the room, handing Brem his mug of stew; I began to gather together my bits and pieces.

'What the ----- are you doing?' said Brem weakly.

'I've been told to report outside to go up to Bandung; there's a sort of press gang of NCOs out there; anyone who is able to stand is deemed fit for active service.'

'You're not fit, you stupid -----.' said Brem. 'Lie down and turn your face away from the door, no one will recognise you in this light, even if they bother to come searching the rooms.'

I consoled my conscience by telling myself that I was not really fit and would probably have buckled at the knees before going very far. It was not until much later that I realised Brem had probably saved my life with that one piece of good advice. Of those that went to Bandung none escaped either death or capture.

In retrospect, it was lucky I had been taken sick at just that time in our escape; had it happened in Sumatra I would just have been left behind in a hospital that must now have been overrun; had I remained fit then I would have gone to Bandung. As it was we were able to lie up, albeit uncomfortably, during those days when the illness gripped us without losing out on our prospects of escape. During the few minutes we felt like talking we discussed our chances of still getting away to a place of comparative security.

'I reckon we had better stick close to the Aussies,' I suggested. 'There's quite a few of them in these rooms; they are nearer to home than we are, and pretty desperate to get there, particularly as their continent has been threatened by the bombing of Darwin.'

'Could be right,' responded Brem. 'There doesn't seem much chance heading north into the Java Sea, even if we get the chance, the Jap Navy must be flexing its muscles there; best to try for the south coast, and ship across the Timor Sea.'

We kept down our stew and awoke next morning feeling a little better. It was 22 February and somehow there was an air of foreboding that I could not begin to describe; I felt in my bones that this was going to be a day of destiny; the climax of our escape.

We dared not put our heads outside the door during the morning for fear of being rounded up by the press gangs. By midday hunger drove us to chance our arm. It was good just to feel hungry again. The coast was clear this time and we were able to get some sausages and bread, and tea to wash it down. It stayed down this time.

By three o'clock in the afternoon we were even feeling well enough to contemplate going out on the town to get a real meal. At that moment Sergeant Levy appeared in the doorway, just like the genie; but no-one had rubbed the lamp.

'There's a convoy of trucks leaving here for the docks at 16.00 hours,' (always used the twenty-four hour clock, did the sergeant). 'There's a P & O liner put in to the quay on its way to repatriate Aussies from the Middle East. The ship's less than half full and will take any servicemen who can get on board before dusk. You'd better be there.' He turned on his heel and left to see who else he could round up.

'Best do as he says,' said Brem, turning to me. 'Always trust a Jew for looking after his own skin. We should think ourselves lucky he's trying to help us too.'

'I'm not so sure we shouldn't keep close to the Aussies.' I think I was still nursing a hope that we might reach the magic continent of Bradman and Ponsford; I might not get another chance.

'Don't be a -----,' responded Brem vehemently. 'A bird in hand, you know.'

So we threw our few belongings in our side bags and made our way out to the courtyard where the trucks were already filling up. It was good just to be on the move again and doing something positive.

The city of Batavia was inland by a few miles, being linked by water to the main docks by a canal. The road ran flat and straight alongside this canal. As we made our way steadily along the road, the dust billowing up from the wheels of the trucks, still I could not shake off the sense of foreboding; something dramatic was going to happen, and soon.

I could only think it would be the aerial armada once again. The great liner tied up to the quay must be a sitting target, and there was no quick escape for the ship, which surely would be doomed. There was no Allied fighter force left to dispute Japanese supremacy of the skies; if they could sink two great battleships such as the *Prince of Wales* and the *Repulse*, moving fast in the open sea, what chance had our cruise liner tied up to a jetty?

I cast these gloomy thoughts aside as I put a foot on the bottom of the gangplank. At least there was still hope. Had I been a religious man I would probably have prayed to God.

Chapter 26

There was some feeling of security just being on the deck of a big ship, with brave and professional sailors to look after us. Literally we were all in the same boat; if we were attacked some would probably survive. With my usual inborn optimism I still kept thinking it would be the other man who would be blown up or drowned. This time it was not up to me, or to Brem, to make the decisions; that was quite out of our hands.

Once on board, with a couple of hooks in the mess deck ceiling earmarked for slinging a hammock, I was able to indulge in what I had needed for several days – a good shower bath. It was only salt water but who cared; I felt a new man afterwards.

Having downed a meal from the galley I made my way up on deck. It was then that I realised somebody's prayer to God had been answered. It was the reason for my sense of foreboding earlier in the day; the feeling that something sensational was going to happen. Had I looked up to the sky as we made our way down to the dock I would probably have realised how leaden was the sky; a storm of great magnitude must be brewing.

It was the reason why no Japanese bombers had appeared that afternoon to annihilate the sitting duck, the troopship *Orcades*, as she completed her act of mercy in Batavia docks. No aircraft could possibly have survived in the storm that rolled in from the Java Sea, where the Japanese high fleet was lying in wait.

I had never seen, nor am I likely ever to see again, a storm of such tremendous violence. The sky all around was one continuous flickering of lightning. Several times each minute shafts of lightning speared down on to the masts of the ships in the dock, on to the tin roofs of the warehouse sheds, or just plunged into the water with a vicious sizzling noise. The masts of the *Orcades* were hit several times. Rain came down seemingly in one great sheet of water.

185

Throughout this great natural turmoil gallant orderlies were struggling to manhandle stretcher after stretcher from ambulances on the dockside up the gangplank. Blankets covering the patients were completely saturated before they could reach shelter in the ship.

By ten o'clock the last of the sick and wounded were aboard and we cast off from the dockside. It was a moment of great relief to be leaving Java in the eleventh hour of its freedom; but for us the worst might still be to come.

The great storm, which rendered flying impossible, was no great deterrent to a big ship such as the *Orcades*, merely an extra hazard.

As we headed out to the open sea a disemboweled voice broke loud and clear over the Tannoy system. It struck chill into my heart then and still does when I think back on it. 'I am the captain of this ship. The Japanese Navy is out there in strength in the Java Sea, presumably waiting to pounce on Java at the earliest possible moment. We are going to attempt to run the gauntlet between the enemy fleet and the island of Java, keeping as close inshore as we dare, hoping this storm and darkness will provide sufficient cover. By first light tomorrow morning we should be passing through the Straits between Sumatra and Java into the Indian Ocean. If anyone is seen lighting up a cigarette on deck my officers have orders to shoot on sight.'

The Tannoy system clicked and was silent; so too were all the men aboard. We knew that he meant every word. But here was a very brave man; we knew that if anyone could get us to safety he could.

Sleep was not easy that night; tension was heavy around us, to the extent you could almost feel it. I was up on deck as dawn was breaking. I could make out land close by on the port side, perhaps only three or four miles off; and again about the same distance away on the starboard side. That must be Sumatra; we were moving through, and at full speed, the Straits at their narrowest part. Looking back to the port side I could just make out the railway jetty where we had landed in Java only the week before.

The thought went through my mind, as I am sure it did for many others, that if a Japanese informer was anywhere onshore our cover would now be blown. The next two or three hours would be critical as the Straits widened out and we moved out of sight of land. Once in the Indian Ocean a zigzag course could be steered.

The *Orcades* was going flat out, the bows churning great frothing waves on either side. Throughout the morning we bit our fingernails. Surely we had been seen by some little Oriental spy on either island. I visualised him running back to his hidden transmitter in a dark corner of a room, rapping out his message to the admiral in charge of the Japanese invasion fleet. We did not know just how far away were the enemy's aircraft carriers, we merely knew that every minute westward took us nearer to the range limit of the Japanese dive bombers.

It was not until later that we learnt that the planes from the Japanese carriers were busily employed elsewhere: they were knocking hell out of the docks we had just left. There was little doubt in our minds that the attack would have been carried out the day before had it not been for the violent tropical storm. An act of God had saved us.

By afternoon we were out of sight of land and began a zigzag course into the Indian Ocean. The men began to relax, laughter could be heard again as spirits began to rise. Up to now we could only think about getting out of the jaws of the Japs. That had seemed so unlikely that no-one had dared even to think about where we might be heading to land. Rumour began to fly around the ship.

As there were Australian servicemen on board when we embarked it seemed probable that we were heading for Down Under; we were probably not much more than a thousand miles from Perth. The Australians seemed a pretty surly bunch on the whole. We were told that they had been in the Middle East when the Japanese invaded Malaya and bombed Pearl Harbour; when Darwin was bombed the threat to their homeland was all too apparent. It had long been said that Japan coveted Australia for its potential mineral wealth, and its wide open spaces for the teeming millions on Honshiu to colonise. In Cairo the Aussies in the Eighth Army demanded to be repatriated.

Hence the *Orcades*, newly arrived with reinforcements from Britain, was despatched south-eastwards across the Indian Ocean. It could not have been a popular move, from the Aussies, point of view, when they found themselves heading northwards again, and then docking at Batavia. I can't imagine there was a great deal of compassion for us poor souls, who would have been abandoned to the enemy without the courageous action of the *Orcades'* captain, a very brave man, although he would have been acting on instructions from the War Cabinet. Anyhow, we 'Singapore Harriers', as the Aussies nicknamed us, far out-numbered them, although they were physically much fitter.

187

As dusk fell we knew we were safe from attack at least for the next twelve hours.

A strong rumour, no doubt started by some super optimist, passed from lip to lip that we were heading back to the UK. Personally, I thought it to be unlikely; my conscience told me I had really done very little in almost a year since leaving home. Since the Phoney War ended with Hitler's Blitzkrieg in Europe, less than two years previously, my contribution to the war effort was almost nil. What I had done in Malaya had been nullified in a very short time by the Japanese. If my war efforts so far were any yardstick, the hostilities would last for a hundred years.

My own thoughts were that we would be dumped at the most convenient spot on the Indian sub-continent, in order to try to prevent the Japs subduing the Indians, then marching across the Asian continent to link up with Rommel, who should have taken Cairo by then.

For a full twenty minutes the next day I thought I had blown it all. I found myself trapped below the water line, all on my own behind the closed bulkhead doors. I heard the alarm bell summoning all hands to lifeboat stations just as I was taking a shower, at the same time as giving my shirt and shorts a wash out with salt water soap.

I should have remembered the similar circumstances in the café at Taiping, when the building was evacuated rapidly as Jap bombers were sighted and I was set on finishing my ice cream sundae. That nearly cost me my life; but here I was doing the same sort of thing again. I turned off the water, dried myself quickly, wrapped my towel round my waist and, picking up my sodden clothes, made a dash for the bulkhead doors. Too late: operated by remote control they were just rumbling together as I reached them. I must say that I had not expected that to happen, but there was nothing I could do other than wait. I didn't much like the idea of dying, particularly without anybody knowing about it. If the ship was torpedoed and sunk I would simply go down with it; like the pea in a whistle, I was trapped.

The minutes ticked slowly by with no sound other than the throbbing of the ship's engines. After all the past three months, with oblivion a hair's breadth away so many times, surely my luck had not deserted me now, when salvation seemed so near at hand. Luck is a funny thing; the more you have of it the more you seem to expect: at least, that was my experience.

Whether the call to boat stations was a false alarm or just a practice I never found out. I was only thankful when after some fifteen very long minutes the bulkhead doors rumbled open again.

'Where the ----- have you been?' exclaimed Brem, as I emerged blinking into the sunlight.

'Just having a shower and doing my *dhobi*,' I replied feebly.

'You stupid bugger, everyone was supposed to be standing by their allotted lifeboat waiting to hop in as they were lowered.'

'Oh well, I'm still here.'

'Yes, I don't suppose we can get rid of you that easily.'

By the next day, steaming steadily on a course that was taking us north of west, it was evident we were not aiming for Australia; nor were we heading for the Cape of Good Hope, and beyond it Blighty. It seemed certain now that we were heading either for India or Ceylon.

For the next two days we continued on our course, every nautical mile taking us further away from the main forces of the enemy, although the potential threat of a submarine's torpedoes was ever present.

Late in the afternoon of 27 February we sighted land on the horizon to the north-east. As we drew nearer I could just make out a line of mountains in the far distance, with the unmistakeable dunce's cap of Adam's Peak in the middle. So it *was* going to be Ceylon that would provide our immediate haven.

That evening at meal time the skipper addressed us again over the Tannoy. 'At first light tomorrow we shall be moving into the docks at Colombo; all those who boarded at Batavia are to be ready to disembark.'

Just that one terse statement; nothing about 'Hope you enjoyed the trip,' or 'Wishing you good luck, chaps.' This captain, whom we erks never actually saw, was the strong silent type. I think that we all would have liked the opportunity of thanking him for saving our lives.

I turned to Brem as we leant on the deck rails of the upper deck and gazed across the water that separated us from the shoreline of Ceylon. 'So this is it, we've made it.'

'For the time being, at least,' replied Brem, giving vent to his natural Caledonian caution. 'I don't suppose Jappo will let us go as easily as that; there's still a long way to go if we are going to win the war.'

'I don't think it was a question of Jappo letting us go, we just had incredibly good luck, enough to last for the rest of our lives.'

189

'Let's hope that there is a rest to our lives,' said Brem.

We fell silent, taking in the beauty of the scene as the light of the full moon danced upon the rippling water. My thoughts turned, as I believe Brem's did too, to those happy days of our great escape when we first met the Wong girls in Penang and our friendship grew into love. I felt a warm trickle down my cheeks as my thoughts moved on to dwell on those two days of passion spent on Love Island. It could now never be more than just a memory which would probably fade with time. But to think of it then still brought a lump in my throat and an ache in my heart.

At dawn on the last day of February 1942 the *Orcades* slipped quietly into the harbour at Colombo and tied up. It was to be almost the last time she docked, for within a few weeks she was sunk by a single torpedo from an enemy submarine.

As our motley band of some eighteen hundred shuffled down the gangplank in all sorts of bedraggled clothing, hope was beginning to lift our heads again. The fact that we had been dubbed 'The Singapore Harriers' did not mean that we could not turn round and face the enemy when the time came.

We did not know then that it would not be many weeks before we would be put to the test again under enemy bombardment. But that is another story.